Come Back to the Farm

Books by Jesse Stuart

MAN WITH A BULL-TONGUE PLOW
HEAD O' W-HOLLOW
BEYOND DARK HILLS
TREES OF HEAVEN
MEN OF THE MOUNTAINS
TAPS FOR PRIVATE TUSSIE
MONGREL METTLE
ALBUM OF DESTINY
FORETASTE OF GLORY
TALES FROM THE PLUM GROVE HILLS
THE THREAD THAT RUNS SO TRUE
HIE TO THE HUNTERS
CLEARING IN THE SKY
KENTUCKY IS MY LAND
THE GOOD SPIRIT OF LAUREL RIDGE
THE YEAR OF MY REBIRTH
PLOWSHARE IN HEAVEN
GOD'S ODDLING
HOLD APRIL
A JESSE STUART READER
SAVE EVERY LAMB
DAUGHTER OF THE LEGEND
MY LAND HAS A VOICE
MR. GALLION'S SCHOOL
COME GENTLE SPRING

For Boys and Girls

PENNY'S WORTH OF CHARACTER
THE BEATINEST BOY
RED MULE
THE RIGHTFUL OWNER
ANDY FINDS A WAY
OLD BEN

Jesse Stuart

7103364

COME BACK TO THE FARM

McGRAW-HILL BOOK COMPANY
New York   St. Louis   San Francisco
Düsseldorf   London   Mexico
Sydney   Toronto

Contents

⚡ Appalachian
Patriarch ⚡

"WHAT do you say, Uncle Peter," I say as I walk up Uncle Peter's porch. He is sitting on the porch, barefooted, fanning with a bundle of leafy sourwood sprouts.

"Can't say anything, my boy," he says. "Times are good. I'm the happiest man in th' world."

He laughs. "Ahhhhhhhhhhhhhhhhhhhhhhhhhhhhhhh."

Uncle Peter slaps his knees with his big hands and laughs. He laughs and he laughs. He mocks the wind blowing through the dead grass by the garden palings.

"Ahhhhhhhhhhhhhhhhhhhhhhhhh! Haaaaaaaaaaaaaaaaa! Haaaaaaaaaaaaaaaa! Just so happy," he says. "Ahhhhhhhhh-hhhhhhhhhhhhhhh."

Uncle Peter slaps his knees again and laughs. Then he says, "We got you this time. We got you, old boy. It's took a long time to get you. But as th' old fellar says, 'We got our bacon.' We have our bacon. Ahhhhhhhhhhhhhhh-hhh! Haaaaaaaaaaaaaaaaa! Haaaaaaaaaaaaaaa! Ahhhhhhhhhh-hhh! Haaaaaaaaaaaaaaaaaa!"

Uncle Peter is a big man. His hands are as tough as grapevines and as solid as bank-rock slate. His face is covered with curled ragweed beard. His eyes are two black pools of stagnant water. His sturdy legs, gnarled and twisted like middle-aged black oaks, hang limp from his rocking chair. His pants are short and show his hair-covered shin bones. His big bare feet are as brown as two rocks.

"No hair on th' top of my head," says Uncle Peter. "Hair and brains won't mix. Ahhhhhhhhhhhhhhhhhhhhh! Ahhhhhhhhhhhhhhhhhhhhh!"

The wind keeps blowing through the ragweeds by the garden. Uncle Peter is mocking the wind in the weeds the way he laughs. Uncle Peter draws a whiff of smoke from his long-stemmed corncob pipe. He blows it into the air. He blows another cloud of wind-blue smoke into the air to overtake the cloud of smoke he just blew out.

"Just comin' into life about th' time I haf to die," he says. "I'm almost too late to receive th' benefits. Just what I was tellin' your Aunt Mallie. She bore me eight children. Heaven has come to th' earth. The end of time is near. The earth will be made into Heaven. You know I always prophesied it would. Wish it had a-come sooner."

Uncle Peter blows out another cloud of wind-blue smoke. "Your pa's th' biggest fool this country has had in years," says Uncle Peter. "Won't 'sign,' will he? W'y a man that won't 'sign' is a fool. He can make a cross if he can't 'sign' and get somebody to sign fer 'im. It's there fer 'im to get if he'll 'sign' fer it."

Uncle Peter slaps his big hands on his legs. The dust

flies. His big bare brown rock-colored feet scoot clumsily on the puncheon floor.

The wind blows through the ragweeds by the palings. It rattles the rusted hoes on the palings. The hoes, unused, are rusted now. Their keen edges do not slice the rich loam on the hills. They do not whack the sassafras sprouts that take the corn. Uncle Peter is rock-rock-rocking away. Let the wind blow. Let the hoes rust on the garden palings. Let the old scythe blades rattle in their rotting sneads. They do not cut the oats this year. There are no oats to cut. The good earth did not get to swell their kernels in the warm loam.

The wind beats against the ribs of the unfruitful weeds! The wind moans over the empty fields of autumn! The wind is trying to mock Uncle Peter as he sits and rocks. The wind ought to be ashamed of mocking Uncle Peter! Uncle Peter laughs and scoots his big bare feet over the puncheon floor. He blows out clouds of smoke from his corncob pipe. The smoke swirls over the weeds by the garden palings.

"You ought to see my new barn," says Uncle Peter. "I've got a new barn, but I ain't got very much to put in it. Don't need much of nothin'. Ahhhhhhhhhhhhhhh! Ahhh-hhhhhhhhhhh."

His big bare feet tramp the clusters of dead grass where the potatoes have been dug below the barn. It is a little patch of potatoes.

"I ust to tend a whole hillside in Irish taters and a bottom in sweet taters," says Uncle Peter, "but now I've 'signed.' "

We walk up toward the barn through the potato patch. We cross the rusted barbed-wire fence into the barn lot.

"Here it is," says Uncle Peter. "See, it's a purty good

barn. Old Jake Sperry said he wouldn't put th' posts in th' ground though. 'Don't make no difference,' I told him. 'I'm just buildin' it fer as long as I live nohow.' I'm not buildin' fer no future. I'm here on borrowed time. Time borrowed ain't like money. A body don't haf to pay it back. That's th' reason I left th' posts in th' ground. By th' time they rot off I'll be a gone goslin'. I'll be sleepin' right up there on th' pint. That's where I aim to be buried. Right up there among th' pines."

"I believe I can see holes in the roof," I says. "It looks to me like the sunlight is leaking through the barn roof."

"Right you air," says Uncle Peter. "Old Peter Shelton's not buildin' fer th' future. I got some tin that had been used. There's holes in it. Won't be much rain come through. Not like that old barn I ust to have up here. When it rained it was like pourin' water outen a boot in here. Cattle just haf to stand in here and shiver and shake. A lot better now. It'll last me my lifetime. Just climb up th' ladder and look at th' hay I cut along th' creek banks this year."

Two wagon loads of dead grass are piled up against the crossbars. Dry grass for the mules and the cattle. Winter is nearly here and the hills will be barren. The wind will whip across the fallow fields and mock the rockers of the rocking chair.

The great trains of crows will follow the lean cattle to the blue stream of water. They will fly above them and wait for hot dung with broken grains of corn in it. This winter there will not be any golden grains of corn in the dung. The crows must do without. This winter they will eat salted bull grass. This winter they will eat only roughness. It will be a hard winter. The redbirds and the crows and the blackbirds will not fight over the hot steaming piles of dark brown dung on the blue-glistening snow by the water hole. Dark trees, barren of leaves, against the sunset on a white mountain world! Hay in the barn, maybe enough for one cow. Tough-butted white oaks with branches of multicolored leaves and a wind that whips them with a disconsolate wail.

"Don't care for winter," says Uncle Peter. "I don't care nary bit for winter. I'm 'signed' up. Your pa is crazy. Just works all th' time. That's old Ferdinand Farmer. He come down here the other night and he says to me, 'No wonder you ain't got no meat in th' house. No wonder you ain't got meal in your barrel and not a poke of flour in your house. You're a sellout. You know you are. No wonder you've got five old hounds and you ain't got a hog on th' place.' That's the way your pa looks at things!"

My pa is a working man. He will work until he dies. He has asked the hills for bread. The hills told him, "Bread is here. Come and get bread. You will have to get it by the sweat of your brow."

Bread is here for the people. They have not starved. Food is here among these hills same as the sprouts and the rocks are here. Food is here eternal as the rocks and the trees. Food is here eternal as the hills. We must grow the food. We must plant our fallow fields where the ragweeds grow and the broom sedge and the rabbits hide and the quails nest.

"Ferdinand Farmer is a working man," the hills will tell you. "Ferdinand Farmer is stubborn as a rock. No rocking chair on his porch where the wind keeps time with the worn-out rockers. Not any rocking chair rock-rock-rocking away. Wind among the dead weeds by the palings does not rattle his hoes. His scythes do not hang on the palings. His plows have not rusted in the yard. He does not 'sign.' "

Uncle Peter has "signed." Scythes on the palings have not cut the oats on the hill. It will not cut them for another year. Maybe two more years. There are the rusty plows by the gate. They will not furrow the earth for another year. Maybe two more years. Uncle Peter has "signed." Corn grows on clean white sheets of paper now. It is not the kind of corn for hogs. It is not the kind of corn for bread. It is not the kind of substantial corn for life.

The great fields of corn, green in the sun, pretty beneath the July and August moons, are tall over the mules' backs. Great fields of bread prettier than a whole field of bread on a slip of paper. More substantial too.

The furrows have welded together where the plows have been idle so long now. They have welded together like molten steel. The broom sedge grows here, the greenbriers and the saw-briers. The rabbits hide and the quails nest in the briers and the broom sedge. These are the receipts for bread. There is not the smell of corn here. There is not the honor of sweat. There is not the substitute for sweat either.

"Hot as a roasted tater," says Uncle Peter. "Wait a minute till I break me a brush so I can fan. Little stiff where I used to work at a sawmill when I was sixteen years old. Worked back upon Bruin. Pap nearly worked me to death. He was the one who killed me. Back me up against the upper side of a tree. Make me saw till we'd cut a tree six feet through. It broke me down. I've never been any account since."

Uncle Peter breaks a big poplar sprout. He fans his nut-brown face. The beard on his chin works out and in. Uncle Peter fans with the sprout. He smokes his corncob pipe.

"Your pa is a fool," he says. "Old Ferdinand ought to be 'signed' up. He ought to 'sign' his name. That's th' only way to live. Think I'll walk across th' hill someday and tell him he ought to 'sign.' Wonder what old Ferdinand would think if I'd walk across th' hill to tell 'im he's a fool. He don't haf to do all this slavin' around like he does. He could set out on th' porch and smoke his pipe. He don't haf to work outen th' hot sun like he does with th' snakes and th' lizards to make a livin'.'"

We walk back across the potato patch. The sun is coming over the September hills. Uncle Peter fans with the poplar sprout. In front of us is Uncle Peter's house with shingles cupped up at the ends on the roof.

"Put 'em on in th' light of the moon," says Uncle Peter. "See what has happened. Turned up on the ends. Plant taters in th' light of the moon and they grow on top o' th' ground. It don't matter to me if they grow on top of th' ground or under th' ground or in th' moon! Don't matter at all to me! Ahhhhhhhhhhhhhhhhh! Ahhhhhhhhhhhhhh!"

The log house is before us. The yellow daubing is dropping from the cracks. It leaves the blocks and sticks of chinking between the logs stained with yellow mud. The hound-dogs are sleeping on the porch. The smoked-globe lantern is hanging on a rusty nail on the porch post. Old coats are hanging on the porch wall. Moss is growing on the shingles.

"W'y, you know," says Uncle Peter, "I found a hen's nest th' other day up there in the moss on th' roof. It had twenty-one eggs in it. A egg rolled off and broke. That's w'y I found it."

"Th' government has my old place here now," says Uncle Peter. "They loaned me more money than my place was worth. I'll keep th' interest up until I die. My boys can

« 7 »

help me do that. They can dig coal and do that. I want to hold on to these hills until I get too old to fox hunt. When I get too old to fox hunt I want th' Master to call me home. I ust to farm these hills. But life is easier now. I 'signed' up."

"I didn't buy these overalls n'r this blue shirt," says Uncle Peter. "I got a pair o' shoes I didn't buy but they squeeze my feet. I don't like shoes nohow fer summer. Old Ferdinand is a fool. I get paid fer not raisin' tobacco. I get paid fer not raisin' corn. I get paid fer not raisin' cane. I get paid to let these old hills take a rest and to take a rest myself. I did get paid fer not raisin' hogs. I'm gettin' money fer th' things I have done. I'm takin' it easy."

Uncle Peter climbs upon the porch. He falls into his rocking chair with a plump. He refills his corncob pipe.

"You ought to have your pa to come over," says Uncle Peter, "and try my rockin' chear. I'll bet if he'd ever get his old boney carcass in it once you couldn't punch 'im out with a ten-foot pole. Ahhhhhhhh."

Uncle Peter slaps his legs with his big hands and laughs. He blows his smoke toward the garden again. Uncle Peter looks at the hills above the log house. He can see sprouty fields where the corn used to be. He can see the oak trees on the hills, the saw-briers and the great rock ribs that bulge from the skin of the earth. He can see the fields that have made him bread on the hills that were his own. These hills hold his blood, his life, and will hold his dust.

"Ahhhhhhhhhhhhhhhhh!"

I leave Uncle Peter laughing in his rocking chair. I walk up the hollow and over the hill home. A lazy wind hits my face and the sun is warm.

Why Menifee
Wasn't
Our Country

"WHAT I'm goin' to tell you is not the reason I left the Lickin' Country," Fonse Timberlake said. His words hissed from the gaping hole where his four front upper teeth were even with the gum line. The wind pushed his beard, as reddish-brown and soft as summer love vines, against his lean slabby cheeks. "I liked the Lickin' River 'cause it was the best place to fish I'd ever found. I liked Menifee County, too, 'cause there were five sawmills—and they wanted lumberjacks.

" 'Cause I'd heard about the Lickin' River and the good fishin' there under the cool shade of the red elms beside them mossy cliffs where the Lickin's waters swirl and eddy," he said, with hissing words, "I rode my white pony from Morgan County over into Menifee and into the Lickin' River Valley where I found work over at the mill. I found me a little three-room shack beside the river, with some seven acres of ground, and I bought me the shack and acres for sixty-eight dollars. I paid twenty down and I had a year to pay the balance—four dollars comin' due at the end of each month.

"Then I moved my wife and our four young'uns on a damn jolt wagon with all our house plunder into the Lickin' Valley in Menifee County," Fonse continued. He pulled a little cloth sack of crumbled tobacco leaves from his hip pocket and started pouring the bright crumbs into an unevenly torn piece of thin brown wrapping paper. "The road from Morgan to Menifee was rough enough to jar a body's kidneys loose, a-ridin' in a jolt wagon without springs. We had to stop all along that rocky crooked road and let Hiram and Little Fonse down. And Arabella had to take little Subrina from the wagon every mile or so, and then change the diaper on little Draxie. Often I had to stop the team in the middle of the old lumber road and let that white pony and the old sorrel mare I borrowed from Jasper Higgins git their wind. Once when I did this, I killed two black snakes with one rock. Arabella took the little girls behind the green wall of bushes on one side of the old log road, and I took Hiram and Little Fonse and went the other way. I'd heard my pappy and mammy talk about this very same thing when I was a little boy. What they said about Morgan County then was just like what I found in Menifee and the Lickin' River Valley country."

Fonse pressed the bright burley crumbs down with his index finger and folded the brown paper gently over the tobacco so he wouldn't waste a little crumb of the precious leaf. Then he moistened the paper with his tongue and pasted the two torn edges into a cigarette that looked like a rooster's bill, with one big end and a small sharp end and a little rainbow curve.

"Well, we got to the shack that day and we fed the pony and the sorrel mare," he continued. He pulled his hat from his head and took a match from the hatband, a place where lumberjacks kept their matches to keep them dry. "Then we set up our cookstove. Arabella carried one side and I carried tother. We set the stove on four rocks Hiram found—they was all about the same size and thickness. There sure was enough rocks to choose from around that there shack. While Hiram was choppin' wood for the stove with a double-bitted axe, I carried one of our beds in and set it up so we could lay Subrina and Draxie down, 'cause they were so tired from thirty miles of joltin' over rocks, ditches, and logs in a springless jolt wagon they needed sleep. Little Fonse carried wood inside and made a fire in the stove, and Arabella started supper while our oldest, my eight-year-old Hiram, worked with me like a little man. We got the house plunder from the wagon into the shack and had that table set and dishes on by the time she'd cooked vittles to fill our empty stummicks. When we'd et a big supper, I smoked and then we went to bed and slept like saw logs."

Fonse at last flipped the match head with his thumbnail, making a blaze of fire shoot forth, and he held it to the little end of his rooster-bill cigarette. He inhaled, then exhaled a cloud of smoke that streamed from each nostril in long blue lines and thinned on the summer air.

"Well, sir, it was the next mornin' when it happened," Fonse went on. "You know how young'uns like to play. Little Fonse found a loose plank in that kitchen floor, and he raised it up and looked down. See, in the whole of Lickin' River Valley there's not much *level* land and there wasn't any of it where our shack stood. It set on the side of the riverbank and was underpinned with field rocks, 'cause the Lord knows there was plenty when they built the house and a-plenty left then. The lower-side underpinnin' was a rough rock wall higher than your head, while the side next to the hill wasn't no more than eight inches high.

" 'I see 'em down there,' Little Fonse hollers. 'I'll get me a string and I'll ketch that there big'un.'

"Well, sir, we paid no attention to what he said. He was six, but he had some man ways. So he got him a string off'n a box or somethin' and tied a loop and let it down in that there hole where he'd moved the plank over. 'Hiss, durn you, hiss,' he says. 'I'll make you somethin' for somethin'!'

" 'You come on to your breakfast, young man,' I told him. 'Quit playin' with somethin' under the floor this early!' And about that time he started pullin' and heavin' same as I did once when I ketched me a forty-two pound mud cat from the bottom of a deep hole in the Lickin'.

" 'I got 'im!' Little Fonse screams. 'I got the loop smack dab over his old big rusty head! Squirm, you old devil, squirm! Hiss all you durn please!'

"Well, sir, I'd set down at the table ready for my sow bacon, hot biscuits, eggs, and black coffee, and I paid no mind to Little Fonse, specially after I smelled the coffee. It was Arabella who looked over just as he was about to bring that big squirmin' snake—a-rattlin' to beat the band—up through that there hole in the floor. Arabella she let out a scream, jumped up, and took off toward Little Fonse. 'Let it back, Little Fonse,' she screamed. 'Let it back!' Then I jumped up too, just in time to see the big rattlesnake Little Fonse was a-heavin' to fetch up onto the kitchen floor.

" 'Ah, shucks!' Little Fonse said when the string broke and his snake went back down under the floor. 'I lost 'im, but I'll get 'im again.'

" 'No, you won't,' I said to 'im. 'No, you won't! Now you take this here from your pappy who's been through enough trouble in his day to break a jolt wagon down. You come on to your breakfast and dry them tears—no use cryin' just because you didn't get that there old rattle-snake! Come on and let's eat breakfast, 'cause we're all hungry people.'

"Well, sir, Arabella, she was unmoved as a red elm be-side the Lickin'," Fonse continued, sending another cloud of light-blue smoke toward the holes in the roof. "She sat back down in a chair close by the stove where she could reach the coffee biler. Little Fonse was awful disappointed, but he dried the tears from his eyes with the backs of his hands and he pouted and sniffed as he sat down to eat his bacon, biscuits, and eggs.

" 'That old snake, Pappy,' he said, snifflin' like a rabbit smellin' green clover in the early spring, 'he's near big enough to swaller one of our hens or maybe our old rooster, and what will we do without a rooster to crow and wake us up at four? Pappy, he was the old big 'un among a lot of lesser-sized 'uns. And the lesser-sized is bigger than any snakes we ever seen in Morgan!'

" 'Now, my son, let me tell you somethin',' I tried to explain to Little Fonse. 'The best thing to do with them there snakes under the floor is to leave 'em alone. I'm a-tryin' to give you good advice.'

" 'Your pappy is right, Little Fonse,' Arabella said, tryin' to reason with him. 'When you go a-stirrin' up trou-ble with them rattlesnakes you've got trouble on your hands. That snake wasn't a-botherin' you. He wasn't a-botherin' any of us. Now he knows he's got enemies up above 'im!'

" 'Supposin', Little Fonse,' I says, 'that we lived down

on the dirt and somethin' lifted a plank above and made a little loop in a rope and dropped it down over your neck and lifted you up bodily into the air, and you was a-kickin' and a-squirmin' for your life, but, luck for you, the rope broke and you went down to your home and loved ones again. Wouldn't you always be juberous of that family above you?'

" 'I guess I would, Pappy,' says the little feller. 'But I have allus thought a snake was my enemy. I had 'im if the string hadn't broke. The way I had that string around his neck I could have got 'im by the throat with my hand and he couldn't have bit me! I could have choked the daylights outten 'im!'

"Little Fonse grinned when he talked about his a-havin' that old rattler. 'Now, my son,' I says, 'as long as them rattlers down under this floor leaves us alone, I say we leave them alone. But, Little Fonse, if any snake ever tries to come up on our floor we show him no mercy. Then he's our enemy and we'll git 'im. I've allus heard it was bad luck to bring a gooseneck hoe into the house, but I'm goin' to bring one in right now. And if one of them jaspers down there show up on this here floor, cut 'im to pieces!'

"I got me a gooseneck hoe and then I says, 'Now, let this hoe set right here in the kitchen!'

Fonse made and lit another cigarette.

"Well, I thought Little Fonse was satisfied with my idear," he continued while the wind pressed his red beard against his face and the fire in his cigarette was whipped into a bright glow. "We went on and we et our breakfast and got up from the table and stretched ourselves. When I went over to put the loose plank back I got down on my knees and looked down in that there hole. Little Fonse was

right. The place must have been comfortable and cool
'cause it was alive with rattlesnakes—old residenters,
middle-sized 'uns and young'uns. I guess to have got 'em
all at once, if they'd turned out to be our enemies, we
would've had to move the plunder out and set fire to the
house. Arabella got down and looked through the hole too,
and she agreed with me. We had a big family of unfriendly
snakes below us, but we'd talked it over among ourselves
and agreed that if they didn't bother us no more we
wouldn't bother them none. But I took the hoe and filed it
sharp as a razor. I told Little Fonse, Hiram, and Arabella
what to do if one of them jaspers came up to us for a visit.
Hiram looked everywhere to see if there was a crack between the planks or any knothole big enough for one of
them to get through to us. He and Little Fonse just didn't
like rattlesnakes that close. Then on the outside of the
shack Little Fonse found a slick path worn from a hole
under a cliff to a hole under the underpinnin' of our
shack. I wondered when I went to the sawmill that day if
the old rattlesnakes started to go between our shack and
the rock what would happen if Little Fonse saw them! He
might tie into 'em with hoe, club, rocks, or anythin' he
could lay his hands on and make them meaner enemies
to us.

"That day when I worked at Rufus Pratt's sawmill, I
worried about Little Fonse back home," Fonse said, talking fast with his burning cigarette in his hand. "I didn't
worry so much about Arabella, Hiram, and the little girls.
But atter Little Fonse had once disturbed the rattlesnakes,
I thought it would spell trouble in two ways. Little Fonse
would be atter the snakes while they'd be atter us.

"Every mornin' I went to work at the sawmill for a

couple of weeks," Fonse continued, exhaling another cloud of smoke, "I thought I'd go home some afternoon and one of my family would be hurt. Still not a thing happened. Atter two weeks at the mill, Lester Pratt sent me to Red River, on a small fork of the Lickin' River, to cut timber. An' honest, if I do say it for myself, I passed rattlesnakes in that country and they didn't offer to bother me and I didn't offer to bother them. I could've cut them in two with my ax, but I didn't. Menifee was their country and Morgan was mine. So I left them alone and they didn't bother me none. They seemed to understand. I had nothin' against them and that was the reason, maybe, they didn't have anything against me. Little Fonse had started all the trouble.

"I'd been cuttin' timber about a week when I went home one evenin' and somethin' had happened," Fonse said, shaking his head sadly. "When I went home I found Little Fonse was out playin' with a rattlesnake head! Honest, it was a lot bigger and broader than Little Fonse's hand.

" 'Arabella, look what our young'uns are a-playin' with,' I said. She was out with a gooseneck hoe diggin' in our rocky garden.

" 'What is it?' she asked. 'A big copper-colored buckeye?'

" 'A copper-colored buckeye, my foot!' I told her. 'It's the biggest damn rattlesnake's head I've ever seent! I spect Little Fonse's the one who kilt it. I'll see if he did.'

"And sure enough I asked 'im, and he said he was a-playin' and the big snake was a-crawlin' from the hole under the rock to the hole under our shack. Little Fonse, he said the big snake wouldn't get otten his way when he was playin' so he got the hoe and chopped off his head.

Then, I ast Little Fonse where the rest of his body was and I counted nineteen rattlers. So, Little Fonse had kilt one of the old residenters and this sure meant trouble.

" 'Arabella, we're in fer it,' I said that night at the supper table." Fonse's words hissed like a bluffing black snake's warnings. " 'Them rattlesnakes will be atter us now. Watch the slick-worn path between the shack and the cliff and watch all over the yard. Watch the house, 'cause one might want to slip up to see what we're a-doin'. Menifee is rattlesnake's country, and Little Fonse he started trouble with 'em. He pulled one up by the neck and he cut one's head off with a hoe!'

"Well, sir, it wasn't a week later. I'd laid the law down to my family at the supper table about our a-tryin' to take over, when Little Fonse and Hiram harnessed a pony and hitched 'im to an old sled." Fonse's words came as fast as a winter wind in the leafless trees. "They put a box on that sled to fill with chips to burn in our stove. Then they went to the timber woods where Lester Pratt's men had made crossties. I was back home from the timber woods when they got back to the shack with a load. They'd not even bothered to put chips in the box. I saw Hiram ridin' on the front of the sled drivin' the pony, and Little Fonse was standin' back beside the box a-holdin' to it with one hand and a-slappin' somethin' with the other when it tried to get out of the box. I figured right then somethin' was wrong. So I went out to the path to meet 'em. And when Little Fonse stopped the pony and I jumped on the sled and looked into the wood box, I never saw a rattlesnake as big in my life. It was tied with a string around the neck, and the string was tied on either end to the box. When the old rattlesnake jumped up and tried to get out, Little

Fonse boxed him first on one side of his hard head and then t'other with his hand. He was a-sayin', 'You stay in that there box! You stay in that there box! I said for you to stay in that there box! I mean it!'

" 'It's more trouble,' I said to Arabella, when she came runnin'. And it sure was more trouble.

"One evenin' in August when Subrina went over to the little table where we kept the water bucket," Fonse went on, his words hissing now like steam from a teakettle spout, "I heard a warnin' like the rattlin' of many little bells. Subrina'd gone to get a glass of water for her mammy. I was the first up from the table, then Little Fonse, then Hiram and Arabella, in that order, while I grabbed the hoe from the kitchen corner. Just as Subrina jumped back like a young bird tryin' to get away from a black snake, I let the sharp hoe fall, and off went the head of a rattlesnake old enough to vote. 'See what you've started, Little Fonse?' I said. 'You've got us into it with all these Menifee County rattlesnakes. You look out, young'uns, from now on!'

"Then, I had to do somethin' I didn't want to do, 'cause I made every shell I had brought with me count for a squirrel, rabbit, young coon, or a ground hog," Fonse continued. "But on this very evenin' I didn't wait to finish supper—not since this big rattlesnake had come up from its room downstairs to get us. I went to the trunk and I got the shells for a single-barrel, twelve-gauge, full-choked, mule-kickin' shotgun. Arabella lighted the lantern and Little Fonse, who liked the smell of powder, lifted up a loose plank. Arabella held the lantern down, and I started shootin' rattlesnakes. Every time I aimed at one's head and fired, his body squirmed like an eel in the Lickin' River mud. Then he flopped over with his belly up. So one by one I turned their bellies up, while Little Fonse enjoyed the smell of burnin' gunpowder. No matter how many I kilt, the other snakes wouldn't skeer. They stayed right on and waited for the shells I hated to waste on 'em. But now I believed it was better to use my shells than to burn the house. I figured it out and it was much cheaper. But I killed rattlesnakes until my single-barrel was hot. I let it cool a bit and then started shootin' again. I didn't leave nairy a rattlesnake. Little Fonse had a lot of fun usin' my frog gig fetchin' 'em up and puttin' 'em in a washin' tub. Arabella and I carried out two tubs of rattlesnakes that were heavier than the cookstove we'd carried in together. I didn't stop shootin' until every rattlesnake under that floor was dead. Didn't want to take no more chances. I thought it best to get 'em before they got one of us.

"But this wasn't the reason we moved away, 'cause October had come and all the snakes in that country had gone to sleep," he concluded. "Our war with the rattlesnakes was over until next spring. The reason I left: a man come and claimed the floor in our shack. Then I went back to the man I bought it from and asked him if it was the truth that when I bought this shack and the acres, I didn't get the floor. He asked me if the floor was nailed down. Then I remembered how Little Fonse pulled a plank up any time he wanted to look down to see what them rattlesnakes were doin'. Sure enough my floor wasn't nailed down and I didn't own it. That was an old custom we'd had in Morgan County long ago, and I didn't like it. So, here we were supposed to start livin' on the ground floor where the rattlesnakes used to be. So I sold my shack and seven acres for twenty dollars less than I paid for it, and I bought me an old plug horse to work with the pony in the jolt wagon to take us back to Morgan. No, it wasn't the rattlesnakes that whipped us out. We didn't like it 'cause we didn't own the floor. The very day we left for Morgan where cliffs weren't so high and the rattlesnakes never lived to be old enough to vote, Little Fonse, he happened to think of a pretty good'n. 'Because the floors ain't nailed down is the reason that them old rattlesnakes can get into the shacks,' he says as we drove back over that jolty road. 'We're goin' back to Morgan where the floors are nailed down and where we can go to the water bucket in the kitchen to get a drink of water without hearin' an old rattler shake his dry bones like little bells a-tellin' us that this here is his country, and fer us to git!' "

Give Charlie a Little Time

"**P**A, you never know when one of these cows is going to kick the bucket out of your hand," Finn said. "You never know when one is going to kick you over. You never know what is going to happen in this barn lot. I have to tie every cow on this place before I can milk her. I go to the pasture to hunt the cows night and morning and I never know where I'll find them. Half the time I find them in a neighbor's pasture. No wonder we don't get any work done in the fields. We spend half our time hunting and milking the cows."

"I'll tell you what is wrong," Pa said. "We need a bull in this pasture. Eleven cows and five heifers on this place and we've not got a bull. When we get a bull among them they will tone down. You won't see them flying over these high barbed-wire fences like a bunch of setting hens. You mark my word!"

"I hope you get a bull soon," Finn said. "I'm tired of trying to milk these cows. We've got the meanest cows I've ever seen."

"Erf's bringing a big white-faced bull down in the morning," Pa said. "When Erf Bailey tells me he's sending a good bull, I expect to get the best. I've had a lot of dealings with old Erf and I've always found him a man of his word."

"That's the best news I've heard around here," Finn said. "If these cows ever get quieted down so we can milk them, we can get a lot more work done. I can't get away from this barn until ten o'clock every morning. I never know where to look for these cows. I go to the pasture and hunt half of the morning and then I find them in somebody's pasture. And there's not a bull in a pasture that joins us."

The next morning we heard the truck roaring up the Hollow. Finn, Pa, and I went down the yellow-clay bank below the house to meet the truck. We stood at the gate at the foot of the yellow-clay bank and waited for it. We saw Erf driving slowly around the bend in the road, saw the truck lumbering this way and that and the big white-faced bull skidding from one side of the truck bed to the other. Erf had a rope tied around his horns and tied to a slat on the truck bed. Erf was smoking his pipe and driving slowly up the rough road.

"Road's a little rough, Mick," Erf said, stopping at the gate and getting out of the truck.

"Yes, Erf, the road's a little rough," Pa said, "but we need a bull worse than anything on this place."

"You have him here," Erf said. Erf was a short thick man with squinty eyes, big calloused hands, and he smoked a big pipe. He pulled the pipestem from between his gold-

crowned teeth. He winked at Pa when he said the bull was
a good one.

"He looks like he's all right, Erf," Pa said. "I'll take
your word any time. You know we've traded many a time
and just told each other about what we were trading! We
have traded sight unseen, and I've always been satisfied
with the trades."

"That bull's eye is a little bad," Erf said. "I think some
wild boy shot him in the eye with a slingshot."

"That's too bad," Pa said, "that a bull pretty as that one
is disfigured like that. But this won't make any difference.
We're needing a bull here. We need a bull worse than
anything on this place. And I wanted a white-faced
bull."

"You have just what you need, Mick," Erf said.

"Just back your truck right up against that bank there,"
Pa said. "We'll let him walk out in the pasture. Here's a
good place to unload him. He's in the pasture here."

Erf backed the truck against the bank. Pa climbed up in
the truck bed and untied the rope from around the bull's
horns. He patted the bull's head.

"What's his name?" Pa asked.

"Charlie," Erf replied.

Charlie leaped from the truck bed upon the little bank.
He walked out across the pasture with his head high in the
air and turned to one side.

"That bad eye bothers him," Erf said. "I believe he's
just got one good eye."

"That's all right, Erf," Pa said. "I'm pleased to get
him."

"So am I," Finn said. "I'm getting tired of looking in
everybody's pasture for our cows."

"That will end now," Erf said. "Well, Mick, I've got a

lot of work to do and I must be on my way back home. Let me know if the bull isn't what I said he was. He might be a little cowed at first. He's been in the pasture with a bigger bull and the bigger bull shoved him around."

"He'll be the kingpin here," Pa said. "What is a farm unless it has a good bull on it? It's not a farm to me! I'll never let my farm go this long again without a bull on it."

Pa looked pleased as he watched Charlie walking out across the pasture with his head high and turned to one side.

"Shame about that bull's eye," Pa said.

"It is that," said Erf getting back into his truck. "Too many wild boys running around with slingshots. Too many boys without any raising these days."

"No use leaving now," Pa told Erf. "You'd better stay and have some dinner with us."

"Thank you, Mick, but I'll have to be getting home for beans," Erf said. "I've got more work to do than I'll ever get done."

"Come and see us, Erf," Pa said.

"I will, Mick, and you come and see us," Erf said.

Erf lumbered slowly down the rough road in the big truck. Pa stood and watched Charlie running over the pasture with his head in the air.

"Do you reckon we'd better drive him to the cows?" Finn asked Pa.

"That's a foolish question," Pa said. "That bull will go straight to the cows."

"I'm not so sure about that," Finn said.

"Son, you've not lived long enough," Pa said. "I know the nature of a bull."

Pa, Finn, and I walked up the road toward the house. We left Charlie free to roam over the pasture.

"You know we got too much work to do," Pa said. "We don't have time to go over the pasture rounding up the cows and putting a bull with them. That's their job to get together. They'll get along all right. We've got to get the new-ground corn plowed out this afternoon. We've got a lot of black-locust sprouts to cut out of the corn too."

We had just got out of the cornfield when Collins Hoffman hurried up the yellow-clay bank in front of the house. He was wheezing on his pipestem and almost out of breath.

"Mick, have you got a bull on this place?" Collins asked.

"Yes, we have," Pa told him. "We just got him this morning."

"Is he a big white-faced bull?" Collins asked.

"Yes, what's happened?" Pa asked. "Come, come, Collins, tell me what has happened."

"He's down there in your soybeans below the old Chatman house," Collins said. "He was just mowing them down. I couldn't do a thing with him."

"That's funny," Pa said. "Maybe Erf Bailey forgot to close the gate when he left with the truck."

"No, the gate was closed, Mick," Collins said. "I know it was closed for I had to open it as I came up the Hollow."

"That's an awful high fence for a bull to jump to get to soybeans," Pa said. "Looks like he'd have found the cows in the pasture."

Pa, Finn, Collins, and I hurried down the Hollow to the soybean patch. Charlie was out in the middle of the patch helping himself. When he saw us coming he held his head high in the air and turned his good eye toward us.

"We'll put him back in the pasture," Pa said. "This time we'll put him with the cows. I guess he's used to a lot of cattle and he thought we'd put him in the pasture by himself."

Finn opened the gate. Pa, Collins, and I drove Charlie up the road. He didn't try to get away. He followed the wagon road through the gate. We closed the gate behind him.

"Much obliged to you, Collins," Pa said. "I'm glad you found him and came and told us. He would have been a lost bull if he'd ever got back in that wilderness above the bean patch. He could have gone for miles and miles and never heard a cow bawl. I'm awful glad you found him. Maybe I can do as much for you someday."

"It's all right, Mick," Collins said, refilling his pipe.

"You'd better go back to the house with us and eat some supper," Pa said.

"No, thank you, Mick," Collins said. "I've got to be getting home. I've got a lot of work to do."

"Come and see us," Pa said.

"I will, thank you," Collins said. "You come and see us."

Collins walked down the road smoking his pipe. Pa, Finn, and I drove Charlie toward the barn.

"That bull is a cowed bull," Pa said. "I can tell he is cowed. He's not bellowed a time since he's been here. If he has, I've not heard him. Go hunt the cows, Finn, and fetch them to the barn. Let's put Charlie with them. He'll feel more contented then."

Pa and I drove Charlie to the barn. When Finn drove the cows to the barn, Charlie saw them. He turned his head to one side and looked at them with his good eye.

The cows gathered around Charlie and looked curiously at him. We could tell the cows were glad to have Charlie in the pasture.

"That bull will never get out again," Pa said. "I still believe somebody left the gate open and let him out. I don't believe he's of a nature to jump over a fence as high as that fence down there. And we'll not have any more trouble with our cows sailing over the fence. All that has ended now."

When we left the barn the cows were still gathered around Charlie. They were kissing his face with their scratchy tongues. They were making over Charlie. They had him surrounded. All we could see of Charlie was his fine pair of horns. But we never heard Charlie bellow. He just stood among the cows contentedly and let them make over him.

"The cows are a lot easier to milk already," said Finn. "Just to have a bull in the pasture makes all the difference in the world."

When we milked the cows Charlie stood in the barn lot and chewed his cud. The cows seemed contented now. When we went to the pasture we found them always gathered near Charlie. When we drove our cows up to the milk gap, all we had to do was to drive Charlie in front and all the cows and the heifers followed. There would be a long line of cows and heifers walking around the path toward the barn in single file. Charlie's horns were so broad that the tips of his horns often hit the brush on both sides of the path as he walked through the woods toward the barn.

"He's a fine bull, but he never bellows," Pa said. "I'd like to hear him bellow just once. I'd be tickled to see him paw the dirt. I like to see a bull be a bull!"

We'd not had Charlie more than five days when I looked at Pretty Thing's eye. I was milking her and I noticed she held her head one-sided just like Charlie did when Erf brought him up the hollow in the truck.

"Finn, Pretty Thing's got the pink eye," I said.

"Something is the matter with Roan's eyes, too," Finn said.

"Good heavens, all the cows have the pink eye," I said.

"That's the bad boy who hit Charlie in the eye with a slingshot," Finn sighed. "What will Pa say about this?"

"It won't be the bull's fault," I said. "A bull is never at fault with Pa."

We milked the cows and turned them back from the barn lot to the pasture. The cows couldn't see the grass. They just had to feel for it with their noses against the ground.

"No wonder these cows are failing with their milk," Finn said. "They can't see to eat."

We took the milk to the cellar and strained it into milk crocks.

"Pa, did you know what is the matter with that bull?" Finn said.

"No, what's wrong with him," Pa replied.

"He wasn't shot in the eye with a slingshot," Finn said. "He's got the pink eye and he's given it to all the cows."

"Too bad. I hope none of them lose an eye," Pa said. He wasn't disturbed about this. "You boys just flip a little salt in their eyes. It's the best remedy I know for pink eye. Too bad about old Charlie! I'll bet Erf didn't know he had the pink eye. Erf would never have let us have him if he had known."

Charlie hadn't been in our pasture a month before we missed him one morning when we went after the cows. We looked all over the pasture for Charlie. We combed the woods for him. He just wasn't in the pasture.

"I don't see, boys, how that bull ever went over that fence any place," Pa said. "That's the best pasture fence on this farm. It's seven wires high all the way around. You might find him over with Holbrook's cows. They just come up to the fence and snort around. I'll bet old Charlie's gone over the fence to them. Fred Holbrook hasn't had a bull in his pasture for the last two years."

"Our cows used to get out all the time," Finn said. "Now our bull has started getting out. Our cows are peaceful now. I never see one sailing over the fence like setting hens. It was because we didn't have a bull our cows got to be such rogues."

"We'd better go over in Fred Holbrook's pasture to see if Charlie is over there," I said.

Finn and I walked over the hill. We walked down the Hollow. We looked for Holbrook's cows. We found them standing by a hole of water under the shade of a grove of poplar trees. Charlie was with them. He was standing contentedly under the poplar shade chewing his cud.

"Here's our bull," Finn said.

We started driving Charlie up the Hollow along the cow path in front of us.

"Boys, you're not taking my bull off," said a voice from Fred Holbrook's apple orchard upon the slope above the Hollow.

"Yes, we are taking him home, Fred," Finn said.

Fred stood under the apple tree with a sprouting hoe in his hand.

"I didn't know there was a bull in this Hollow," Fred said. "I know we needed one. I was just wondering where I was going to get one and I found this big fine white-faced bull in my pasture. My cows are all going to have white-faced calves. Now, I'm tickled he got into my pasture!"

"If Charlie was a scrub bull Fred wouldn't have liked for Charlie to get with his cows," Finn said in a low voice.

We drove Charlie up the Hollow and turned him into our barn lot. From the barn lot, we turned him back in the pasture.

"Our cows haven't done no good with their milking since they got that pink eye," Pa said. "Their eyes have cleared up too. All the cows are well enough, but they're not milking to do any good."

Charlie hadn't been in the pasture a week before we missed him again one morning when we went after the cows.

"I guess he's over about Alf Madden's this time," Pa said. "Alf's not got a bull and he's got four cows. I'll bet Charlie's heard a cow bawling and he's gone over there to her. If Charlie keeps on he'll start bellowing and pawing the dirt one of these days."

"He doesn't need to bellow," Finn said. "Why do you want 'im to bellow?"

"He's not a bull until he bellows," Pa said. "That's the marking of a good bull. I like to see one bellow and paw the dirt!"

"Pa, you ought to go around through the woods pasture to see what old Charlie's done already," Finn said. "At every old rotten tree that he couldn't butt over he's pawed out a hole big enough to bury himself in. I saw him out there taking run-and-gos at an old snag! He hit it hard enough to crack his skull. I thought he would. And finally, Charlie butted the snag over."

"That's the marking of a good bull," Pa said.

Finn and I crossed our orchard and went over to Alf Madden's pasture. We walked down the hill to the Hollow. We hunted up and down the Hollow until we found Alf's cows. They were standing under the shade of a beech grove.

"Here's Charlie," I said. "I don't see how he ever got in this pasture. He had to get out of our pasture and cross our hog pasture and then the two fences around the apple orchard. Then he had to get into this pasture. He had to cross seven fences to get here."

We had to take Charlie down past Madden's toward the highway and then bring him back up the Hollow home. We couldn't get back across the fences without cutting the new wire.

"A lot of trouble to you boys," Alf Madden said as we drove Charlie down past his house, "but I'm glad he got in my pasture. I've not had a bull in my pasture this summer. This saved me the trouble of looking for one. My cows ought to get some good calves from that bull."

"Where did you find him, boys?" Pa asked when we drove Charlie home.

"Alf Madden's pasture and we had to bring him all the way around the highway and up the Hollow to get 'im home," Finn told Pa.

"He's lost a lot of weight but I don't see a blemish on him," Pa said. "He's not cut himself getting over the fences."

We put Charlie back in our pasture. The cows were glad

to see Charlie back in the pasture. When they stood under the shade on hot afternoons, the cows would gather around Charlie and kiss his face. Charlie would stand contentedly and chew his cud.

Charlie stayed a couple of weeks in the pasture this time. He gained weight. When Charlie gained weight, our cows gave less milk. One morning when we went after the cows, Charlie was gone. We always had trouble driving the cows to the barn lot to milk them when Charlie was gone. We always got Charlie in front and drove him to the milk gap and the cows followed. We asked Jess Crumb if he had seen a strange bull in his pasture. Jess said that he hadn't. We asked Charlie Artner if he'd seen a strange bull in his pasture. He said he hadn't but he needed one badly. We asked Frank Brown if he'd seen a strange bull in his pasture and he said he hadn't but he needed one badly. We asked Adam Tar if he had seen a strange bull in his pasture. He said he hadn't but they needed a bull with their two cows and four heifers.

"There's a lot of pastures here yet for Charlie to visit," Finn said. "He'll find all of them before the summer's over. This will be more trouble for us."

We had been all over our farm looking for Charlie. We had visited all our neighbors whose land joined our land. We had left out Crump's little farm. It was across a boney hill, the last place we thought we would find Charlie. When we came to the house without Charlie, we found him with our cows as we crossed the pasture going home.

"Do you suppose Charlie's been out and got back by himself?" Finn asked me, "or do you suppose we overlooked him in our pasture and he's not been out at all."

Pa met us when we walked up to the house.

"Boys, did you know that bull got back to Crump's place

someway," Pa said. "John Crump came over here this morning scared to death. He was afraid of Charlie. I told Old John that Charlie was harmless but I had to quit plowing and go after that bull. I've nearly run my legs off getting him back into the pasture. Charlie will leave his white-faced calves at Crump's."

"It's a good thing," Finn said, laughing. "We'll have some half-breeds instead of scrub cattle around these parts."

"That's what I tried to tell John Crump," Pa said, "but Old John didn't want his cows to calve. He wanted to milk them. Now they will go dry. John was sore about it."

Charlie had been gone three weeks again. Finn and I didn't bother about trying to find him. Pa went to town on Saturday and he saw Charlie Artner in town.

"Say, Mick," Charlie said to Pa, "I think your bull is in my pasture. He's been over there about three weeks. I needed a bull but I don't need one any longer. I thought I'd tell you so you could come and get him. Now he's not bothering anything and if you want to leave him it's perfectly all right with me. I was just a little afraid he'd get out of my field to some of the neighbor's cows and keep on going and going from one pasture to another!"

"That's just what he's doing," Pa told Charlie. "How did he ever get to your place is more than I can understand. He had to cross my cornfield, wheat field, and tobacco patch. He had to cross a half a dozen good fences. But fences don't mean anything to him. And I don't see how he could hear a cow bawl that far away."

"Guess the wind was blowing toward your pasture from my pasture," said Charlie. "Wind will carry the sound, you know."

« 3 3 »

"That bull's got good ears then," Pa said. "I've never seen a bull like him. And I've not heard him bellow since I've had him."

Finn and I had to go to Charlie Artner's and bring Charlie around up by the covered bridge and up Womack Hollow and back home. We had to take him seven miles around when it was just three miles across the hill the way he had gone. We didn't want to cut our fences to get him back home.

"That bull looks bad again," Pa said. "I think Old Charlie has about fifteen cows and heifers over there and doesn't have a bull."

"Charlie has got only three more places to visit," Finn said. "Then he will have visited all of our neighbors' cows. He just has to visit Jess Crumb's, Frank Brown's, and Adam Tar's pastures and he'll have all!"

The next week he got in Adam Tar's pasture. He visited three days with Adam's cows and heifers. As we drove him home, we just turned him into Jess Crumb's pasture and left him two days. We went back and got Charlie and brought him home. We thought he'd forget about Frank Brown's pasture. But Charlie must have heard the call on the wind and he immediately responded. It was the middle of August now and Charlie was gone again.

"He can't be but one place," Finn said. "He's in Frank Brown's pasture. We'd better leave him there a week or two. Frank's got seven or eight head of heifers and cows in his pasture. Give Charlie a little time there. Charlie's never visited a pasture yet where there's ever been the second call for him."

"It's strange Charlie never comes home after he's been on a lark until we go after him," Pa said.

Finn and I had been mowing grass in the meadow below the house. Pa was chopping black-locust sprouts from the new-ground corn back up the Hollow from the Chatman house. We had unhitched the mules from the mowing machine and we were getting ready to eat when we saw Pa coming up the yellow-clay bank below the house. Pa was walking with quick steps and swinging his arms as he walked.

"Boys, I want to tell you I've had a narrow escape," he said.

"How was that, Pa?" Finn asked.

"That damned bull," he said.

"What happened?" Finn asked.

"Much as I have thought of that old rascal," Pa said. "I was coming down that narrow road back of the Chatman house. I guess the bull was coming from Frank Brown's pasture. I don't know. I was looking down at the path. You boys know how I walk sometimes—with my head down. I just happened to look up and couldn't believe there stood Old Charlie. But he had his head turned to one side looking with one eye."

"Charlie you know has been as gentle as a dog," Pa talked as fast as a blowing wind. "I could always go up and catch him any place in the pasture, rub his nose or his hocks and he would stand like a kitten. I spoke to him like I had always done. He started snorting and he held his nose down to the ground and blew sticks away! He pawed the earth and then he bellowed and made at me right in the narrows of the road. I was just lucky enough to side-step him and take to the brush. He wheeled and took after me. I made it for a little limby black gum that I went up like a cat. I just did get away from him in time."

"How long did he keep you up the tree?" Finn asked Pa.

"I've been up the tree all morning," Pa said. "I've not got to do a bit of work. There's going to have to be something done with that bull! I don't believe he ever would have left the tree if it hadn't been for a cow bawling in our pasture. He left the tree and I still stayed up there until I watched him walk over to the fence and go over seven wires just like it wasn't there. He never even tipped the top strand with his hoof."

"I didn't know he's like that," I said. "I would have been more careful around him."

"It would pay you to be, Shan," Pa said. "I was going up that narrow road and he was coming down. One of us had to give the road to the other. It's the first time I've met a bull on a path like this. He won't give a inch of road to anybody."

"You didn't have red on you, did you?" Finn asked.

"Just my face is tanned red from working in the fields," Pa said. "It's not the color of red that disturbs a bull."

"What are you going to do with him?" Finn asked.

"I'm going to take him back to Erf," Pa said. "I'm not going to take time to send for Erf to come with his truck to get him. I'm going to put a ring in his nose and take him back home this afternoon. Something else I've not told you boys about. That bull hasn't been properly weaned. When that cow bawled he went to her just like a calf that was never weaned. I walked over in the pasture and I caught him. No wonder the cows don't do any good milking when he's in the pasture with them."

"How can he get to the cows with horns as long as he's got," I asked Pa.

"Turns his horns to one side," Pa said. "He's been milking all of our cows but one and she wouldn't let him. I stood right there and watched him. I know what I saw with my own eyes is the truth."

"There'll certainly be enough white-faced calves born in this neighborhood," I said. "Next spring we'll see white-faced calves with every cow and heifer in this neighborhood."

"To think when our bull went to the other pastures then came home to us as poor as a snake," Pa said. "No wonder he soon gained in weight. He had plenty of milk to drink. Think of all the time we've lost from our crops running after Old Charlie."

"He's been a Pharaoh's plague to our cows," Finn said. "He gave them the pink eye, relieved them of their milk, and wasn't a bit loyal, but they love him."

"Are you going to take him back to Erf Bailey?" I asked Pa. "We've never had a bull like him."

"I know it," Pa said. "He's a real bull! He's a great one! I hate to see him go. I know he's got faults but I hate to see him go!"

Then Pa's face looked real bright and his eyes sparkled. He always looked like this when he had an idea about something.

"I've always wanted to do something for this community," he said. "I've not been able to do it! Now I have the idea!"

His eyes sparkled brighter. A smile came over his face.

"What is it, Pa?" I asked.

"I'm going to keep Old Charlie at all cost," Pa said. "It was an awful thought I had about taking him back. He's a great bull—the only one I've ever owned that can do it!"

"What's that, Pa?" Finn asked.

"He can lift the scrub cattle in this community to a higher level and make our farmers more prosperous. By keeping him I can help this whole community. I'm going to keep him. I'm going to do my bit for my community and neighbors in my day and time."

℥ *Maybelle's First-born* ℥

"**H**ow do you feel, Maybelle?" Tangie asked.
Her face was pink and dotted with little
beads of perspiration white in the morning sun.
She had walked up the path through the dew-wet grass
where little blades had caught between her toes. Damp
dust was sticking to her bare feet. Tangie was my sister-in-
law. She was Dave's youngest and his last unmarried
sister. Tangie was sixteen, very tiny, wasp-waisted, with
very large blue eyes and sharp cheek bones. Dave had
five sisters and Tangie was the smallest and prettiest.
And she was terribly interested in me.

"I had a bad night last night," I told her. "And it looks
like I'm going to have a rough day."

"Looks like God would have given us perfect parts for
our bodies, Maybelle, so we wouldn't have all this pain
and misery," Tangie said. She stood there looking at me

with sadness in her large blue eyes. "Looks like God would have given us good teeth."

"But He certainly didn't give them to me," I said. "My tooth is giving me plenty of trouble."

"I know," Tangie sighed. She looked at me as if she wanted to do something but she couldn't. "I know it's awful, Maybelle, the pain and misery you're having. I believe the swelling has gone down."

"Not that I can tell it," I said. I put my hand on my jaw and the swelling felt as big as a goose egg. "I've never had a tooth like this one. I had a bad tooth once and Doc Fitch pulled it. He was a body doctor and not a tooth doctor. He didn't do a thing but stick the forceps back and get a-hold of the tooth and pull it out. I thought my time had come for a minute. But soon I felt fine without all that pain. I wish I had this tooth out!"

"Yes, but your time of delivery is near at hand," Tangie said. "You know how Ma and Pa and all Dave's sisters and brothers feel about your goin' to a tooth doctor now! After your delivery go to a tooth doctor and have something done to that pizened tooth, but don't go now! You want your child to be born normal, don't you? You pull your tooth now, your first-born will have a cleavage in the roof of the mouth! Don't take chances, Maybelle. Pa and Ma've always gone by the signs. And there are ten of us all a-livin' and not a one afflicted in body and mind!"

"But I'm a-goin' to be afflicted in body and mind if I don't get rid of this pain, Tangie," I said. "You don't understand how painful a little tooth can be!"

It was eight in the morning. I'd walked up from Dave's Pa and Ma's home where he had brought me in my affliction so his mother could help me. I'd not wanted to leave our own two-room little house on the ridgetop. Dave believed I might be safer down in the valley so if I had to be carried out it would be easier going down the wagon road in the valley than to try to carry me on a set of bedsprings down a winding narrow path from the mountaintop. And whether I believed in "Ma" Adams' remedies or not, I had to accept them.

Since last night was a bad one for me, "Ma" Adams decided to change her remedy. Last night I had a big piece of fat pork bound to my jaw to "draw" the swelling. But it didn't draw the swelling and it hadn't stopped the pain. This morning at seven "Ma" Adams had brought me up to the white oak shade trees where she had always done her family wash in summer months. And here she had sat me down in a rocker. She filled a lard can with ashes taken from the wood furnace where she built fires to boil her clothes. She poured hot water down among the wood ashes, almost too hot for me to stand, and she had me sit in the rocker with my feet and legs up nearly to my knees in the hot wood ashes to draw the pizen from my tooth and the swelling from my jaw.

"I don't want your first-born to be afflicted, Honey," she said. "The cleavage in the mouth is a terrible thing. When a young child with cleavage tries to talk it goes 'yam-yam.' And to hear one is a pitiful thing. Maybelle, you're the wife of my son, Dave! Suffer now with that tooth and have a healthy first-born! And there are ways to prevent such if we apply the old-time remedies. Wood ashes from the Kentucky oaks is a powerful medicine. The ashes will not only draw the swelling and ease the pain but they will almost draw the tooth from your mouth."

I'd been suffering day and night with my left eyetooth,

the same tooth, so Dave told me, in a horse or mule's mouth that sometimes had to be knocked out with a chisel to keep the animal from goin' blind. I wondered while I sat there if I might not lose my right or left eye. And I thought about how a little thing like a tooth could cause so much trouble and maybe cause me to lose my eye or maybe cause my first-born to have an affliction. It was about ready to be born, for every time I put my feet into the hot ashes in the lard can it gave me a lot of trouble.

"Must be a boy," I thought. "No little girl baby can kick that hard. He can't be afflicted the way he can kick."

But I didn't tell my thought to Tangie and "Ma" Adams. I didn't tell Dave and "Pa" Adams when they came in to dinner or at night when the day in the fields was done. It was tobacco settin' time.

My feet and legs felt like they were on fire. "Ma" Adams came and put the fat meat poultice back on the outside of my jaw. She took the light burley tobacco crumbs from her apron pocket and made a little cloth sack to hold them. She put this poultice inside my mouth against my tooth. Since I had the fat pork on the outside and a tobacco poultice inside, I just couldn't understand what swellin' really was now. I doubt that "Ma" Adams knew. She'd been too busy birthin' and raisin' her five daughters and five sons. She had told me more than once she didn't have to worry about a pizened tooth for she'd lost all of her teeth when Dave, her seventh child and my husband, was born. And I'd not minded her telling me this, but when she said I'd be better off without teeth since God hadn't made 'em perfect I couldn't go along with her.

I didn't say anything because she was my mother-in-law and Dave had brought me down off the mountain to the valley to stay in her home. Many expectant mothers who couldn't be carried out had been planted on Laurel Ridge overlooking Laurel Valley. And I didn't want to be planted there when I felt my first-born kicking for dear life to be born and breathe the Laurel Valley air. I'd stand the hot ashes on my feet and legs and the tobacco poultice to my swollen gum and the fat meat poultice to my goose-egg-size swollen jaw. I wanted to live. I was determined to live. I would endure to the end to live.

"If Tangie would only go away and leave me to my thoughts," went through my mind. "If she'd just leave and let me endure my pain in silence."

"Ma wants me to check the water in the lard can to see if it's hot enough," she said.

"Tangie, it's as hot as I can bear," I said. "If it's any hotter it will scald my legs until the skin peels off."

"Better to have your skin peel off, Maybelle, for it will grow again than to have your first-born with the parted mouth roof," she said. "Maybe you remember Sad-Sam Roberts who went from birth to death with the parted mouth roof. His words were hard to understand. He talked with a yam-yam sound and his words went together. Ah, that poor fellow!"

"Yes, I remember Sad-Sam," I said. "And don't you think one minute, Tangie, while sitting here under these trees of a day and lying in the bed at night, I've not given thought to him and my first-born. I'll endure if I can, Tangie, but I don't want any more hot water in the ashes!"

"There is no more I can do now," Tangie said. "I'll be back in the tenth hour. I'll leave you to your thoughts."

"And my misery too," I said as she walked away.

"How pretty Dave's sister is now," I thought. "She will

marry and lose her white perfect teeth and her wasp-like waist. She'll lose them when she starts child bearing and working in the fields beside her husband like I have worked beside Dave. Three years I have worked beside him in the fields before I could conceive to bear us a child."

While I sat in my rocking chair, I thought of how wonderful it would be to be well again and be out with Dave stooping over and setting the green tobacco plants in the long rows. How much better it would be than sitting here with a painful left eyetooth, one that decayed near the gum line and broke off a month ago.

Now, I wiggled my toes in the thick watery wood ashes as I sat and thought about the past. Even when I thought about my baby, the pains didn't bother me so much. I could endure. I knew the water had cooled in the ashes and the pain was less now and I didn't want any more hot water added. I didn't want my feet and legs to scald and peel off. I was having enough pain as it was. And I thought about my own father and mother. I wished they knew about my condition and that they would come and visit me. My mother and father, my six sisters, and my five brothers didn't believe in the signs and the old remedies like the Adamses. While I sat wiggling my toes in the ashes and holding my hand over the poultice of fat meat on my jaw, I felt the pains from my tooth cut through the flesh across my face like darts of lightning cut the sultry air on a summer evening just before a rain. I hoped and prayed somebody would come from my home. I was homesick to see somebody from Three Prong Valley where my people, the Morrisons, lived.

At eleven o'clock "Ma" Adams came. She walked up the path with her sleeves rolled up showing her brown arms.

She had been hoeing in her garden. She was smoking her pipe, holding the long stem firmly between her toothless gums.

She took the pipe from her mouth, looked at me and said, "Honey, how is that tooth?"

"As full of pain as ever," I replied.

Then she stooped over the lard can and dipped her fingers into the dirty wood-ash water. "No wonder," she said. "The water is too cold to let the ashes draw."

"But that hot water," I sighed. I almost cried. "I can't stand it! It's scalded my legs and feet already. 'Ma' Adams, the remedy is worse than the cure!"

"But you must endure the pain awhile longer," she told me. She pointed a chiding finger at my face. "Pulling a tooth of a pregnant woman will sure bring the cleavage of the mouth to the little unborn."

So she went over and dipped a bucket of hot water from the kettle. Steam rose from the boiling bubbling water. When she poured it into the lard can in a tiny stream she was careful for it not to strike my legs. She'd pour and then take a stick and stir the ashes and I began to feel a new warmth and then heat. I began to holler that it was setting my legs on fire.

"Enough, enough," I shouted when she added another pint. "If you pour more hot water into that can I'm a-takin' my feet and legs out of there!"

"Easy, my child," she said. "Endure until the ease comes and the child is here."

"I've endured this for a week," I said. "There has been no letup of the pain! You know I don't smoke or chew tobacco and this poultice on my gum is about to make me sick!"

"I've smoked since I was twelve," she said. "And it

hasn't killed me yet. Can the Morrisons stand pain like the Adamses? Can a Morrison woman have her baby one day and be in the field in two more days?"

"Yes, 'Ma' Adams, she can," I said. "But never has a Morrison man or woman used this kind of remedy for the toothache!"

She filled her pipe with tobacco from her apron pocket, dipped up a living coal of fire from the furnace, and began to puff the blue wind-colored smoke from her long-stem pipe. She puffed the smoke as natural as a minnow breathes water through its gills.

"This will ease the pain," she said as she walked away.

"I hope and pray it does," I said.

I watched the blue trail of smoke follow her as she went back to her garden.

At noon, Tangie brought me mashed potatoes, pea soup, and milk. But I didn't want vittals. The tobacco poultice left a bitter taste in my mouth. I couldn't eat because my mouth was too swollen and sore. When Dave and "Pa" Adams came in from the field, they came up where I was sitting and Dave shed tears when he saw the misery I was in.

"Maybe by tonight you'll be better," Dave said. "Ma's remedies are sure-fire."

"Maybe, Dave," I said.

Dave had to go back to the house, eat his dinner, and go back to the field. Dave had to work. Spring was here. The ground fed us. And we had to be up-and-doing. Instead of his being with me, I ought to be with him. If it hadn't been for my tooth, I would have been with him. I would have worked up to the time of delivery.

We had saved our money for this. We had planned to

have a baby doctor from Blakesburg, Doc Heberlin, until I moved from my home on the mountain down the valley to Dave's home. "Ma" Adams changed our plans.

"Honey, payin' him twenty-five dollars to deliver your first-born is outrageous," she said. "Let Old Effie do it. She only charges five dollars. And she delivered my ten. All sound in body and mind. Some haven't got good teeth but our Lord didn't intend for all of us to have good teeth! Save twenty of the twenty-five dollars and buy you a heifer calf to make you a cow. This will save your comin' off the mountain and carryin' milk from here."

When Dave agreed with his mother on her plan for us, I went along too but it went against the grain. I loved Dave enough to work beside him in the fields in growing season and I helped him harvest our crops in the fall. I did my housework, too. I wouldn't go against him when he took his mother's advice.

"Ma" Adams came out in her slat bonnet to hoe the early young corn, peas, and beans in the garden. She was always punctual. By one o'clock she had finished with dinner, washed the dishes, and was out at work. She helped "Pa" Adams just like I helped my Dave. We women in the hills worked beside our men and we did our housework, cooked the meals, and bore our babies. We were not a lazy breed.

I must have been asleep in all my pain and misery when Rags, "Pa" Adams' hound, woke me up barkin'. As I looked down toward the garden, I saw my sister, Daisy, comin' up the path. "Ma" Adams walked out of the garden with her hoe.

"Welcome, Daisy," "Ma" Adams greeted my sister. "I 'spect you've come to see Maybelle."

"Yes, I have, Mrs. Adams," Daisy said.

"Well, she is in a heap of misery," "Ma" Adams said. "She is sufferin' from a tooth and is ready to deliver. There's danger!"

"Well, I don't know why there should be any danger," Daisy said. "Can't she have her tooth pulled?"

"To pull the tooth now would make her first-born have the cleavage in the mouth," "Ma" Adams said. She knocked the fire from her pipe and put it on top of the gatepost.

"Mrs. Adams, I've never heard that before," Daisy told her. "Where is Maybelle? In the house in bed?"

"No, she's up there!"

"Here I am, Daisy," I said. "I'm glad you've come!"

"Ma" Adams came up the path with Daisy.

"Maybelle, what is this?" Daisy asked. "Feet in a lard can of what?"

"Hot water and wood ashes."

"Poultices on your jaw?"

"Fat meat on my jaw and a tobacco poultice on my gum."

"It's to draw the swelling and ease the pain," "Ma" Adams said.

"How long have you used all this?"

"One week," I replied.

"Has it drawn the swelling and eased the pain?"

"The swelling grows and the pains get sharper," I replied.

"How far is it over the hill to Blakesburg from here?"

"About three miles," I replied.

"I've never heard of anything like this," Daisy said. "Get your feet out of the lard can, take that poultice of fat pork from your jaw, and spit that tobacco out. You're goin' with me if you're able."

"Oh, no," "Ma" Adams said. "You can't take her from here!"

"Yes, I can," Daisy said. "Maybelle is going to the dentist in Blakesburg even if I have to tote her."

"You won't have to tote me," I said. "I can still walk."

"I've walked six miles here to see you, Maybelle," Daisy said. "I can walk three miles more."

"Ma" Adams looked hard at Daisy.

"I'm not foolin', Mrs. Adams," Daisy said. "The Morrison women are great workers and long-distance walkers. And I don't believe in hot wood ashes on the feet to draw the swelling from a tooth."

"All right, Maybelle," "Ma" Adams said, "if your first-born is afflicted, I'm not the cause."

"I'll remember that," I said.

I had my feet out of the lard can of hot ashes. I threw the meat poultice on the ground. I threw the tobacco poultice in the fire. My feet and legs felt good in the cool wind. But the same wind was hot to my face and body!

"Then you're goin' with your sister?" "Ma" Adams said.

"Yes, I'm goin'," I said. "As soon as I get shoes on my feet."

"Don't change your dress, Maybelle," Daisy said.

I eased my feet into my slippers. They were tight but this didn't matter. Not after the hot wood ashes.

"You know the closest way to Blakesburg, Maybelle?"

"I sure do," I said. "Down the Right Fork of Academy Branch."

"Then, let's be on our way!"

« 4 9 »

"To think of the cleavage in the roof of the mouth," "Ma" Adams sighed. "Poor little innocent thing."

"Come on, Maybelle," sister Daisy said.

We walked away and left "Ma" standing by the gate. When I looked back she was getting her pipe off the gatepost. Then she took a last long look at us before we were around the bend and out of sight.

We didn't walk too fast because our path wasn't smooth. There were big rocks we had to walk around. We had to walk downhill and uphill and cross the creek two or three times. In one hour we were in Blakesburg. Daisy took me straight to Dr. Long's office.

"He's a real dentist," she said. "He went down in the gums and pulled the roots of a tooth for me."

"Is Ma Adams right about my baby's being born with a cleavage in the roof of the mouth if I have this tooth pulled?"

"You've heard that talk so long you're about to believe it, Maybelle," Daisy said. "You would have died with your feet in hot wood ashes, a fat pork poultice on your jaw, and a tobacco poultice on the inside of your mouth on your gum. This can't be any worse."

When we walked into Dr. Long's office a woman in white came to meet us.

"Tell Dr. Long it's an emergency," Daisy said.

"Just be seated," she said. "I'll see that he sees you."

She went through the door and came back with Dr. Long.

"Trouble?" he said.

"Plenty of trouble," my sister said. "Look at her tooth."

"Come in here where I can get a look."

He looked as he probed and I flinched.

"It's hard to numb an abscessed tooth," he said. "This has to come out."

"Dr. Long, if you pull this tooth do you believe my baby will be born with a cleavage in the roof of its mouth?" I asked.

"Where did you get such an idea?" he asked.

"Dr. Long, she's my sister and when I came to visit her, her mother-in-law had her with her feet in hot wood ashes in a lard can to draw the swellin' and ease the pain. She had a tobacco poultice on the gum and a fat meat poultice against the jaw."

Dr. Long rubbed the gum in two or three places and then he stuck me with a needle. I'd never had a tooth pulled before. This hurt but not half as much as the hot ashes in the lard can hurt my feet and legs.

"Just a little pain now and some more when I do some probing," he said. "But this is an emergency, all right. Claris, you tell Mrs. Murdock we'll be a little late for her appointment but we'll get to her."

Then Dr. Long said to me, "I don't see how you stood this tooth. How long have you used the ashes and poultice remedies?"

"A week, Doctor," I said.

"I don't see how you've lived."

Dr. Long looked at his watch. "Now, I must do more probing."

When he started probing around it did hurt.

"Yes, I feel that tooth," he said. "Does it hurt?"

"Just a little more," I said.

"You've got good pluck, Mrs. Adams," he said.

Then all of a sudden something seemed to give and pop and there was relief.

« 51 »

"Spit," Dr. Long said. "I've never pulled one like this."

When he pulled my tooth it was like a little volcano erupting. Dr. Long used swabs to clean my mouth. "It's the worst tooth I've ever pulled," he said. When he let me out of the chair, Daisy paid him.

"Are you sick?" he asked. "Do you feel faint?"

"I feel like I've been let out of a cage," I said. "I've been released from a pain cage! I've never felt better! No, I'm not sick. I feel fine. I feel like shouting!"

"I told Maybelle a dentist was better than all the remedies," Daisy told him.

"Now, take this medicine," he said. "Take it as I have prescribed and you'll be all right."

Daisy and I walked back to "Ma" Adams' house.

"She got it pulled, Mrs. Adams," Daisy said. "She couldn't have gone on with that tooth. She's a new woman!"

"Her poor first-born," "Ma" Adams sighed. "It will say 'yam-yam' when it tries to talk."

Daisy left me and said she was walking on to Three Prong Valley. I knew she'd never stay all night with "Ma" Adams.

"I'm a Morrison woman and the Morrison women are used to walking," she said. "Six more miles won't hurt me. The moon and stars will light my path."

Daisy had promised to come back when I was ready to deliver if Dave could get her word. Well, he couldn't get her word. The delivery came too soon. I slept as soundly as a log the first night after the tooth was pulled. Next night the pain came and Dave rode a mule and led one with an empty saddle. He went after Old Effie.

After I'd been in labor fourteen hours I said, "Take me to a body doctor. If you don't, I'm not goin' to make it."

I don't remember when they carried me out on the bedsprings. But they did. And I don't remember when they got me to Doc Heberlin's office and he sent me to the hospital where after twelve more hours I gave birth to a son.

But I remember the first words I said to Doc Heberlin when I came to: "Doc, is my baby's mouth all right?"

"What do you mean, Mrs. Adams?" he asked.

"Is the roof of his mouth all right?" I asked. "Is there a cleavage in the roof of his mouth?"

"No, why do you ask me that?"

"I just wanted to know," I replied.

Then I turned to my man, Dave, and said, "We have a fine son."

Well, I didn't know then but my Dave knew that due to Effie's midwifery I would never have another child. We went back to our two rooms on the mountain top. And I said to Dave, "We will work for this fine strong boy. He must go to school. We'll raise more corn and more tobacco and we'll move close enough to a school so he can go."

And we did. We sent him to the one-room school until he had finished. And we moved again where we rented another and bigger farm. But the school bus came near and he rode it to Maxwell High School. We worked to see that our son got the opportunities we didn't have. And that's the reason today he's one of the young men who has a good job. He is twenty-four and he's a crane operator for the Docco Steel Mills. He makes over eight hundred dollars a month, more than we make working a whole year for a crop of tobacco. Our son has the best job of any man, young or old, among the Morrisons or the Adamses. And if he hadn't had that high school diploma, he never could have applied for a job at the Docco Steel Mills. I had the feeling that remedies and times had changed and youth had to change with them.

✠ *Victory and the Dream* ✠

THIS was Monday morning, in early April, the beginning of my one week's spring vacation from Greenwood High School. I would have a change from Caesar, English, History, Plane Geometry, and Physical Geography, all right. I would be forgetting all about these subjects in my spring vacation. It was just good daylight now and I stood in our barn lot with the leather checklines in my hands to hold back a pair of young frisky mules. They were coming four-year-olds just when they were in their greatest strength of power and work. And I was sixteen, six feet tall, 180 pounds, a right guard on the Greenwood High School football team, played baseball, ran on the track team and walked five miles to and from school. I didn't know my strength either.

My father, a wiry, slender, red-faced man with big blue eyes and a long big nose, stood beside me.

"Now watch these mules, Shan," he said. "You've been in school and not had enough exercise to plow in new ground. These mules can get you down. Plowing will be rough among the stumps in the new-ground field."

My father didn't have to tell me the plowing would be rough in new ground, for I had plowed in new ground before. Under the surface of the ground there was a solid mass of roots from the trees that had been cut from the surface of the land, piled in brush heaps and log heaps and burned so we could have more land for crops. I had helped my father late last autumn, and all winter long on the late afternoons and Saturdays I was home, to clear the eight acres of land. I was now going to plow this land. My father had been called back to his job on the railroad section, after his being off due to lack of work in the winter months. I told him I would plow this new ground, all of it if I could, in spring vacation. He said he thought it was impossible, since one acre per day would be good plowing in new ground. He said I had eight days in plowing, one day in harrowing and one day in planting, with the help of a man for two days to follow me, one day to pack roots from the field and one day to follow with a planter when I laid off the corn rows.

"You know how a cutter plow can shake your shoulders when the cutter or the plowpoint strikes a solid root, a stump or a rock underground," he said. "I wish I could be with you but I can't. I must walk across the hill to join with the boys at the toolhouse. It will be much easier pulling a handcar eight miles up the tracks to my work on the section than to walk between the handles of the plow in that new ground today."

"I don't know about your work," I told him, "but don't

you worry about me. What I worry about is the mules. Will they be able to stand me?"

Then my father laughed loudly.

"Shan, who do you think you are?" he said. "A young Samson? That pair of mules, give them time, follow them if you can ten hours in that new ground and no one will have to rock you to sleep when you get home tonight. You're just out of school and don't have to work that long. I'll say follow them eight hours and you'll be doing a man's work. You could work these mules fourteen hours a day in that new ground, take the harness off them at night and let them go to their water hole, and they'll run and kick up their heels all the way. One mule can pull that cutter plow through the new ground. That cutter plow is a little too much for one mule, but it lacks a lot of being enough for two mules. Well, good luck to you."

He left me in the early dawn in our barn lot while he hurried back to the house to get his dinner bucket and be on his five-mile walk to work. I moved the leather lines and said softly, "Gitup" to my mules, Jack and Barney. They stepped briskly pulling a sled on which I had put the cutter plow, a double-bitted ax, hatchet, my dinner bucket, feedboxes and corn for my mules. The reason we always used a sled on the land, which was harder to pull than a wagon, was because the sled didn't leave tracks like the rims of a wagon wheel for spring rains to run down and make ditches. And the reason I was hauling the plow and not dragging it behind my team was the plowpoint and cutter always broke the skin of the earth and caused ditches. My father never would let us drag a plow behind the mules off a hillside. We had to unhitch the mule from the plow, lead the mule and carry the plow, and this was the reason we never had a ditch on our farm. We protected our land's surface just the same as we protected the skin on our bodies. We had to protect our land, so my father thought, for our land fed our family and our livestock.

It was less than a half mile to the eight-acre clearing. My mules followed the path made by the cattle from the barn lot to the first gate. And when I opened the first gate and drove the mules through, here lay the charcoal-dark earth burnt over by fire when we burned the brush piles. I could see where each brush pile and log heap burned, by a gray-ash thickness against the dark. Now, I put my dinner-bucket bales over a broken limb head-high on the tree at the end of the field. And here I tied the sack of corn up to a branch of this tree. I set my ax up against the tree's gray-barked trunk. I had brought it along, so if my cutter hitched on a root too big to cut with a hatchet, I would have the ax. Then I tied my hatchet on the locust beam of my cutter plow, a plow made for strength and durability. My father had made this plow. Now, I unhitched my mules from the sled and hitched them to the plow. I didn't know how tough the plowing would be but I would soon find out.

There was a small valley in the center of the field. On either side, north and south, there were gentle slopes slanting up toward the ridgelines. On the west end of the field the valley was deeper and there was a perpetual small stream that filled a water hole where my mules would get water. And here was a small spring where I would drink. And here on the north slope is where I would start plowing first—when I drove the mules down with the plow hitched behind them, for here it wouldn't matter if the plow did make a mark, because all this ground would be plowed. Soon my plow was in the new-ground earth and I walked behind the finest young mules in our part, mules who knew more about plowing than most men, and I heard roots snapping underground like small threads. I had that good feeling of strength, a young man with power, plowing wonderful animals imbued with know-how of the plow. I had the feeling that everything was going to go well. I was plowing my first furrows before six o'clock, the time my father was supposed to have walked five miles and reached his railroad-section handcar.

My mules, Jack and Barney, wanted to move steadily along. When the cutter on the plow came up against an object underground, a root or stone, they eased up against their collars to feel whether it would "give" or if it was solid. If solid it could be an underground stump; then it was my duty to lift up the plow and set it point down on the other side of the stationary object. My mules soon learned that I knew how to handle a plow, for now I had faith in myself as never before. Now, we were moving up the dark slope of new-ground hill before the sunrise. And the plow went down and brought up soil that was not as dark as the surface. How wonderful the earth looked where I had plowed. My father wanted corn planted here. After the corn was planted and began to break through the ground, one of us would go through the field and plant beans beside the ground corn, and plant pumpkins seeds around the fertile leaf-rot loamy places. There was no better land in our hill country than good new ground for corn, beans and pumpkins. Soon the blackbirds and the cowbirds had found us and were following the furrow behind my plow. They were busy picking up the worms and bugs while we inched and inched up the slope, cutting roots and turning the rich loam over.

When the morning sun first peeped above the tender-leafed trees, we had plowed a broad strip of new-ground earth. And as the minutes made hours and passing hours climbed toward midday, we gradually moved up the hill. We were plowing faster than I had thought we would. On my wrist I had a small watch, but I could have told time by the sun. When my shadow was short enough for me to step on my head, then it was twelve noon. I watched my shadow as I plowed and when it became short enough for me to step on my head, I checked with my watch and it was twelve noon. Then I unhitched my mules and drove them to their water hole where they drank clear, clean, cool water. In a spring close by where the water bubbled up from the earth, I too drank some clear, clean, cool water. And now we went to the shade tree at the end of the field, where I put corn in the boxes for my mules while I sat on the sled and ate my lunch. At our home our animals were always watered and fed before we ate.

After thirty minutes for noon, my mules and I went back to our water hole and spring for fresh water after our noon meals, then back to the plow. All afternoon I followed behind the plow. And once or twice I wondered if the advice my father gave me about the plow handles shaking my shoulders in the new ground wasn't correct. But now I had a challenge. And my mule team, it seemed to me, seemed to know and accept the challenge too, that we were working for a goal, and a notable achievement. Since my father had begun working on an eight-hour day now, he went to work at seven, ate his lunch at eleven and took an hour for lunch from eleven until twelve, and quitting time was four. If he hurried he could be home by five o'clock. But I was surprised to see him standing at the end of the cornfield smiling at me. I looked at my watch and it was fifteen after five.

"You're moving," he said.

I stopped my mules, who must have felt a little like I did, not as brisk now as they had this morning.

"How much do you think we've plowed?" I asked.

"Over an acre and a half," he replied. I would take his judgment on land. When we cleared a piece of land he could estimate its size to within one or two square rods or under. "Yes, a good acre and a half!"

"I'm going to plow another round," I said. "Then we are quitting for today."

"It's good-looking dirt," he said. He bent over and gathered a handful and looked at it. Then he let it fall between his fingers to the ground. "This will bring good corn, vines full of beans and big pumpkins over the field close enough to walk on."

My father was well pleased with what we had accomplished. The only places on my mules that showed any sweat were under their collar pads and where their harness had fit snugly against their bodies. My father led Barney, and I led Jack back around the road to the barn. Here we took the harness from them, took their bridles off so they could first wallow in the sand then go to their water hole for a drink. When we turned them free, first each lay down on the place where he wallowed and Jack turned over uphill, which was a feat a young animal seldom did and an old one or a tired one, young or old, couldn't do. After they had wallowed, first on one side and then the other, each jumped up and shook the dry sand from his body then took off over the slope toward the water hole kicking up his heels.

"I told you, Shan," my father said. "Ah, I wish I felt as young and as strong as them young mules."

We went inside the barn where I threw hay down from

the barn loft into their mangers while my father counted out eight nice ears of corn to put in each feedbox.

"Well, how do you feel after your first day at the plow?" he asked me.

"Wonderful," I said. "If the weather stays clear we'll get more done tomorrow than we did today."

My father had always fed the mules at our home. He was out of bed at four, dressed and went to feed the mules. My mother was up from bed, dressed, and was preparing breakfast so my father could go to his work early and I could be off to mine. And after breakfast just as the morning light was breaking through, I harnessed my mules and led them to the field. I took them to their water hole and let them drink, then I drove them up the slope and hitched them to the plow. Just a few minutes after good daylight, I was behind my mules and we were moving around the slope. Before sunup, we had plowed a strip of dark new-ground earth around the slope twenty feet wide. We were climbing toward the top of the north side. We were beginning to see daylight among the oaks on the ridge. We could see the blue morning April sky beyond.

Furrow by furrow we climbed up the slope in the coolness of this April morning while I breathed fresh wind that blew across the open new-ground field from the tender-leafed oaks on the high slopes, and from the rustling beech, poplar and elm leaves down in the valley. Overhead the parent birds flew with worms in their bills for their hungry young, some glided on the updrafts of air. I heard cawing in a nest among the tall pines, above the south slope of the new ground where I would be plowing when this side was finished. In this April world birdsongs were in the air. I heard the redbird singing at the far end of the field. Somewhere above me among the oaks on the ridgeline I heard a blue jay scolding. Everywhere wild birds were on the wing. They filled the air with song. This is a good time to be alive, I thought as I breathed deeply of the fresh air. Plowing this new ground would put me into good shape for baseball this spring.

When noon came I had only a strip of about ten feet left before I would have this side done. We had considered this north slope of the new ground about three acres. When I led the mules to the water hole to let them drink and to get myself a drink from the spring, I came alive with the thought: if it didn't rain, I had a chance of plowing, harrowing and planting this field in six days. After the mules and I had water we went back to the poplar shade at the end of the field, where I fed them corn in their boxes. I ate the lunch my mother had prepared for me. It had been a long time since 4:30 when we had eaten breakfast at my home. Now, I felt very much like eating my lunch. After I had finished lunch and the mules had eaten their corn, I watched them rest first one leg and then the other. Mules are smarter than people believe, I thought. They know how to relax their bodies in a little time allowed them for rest.

There is that small strip up there at the top to plow, I thought. We must be on our way to work.

My mules drank slowly of the clear, clean water from their water hole and I drank of the good, clean, clear water boiling straight up from the ground in my spring. Now, up the hill to the plow where I let their trace chains down on their harness and hitched them to their single trees. Now we were plowing again, where the sweep of bright April winds blew over, wind that was cool to our bodies and wind that was good to breathe. Furrow by furrow we inched up to the top. The smaller side of the new ground had been finished in a little over a day and a half. Now, I had a sense of accomplishment which gave me a wonderful feeling, like winning a football game, only this was greater.

Plowing this new-ground field, harrowing and planting it in record time would be a greater achievement than winning a football game. My mules walked down the hill over the plowed ground, while I walked behind, lifting the plow as high as I could to keep it from making a ditch. I couldn't put a ditch here, not now, for this ground was already plowed and it would soon be harrowed and planted. Down in the little valley that separated the north and south slopes of this new ground, we began again at the bottom. And at the bottom of anything I certainly never had any sense of accomplishment. I never liked the bottom except for a place where I had to begin.

By the end of this day we ought to have a showing made on this side, I thought. I had no one to talk to and sometimes I found myself talking to the mules. In high school I was with people. I was with my classmates and teachers and I was always talking. But out here on this new field I walked alone hour by hour.

Gray ash lay on the ground where brush heaps and log piles had burned, and the earth was like a dark skin with gray spots. Furrow by furrow, go to one end of the field, there turn and back to the other with my mules walking steadily along, while the small roots snapped in front of my cutter like white threads. Sometimes my cutter hitched behind a large white tree root, which caused me to take my hatchet from the plow beam and cut the root. The hardest kind of a root for the cutter to snap in two was a locust root, the same kind of wood that my plow stock was made of for durability. It took a sharper blade than a cutter to cut locust roots, and this is where I had to use my hatchet often.

Here my plow turned up the roots of fern, saw-brier and white knotty lumps of greenbrier roots. Two, three and then four o'clock. And now we were making a showing at the bottom of this slope. Very soon my father would be here and I would be glad for him to see. I had the feeling now that I might be able to accomplish a faint dream I had had in the beginning. I knew that one acre a day was considered good plowing in new ground by all the mountainside farmers in my area. I had in the back of my head before I ever stuck the plow in the ground, what if my young frisky mules and I could plow this field, harrow, lay off the corn rows and plant it in my week of spring vacation! This would be a spring that I would always remember.

While I was having my dreams behind the plow, adding furrow upon furrow now on the south slope, while my little wristwatch ticked away the seconds and the sun slanted toward the western hills, I looked up to see my father. He was coming down across the plowed ground on the other side of the small stream. He had a half-moon smile on his face and from one hand he was letting a handful of soft loam sift through his fingers.

"Shan, I can't believe it," he said. "You're really moving this work. You've got the best plow mules and you're the best plowman in this area."

I stopped my mules so that they and I could get our second breaths. The ground where wild ferns had grown here was a little steeper and the pulling of the cutter plow had been a little harder on the mules and on me.

"If the weather stays fair and you keep on going like

yesterday and today, you might set some kind of record here by the end of the week," he said in a pleasant voice. He stepped over the little stream and walked up to where my mules and I were resting.

"How much does it look like we have plowed?" I asked him.

"Very close to two acres, I believe," he said.

"Could we have plowed that much?"

"Yes, very close to it," he replied. "I like the way you handle the mules. You work as a team together. I never hear you holler at them. I don't know you're plowing until I see you."

"I don't have to holler or scold Jack and Barney," I said. "I've never touched one with a line. Best mule team I've ever worked with, but I've not worked with very many."

He stood there beside me, his face was very red, after his ten miles of walking to his handcar and his eight hours working on the railroad tracks. My father didn't have a pound of excessive weight on his five-foot-eight frame. He never weighed more than 140 pounds and not less than 126 after he grew to manhood, yet he worked beside the giants of his day.

"You look tired," I said to him.

"I am tired," he said. "I dogged steel today. You know who was my lifting partner? Slick Timberlake!"

"And he is all man and weighs 260," I said. "No wonder you are tired, lifting beside him!"

"Yes, but I'm proud of you," he said. "You're going to high school. And I didn't have a school in my day to attend. And you will work, Shan! I've got confidence in you, my son!"

This made me feel very good. My mules and I had

enough for the day. It was now 5:30 and time to quit. We had had a good day today. The dark charcoal ash that lay over this field was quickly disappearing. My father unhitched Barney and led him away and I unhitched Jack and we followed.

"You suppose they'll run and kick up their heels again like they did last night?" I said.

"Sure they will," he replied.

When we took them to the barn and took the harness off, they wallowed, first one side and then the other against the dry warm sand and then they jumped up, kicked their heels high into the air and ran toward the water hole. I felt good they were able to do this. I had wondered if my father's young mules could stand as much as I could in my young dream that had come alive. At the end of this second day, I had the feeling of accomplishment. I had more confidence.

Now, on the third day, which I thought might be the decisive one, my mules and I were in the new ground and they were hitched to the plow and I was walking between the handles at five o'clock. I thought we would work more hours today, now that I knew my mules could stand all the plowing I could stand and maybe more. I thought we would take an hour at noon to rest and eat and then plow on until six o'clock. On this third day, plowing when the sun peeped over the trees with splinters of light, and while the April winds were blowing and birds were flying and singing . . . breathing the cool fresh wind of morning, how wonderful it was to be young and able to plow with a mule team, to go to high school and play right guard on our Greenwood High School football team! And now how wonderful it was to have this dream to work for. When I unhitched the mules to get a drink before we ate, plowed furrows reached high upon the south slope.

After I had eaten lunch and my mules had eaten their corn, shelled and mixed with sweet feed for I had a new diet for them today, we had a good rest. I sat on a giant brace root of the big tree and leaned back against its gray rough bark. I watched them, standing by their feedboxes on the sled, relaxing first one leg and then the other. And they seemed to doze with half-closed eyes. But I never closed my eyes and I didn't go to sleep. From five to eleven had been six hours of work. From eleven to twelve we ate and rested. And now, from twelve to six we would be plowing. Back to their water hole and they drank and I drank nearby at my spring. And then back to the plow, higher upon the hill now, I fastened their trace chains to the single trees and we were off.

This was the deciding day. Plowing seemed to grow easier on this south hillslope. My plow ran smoothly with few hitches when I had to lift and reset the point on the other side of the solid stump or rock. Plowing was so much easier that I thought, perhaps there were fewer roots in the ground on the south hillslope. And maybe there were. I would never know, for I didn't have time to examine the earth to see. I was following the plow as my mules pulled it on and on. When my father came at 5:30, he didn't disturb me. He sat at the end of the field and watched my mules and me go and come from one end of the field to the other until six o'clock. The last furrow came when we were going toward the end of the field where he was seated; he got up and walked toward me.

"It's six and time to quit," he said. "You and the mules have had enough. What a day! You've plowed over two acres today."

We unhitched the mules, took them to the barn and unharnessed them and let them wallow. And after wallowing they didn't run and kick up their heels. I didn't either. I went to the house with my father. He was tired and I was a little tired.

"Now, Shan, the sky is clear," he said at the supper table. "I don't think we will have rain this week. And if you average tomorrow as much plowing as you have the last three days, you will almost have the field plowed!"

"What did you say?" my mother said. "That field plowed in four days?"

"Yes," he replied.

My mother couldn't believe it.

"I've talked to Poss Sparks and he can help you on Friday when you'll be harrowing ground," he said. "He'll pick up roots and carry them off the field. You won't have time to do that."

My father had guessed right. On Thursday morning at five, Jack and Barney were pulling the plow at ten past five. And at noon when I unhitched them to go to the foot of the hill for water, I sensed victory. I knew if we finished the plowing today, that it would be an easy task to get the field harrowed tomorrow. Saturday we could get rows laid off, and the corn planted. We had a half hour for noon, then back to the water hole and spring and then to the plow. My mules must have sensed victory too, for they pulled the plow on and on. Time and the big push had not daunted them. And we never stopped, except for the hitches, all afternoon. Furrow by furrow until we plowed the last one at 5:30, I had the greatest sense of accomplishment I had ever had in my life. When my mules and I had reached the sled, my father walked through the gate by the poplar tree.

"It's plowed," I said. "Come take a look at this field now!"

His eyes looked as big as dollars and as bright as morning stars.

"Shan, if I had something I'd give it to you," he said. "I don't have it! I'd like to give you a present. I just can't believe it. No cutting and covering in your plowing! All the dirt is shoveled up as loose as a lettuce bed! What a work you have done here."

"What I've needed," I said. "It's that feeling, that great feeling of accomplishment . . . that I have done something. I've done something maybe no one has ever done before! If it just doesn't rain until we can finish this week, then I'll realize the big dream. And what a sense of accomplishment this will be! It's the big game to win."

I hitched the mules to the sled, for in the morning I would bring the sled back with the harrow on it. This was a harrow that my father had made by making a triangle of heavy yellow locust wood, bolting the pieces together. Then in the center he made a cross of locust wood and bolted it to the triangle. In these pieces he put railroad spikes for harrow teeth. On the triangle end he put a clevis and a double tree into which I could hook the single trees and the mules to them. My father was good at making our farm tools. If he hadn't been good at making them we wouldn't have had any, for he certainly wasn't able to buy them. Now, hitched to the sled, I drove the mules home. We unhitched, unharnessed them, let them wallow and drink. This afternoon they ran toward the water hole but they didn't kick up their heels.

Next morning I was at the field, had watered the mules, had them hitched to the harrow and had harrowed a third of the north slope when Poss arrived at seven.

"Say, what time do you go to work?" Poss asked with a chuckle.

"Five," I replied.

"I'll make up a couple of lost hours," he said.

He began to carry piles of roots from the field and stack them at the closest places on the outside of the field. By nine we had the north slope harrowed and Poss had carried the roots from the field. Now we began work on the south hillslope. And by eleven we were above the bluffs where the ferns had grown. Now we took time out for noon, giving the mules a drink at the water hole and drinking ourselves at the spring. Poss and I took the mules to the sled and fed them while we ate our lunches. He had brought his own lunch.

"Poss, do you have to go home tonight?" I asked him.

"No, I don't," he said.

"Then stay all night with me," I said. "We'll get up early in the morning and we can get this planted, maybe, tomorrow."

"Say, I'll do that," he said. "I'll tell your Pa to stop by home in the morning and tell Pa an' Ma I stayed with you last night so they won't be uneasy. How long did it take you to plow this rooty new ground?"

When I told him, he said, "I'll believe you, but a lot of people wouldn't."

That afternoon we finished harrowing the south side and Poss carried piles of the roots that the railroad-spike teeth in my harrow had gathered until I'd lift the harrow and leave a pile of roots. How smooth the plowed land looked now without roots over the surface. The ground was pulverized with the harrow teeth. Walled in by forest on all sides, here was a beautiful piece of farmland and, if it didn't rain tomorrow, this land would be laid off in corn rows and planted in corn. Now the big field, we called it, eight acres on my father's fifty-acre farm, was ready to be planted. I drove the mules with the harrow to the poplar tree. Poss and I unhitched the mules from the harrow and hitched them to the sled. Then we loaded the harrow back on the sled. And we laid the ax and hatchet on, for we wouldn't need them now. And talk about a sense of accomplishment—I had it now as I looked over this field before driving the mules toward the barn. When we got to the barn at 5:15 we met my father on his way to the field. He knew what had happened.

"Well, boys, I've got the seed corn and the corn planter waitin' for you over there in the corncrib," he said.

After supper Poss and I went to bed upstairs. He lay in one bed while I lay in another just across from him and we talked about baseball. Poss had never finished the eighth grade, but he played baseball on Greenwood's town team. He was one of their young left-handed pitchers. I never knew when we stopped talking and when I fell asleep. The next morning I heard my father's familiar voice waking my mother and then he turned toward the stairs and called for me. And I got up and woke Poss and we dressed and went downstairs to be ready for breakfast as soon as my mother prepared it and my father returned from the barn, where he had fed the mules, hogs, cows, livestock and chickens.

"Good luck to you," my father said as we left the house for the barn.

First we harnessed the mules when it wasn't yet light in their stalls. Then we loaded a two-bushel sack of seed corn on the sled. We hitched the mules to the sled. When we reached the field, light from the east was just breaking. At the poplar tree we unhitched the mules. Poss tied Jack to the tree while I hitched Barney to the cutter plow. I could use only one mule.

"Poss, I want to get this first row with the contour of the hill," I said.

I had been studying Physical Geography under Charles Haylor at Greenwood High School. I had studied about contours.

"This first row is a very important one," I told him.

When I sighted to an object at the far end of the field, I told Barney to get along. I tried to lay off the row as straight as if it had been surveyed. Behind me I heard the corn planter clicking when Poss took a long step and a short one. We were on the move. One row after another. My father had always said if I could do anything well on this earth I could lay off corn ground. By noon we had the north slope planted. Then we turned to the south slope. When I laid off a row, Poss was right behind me with the planter. And by noon we were above the bluffs where the ferns grew. Now, I took Barney to water and Poss went along and unhitched Jack and brought him to the water hole. The mules drank the cool water and Poss and I drank from the spring. Then we went to the sled, fed the mules and ate the lunches my mother had prepared for us.

"Shan, we're goin' to finish here today," Poss said. "Will anybody around here believe you plowed this, harrowed it and we planted it in your spring-vacation week?"

"I don't believe anybody would," I replied.

That afternoon I used Jack to lay off the ground while I let Barney rest. After lunch we watered the mules for the last time in the water hole where the water was cool and sweet. And we drank, ourselves, from the spring. Poss took Barney back to the poplar tree and tied him up so he could rest.

"We've got to get done this afternoon," Poss said. "It won't take us all afternoon."

And it didn't take us all afternoon. We had finished by 4:30.

Now I stood on the side of the south slope and looked back over our new-ground cornfield. I had the greatest sense of accomplishment I had ever had in my life. The job was finished. I had realized a dream, a dream that it could be done. Poss enjoyed my victory with me. He led Jack and carried his planter back to the sled and I carried the plow. The dream was finished. It was over.

We loaded the plow on the sled, put the seed corn we had not used with the plow. Then we hitched the mules to the sled and we drove to the barn. We put the seed corn back in the crib and the plow back in the tool shed. We unharnessed the mules, let them roll in the dry dust, then go for water. My father hadn't come from work yet. Usually on Saturdays he went to Greenwood and carried a sack of groceries home. When he came home at six, I had changed my clothes and was going to walk back across the mountain with Poss and on to Greenwood to see the Saturday-night movie. I had to walk over five miles to see one. But I was as happy as I had ever been. This would be my celebration. I felt there wasn't anything I couldn't do.

There wasn't a subject in Greenwood High School I couldn't pass. There wasn't a baseball game on our schedule we couldn't win. There wouldn't be a football game scheduled in the next two years when I'd be playing for Greenwood High School that we couldn't win. I knew now that I could go to college, even if my father didn't have any money to give me and I had none of my own. I knew that I could and I would find a way. There wasn't anything out there ahead of me, a difficult problem I couldn't solve or an object in my way I couldn't move. I had found that sense of accomplishment. I had needed it as much as any young man alive. Now I knew that I would never be whipped or defeated again. The world belonged to me as it had never belonged before. I had passed the turning point in my life.

☙ *Wild Plums* ☙

Two wild-plum trees, weighted with ripe red plums until their boughs swayed, were beckoning for me to come. I'd watched these trees since last April when they were two white clouds of blossoms. They grew not far from the road where widower George Woods lived. He was now an old man and he didn't have a wife like I had to make wild-plum jelly for him.

"You ought to have spoken a long time ago for the plums," Deanems said. "There aren't many wild plums this year. And since these have grown where anybody who drives past can see them, no telling how many people have asked Mr. Woods for them."

"My grandfather used to know Mr. Woods' father and my father knew Mr. Woods and I know his five sons," I said. "Three generations of us have lived near each other and we've always been friends."

"But just knowing somebody and not speaking in advance for the plums might not get them," she said.

"But it will help here," I said.

"Oh, I hope you get them," Deanems said. "We don't have any more wild-plum jelly. And you know how well we like it."

"I sure do," I said. I could taste wild-plum jelly, just a little tart, spread over half a hot biscuit. I liked to eat wild-plum jelly on hot biscuits on a winter morning, while I looked from our dining room window at the snow-covered hills. Then, I liked to follow the hot biscuit and wild-plum jelly with swallows of good hot coffee made from our free-stone water, drawn by an oaken bucket from out the well in the yard. "I just have to get the plums," I said.

I got in my pickup truck and was off over the Valley Road. I had a two-gallon bucket on the truck floor near my feet. I simply had to have two gallons of plums. I wanted more if I could get them. I drove down the Sandy River Road and turned onto the Big River Highway. After driving a mile down Big River, I looked over to my left and there were the two plum trees bending with fruit. They looked like white clouds last April but now they looked like two red-sunset clouds sitting right down on the ground. And I saw old man George Woods walking down the road, stooped with age, a bucket in one hand and a cane in the other. He was walking toward the plum trees. He was walking toward those two red clouds of ripe-red plums, filled with the kind of juice it took to make good wild-plum jelly. I turned off the main road and drove up the lane just as he arrived at the plum trees.

"Howdy, Mr. Woods," I said in a friendly way. I wanted to be friendly because I wanted some of his wild plums. I got out of the truck. He set his bucket down in the road and extended his hand to me. "You've got some nice wild plums here," I said.

"Yes, I have," he said. "But I don't believe I know you."

"Mick Powderjay's boy, Shan," I said.

"Oh, yes, Old Mick, he was a good friend of mine," he spoke softly. "Too bad he had to leave this world. But I guess we've all got to go sometime."

"My Grandpa Powderjay used to live beside your father in Lantern County up in Big Sandy River Valley. My father and you were friends all your lives. And I know your five sons, Joe, John, Jack, Tom and George Jr. too."

"Yes, for three generations we've been neighbors and friends," he said.

"Well, Mr. Woods, I've come to see if I could buy a couple of gallons of wild plums from you," I said.

"You got some last year from me, didn't you?"

"Yes, I did," I replied.

"But didn't you speak for them in advance?"

"Yes, I did."

"And this year you haven't spoken for them?"

"That's right," I said.

"Did you know I have about twenty people ahead of you," he said. "I can't furnish all the wild plums the people want. If I were a younger man I'd set me a wild-plum orchard and sell wild plums. A lot of people, Shan, in this world are poor because they want to be poor. I could make a fortune from wild plums. Sell them at a dollar a gallon and they go like hot cakes, and one good tree will produce twenty gallons of plums. Not bad money for a wild-plum tree, is it?"

"No, it isn't," I replied.

"I'm past eighty years old now," he said. "It's too late to set a wild-plum orchard, but if I had known twenty-five years ago what I know now, I'd have made a fortune on wild plums. See, frost and freeze never gets them in the bloom in Big River Valley. I have plums here when no one else has them back in the county. I'm so close to Big River here water and fog keeps frost and freeze away. Look on these trees. How many wild plums do you say is on one of these trees?"

"Forty gallons, I'd say," I told him.

"You're about right," he said. "I'm sorry, Shan, I don't have any for you because they're all promised."

"I'm sorry too," I said. "I should have spoken for these earlier. Say if you live and I live until next year I'm speaking for four gallons right now."

"It's a deal," he said.

When I looked up at those red-laden branches, bending, bending dangerously low toward the ground, my mouth watered. "Oh, for just two gallons of those wild plums," I thought. "Just a gallon! Oh, for a half gallon! That good tart wild-plum jelly and hot biscuits would go wonderfully well this winter with good coffee made with freestone water from our well. Sit at our breakfast table and eat wild-plum jelly and drink hot coffee when the snow is on the ground and the cold angry winds go howling over our earth. How wonderful it would be."

"You've got a lot of young plum sprouts under the trees, haven't you, Mr. Woods," I said.

"Yes, enough to set out a young orchard if I were to dig them up and set them," he said.

"Now a lot of people would be afraid to get under those

« 7 9 »

trees and pick up the plums," I said. "They're afraid of snakes. But I wouldn't be afraid of them."

"Talk on," he said. When he looked up at me his eyes had grown brighter. "What about your not being afraid of snakes?"

"Well, you know, Mr. Woods, there are only two snakes that are poisonous in this country, the copperhead and the rattlesnake," I said. "But if a man has enough sense not to kill blacksnakes and just leave the old harmless fellows around they'll take care of the copperheads."

"You're smarter than I thought," he said. "I don't know when I've ever heard a man talk with so much good sense. Talk on."

"Well, I just know a little about blacksnakes," I said. "I know enough that I never kill one. If one's stretched across the road on my farm and I'm driving that way, I stop the truck and make him crawl on. I never run over one with a car. Used to be copperheads were dangerous around our place. We live in a copperhead country. Anymore we seldom find a copperhead. Our blacksnakes have killed them. They're our friends."

"They sure are," he said. His old deep-lined face was smiling now. His dim eyes sparkled with new light. They shone like embers from their deep sockets under his shaggy brows. "Tell me more about blacksnakes. Ever had any more experiences with them?"

"Yes, I've had two fine pets," I said. "A long time ago I caught a big fellow and brought him home to the barn and corncribs. I called him Old Ben. Well, he soon made friends with everybody, even with my mother who wasn't exactly friendly with any kind of snake. Later she was handling that affectionate old reptile like he was a piece of rope."

"That's just wonderful," he said. "What happened to him?"

"We kept Old Ben two years at our barn," I said. "He hibernated near a cliff by the barn his first winter. Came back in the spring. But he didn't get to hibernate the second winter. He made the mistake of crawling into our hog lot and the hogs got him."

"Too bad," he sighed. "Hogs will devour a blacksnake every time."

"Then I had another pet I called Old Jackson," I said. "I have a building out behind the house where I do some book work and one day I looked up and a friendly old snake was crawling in at the door. I thought he'd come in to get a nest of wrens I had in this building, and, maybe he had. But I wouldn't let him have them. When he crawled toward the nest I picked him up and put him on the other side of the room. Since he wouldn't stay on his side of the room I brought me a switch in and I switched him and made him stay on his side. Well the young birds got big enough to fly and after they'd flown Old Jackson came every morning and spent the day with me for most of the summer. Then, my wife and I went on vacation and when we got back Old Jackson was gone. He's never come back and I've looked for him. I think somebody must have killed him."

"Ah, too bad," he said. "Say why haven't I known you before? I mean why haven't I known you better? I didn't know Old Mick had a boy like you. Come on over under the tree and let's get you some plums!"

"But . . ."

"Yes, I know they're promised," he said. "And I don't break my promises either. But I have eighty gallons of plums on these two trees. I can cut down the amount on

« 81 »

some of the others and let you have plums. I feel like giving you all the plums on both trees."

"But, Mr. Woods, that would be too many," I said.

"Not for you if you wanted them," he said. "Since you've told me your stories about your snakes, I'll tell you mine. It's a story about love too."

George Woods picked up his bucket from the road and I got mine from the truck and we stepped over the ditch and stood under one of the trees. A few of the over-ripe plums had fallen and burst, and their sweet plum juice was oozing from their thin red skins. But the yellow jackets and the honeybees had swarmed in to drink this juice. I wondered what wild-plum honey would be like and if it would be as good as wild-plum jelly.

I climbed up, stepping on lower branches until I could shake the tree. I gave it a little shake and the ripe plums rained down like big plump red raindrops. I thought I had shaken too many. The ground was covered.

"You might not have shaken enough," Mr. Woods said when I came from the tree. "We'll pick them up and see how many we have. If we don't have enough you can shake the tree again."

He picked up plums and put them in his bucket and I picked up plums and put them in my bucket.

"Shan, when I was a young man back up in Lantern County, I chose myself a mate, Martha Wells," he said. "She was my bride at eighteen and I was her groom at twenty. She bore us seven sons. Two of our boys died young, and remember George Jr. was killed by a train one night as he was walking along the tracks toward Blakesburg? He was a man of thirty then."

"Yes, I remember that," I said.

"Martha and I lived together fifty years and I lost her," he said. "We were in love with one another from the time we were small childhood sweethearts to the day she died. Oh, how I hated to lose her. I thought I'd die. I didn't think life was worth living. My boys had married off and had families and lived away from here. So living alone and being a lonely man, when Preacher John Morton died, I married his widow. Well four months after we married I buried her beside her husband. She was seventy-four then and I was seventy-five. After her death I was living alone again and a very lonely man. I needed a companion to live out the years with me. And I heard of Tom Jackson's widow, Grace, down at Farlington. So I went down there to see her. She was as lonely as I was and she wanted a companion too. She was seventy and I was seventy-six then. She was living with her forty-year-old son who had never married. I didn't think too much of him from the start but his mother and I agreed to get married. So we were married and we came to that house right up there. And she closed the doors of her house. Willie, her son, came to live with us."

George Woods raised up from his stooped position. He threw his shoulders back so he could stand up straight and tall. And I raised up too and put a handful of nice plums in my bucket. I had just about filled my bucket and he had his bucket about half-filled. Now we stood up straight to rest from stooping over and picking up plums.

"As I have said I didn't trust that no-good son of hers," he said. "He might not have been of sound mind. Anybody that would do what he did I am sure his mind wasn't exactly right. And I am positive that he is the reason that his mother and I are not living together today. She's a widow living in Farlington in her old home with her son and I'm a widower living here in Blakesburg in my old home all by myself. Let me tell you how it happened."

He bent over and began to pick up plums again. And I bent over too and I began to pick them up to finish filling my bucket.

"Back when Martha and I were married I used to kill blacksnakes," he said. "I used to kill them and hang them on the fence in dry seasons to make it rain. Later I learned there was nothing to all that stuff. And I couldn't understand why people just wanted to kill a blacksnake. I couldn't understand why they didn't like a blacksnake. Martha was the same way. She liked them and I kept blacksnakes in my barn to crawl through the hay and get the mice. And I kept them in the corncribs to keep mice and rats from eating my corn. Then, we always had an old pet blacksnake around the house. But as I've told you I lost my Martha."

"Well, I don't know how Preacher John's widow Nancy would have liked my blacksnakes," he said. "I never asked her 'fore we were married after they had hibernated. And she was dead and buried 'fore they were awakened from hibernation by the sounds of thunder and the warm late March rains. So after I put her away to rest beside her saintly husband, good old Preacher John, later in the spring, my two pet blacksnakes, Charlie and Emerine, were awakened by the sound of thunder and the feel of warm soft rain that soaked down to wet them. They awoke from their winter's sleep and came crawling back home. What a joy it was to have them back, for I was a lonely man."

"Another autumn came and in the old days I missed

Charlie and Emerine, for they had hibernated somewhere around here," he continued. "But in the spring they awoke and came back home. I'd had Charlie five years. He was longer than I am tall. I got him over there in Darby's meadow when he ran over the mowed grass away from the mowing machine. I gave young Cyrus Darby a dollar to catch him for me. I never saw a prettier blacksnake. But he was as wild as a buck. After I got him in my hands and rubbed his long shining body he got real chummy. So I brought him home with me, put him in the barn loft to catch the mice. And later he came to the house. And he used to follow me into the basement and later through the house. Everywhere around this place friendly old Charlie followed me. What a wonderful pet he was!"

"Then, one day I was out on Little Sandy visiting my old friend Charlie Greene," he said. "His boy Earl was mowing the meadow and bragging about running over a blacksnake. I asked him the spot and he told me. I walked over where he'd killed the snake and he hadn't killed her at all. And when I picked her up, a nice female blacksnake, almost scared to death, I caressed her with my hand and I said to myself, 'A mate for Old Charlie.' So I brought her home with me and put her with Old Charlie. Well, I think they were mated for life. They took off together and they'd come following me every time I walked out into the yard. And when I brought my third bride and her son, Willie, home with me, my snakes met me in the yard. 'Snakes, snakes,' that son of hers shouted. 'Where is there a hoe, George?' And I said to him, 'They're my pets. You kill my snakes and you'll leave this place faster than you came.' He didn't seem to understand how a man could have pet snakes. And I didn't like the look in his eye when I told him."

I'd filled and heaped my bucket and now I began to help George Woods finish filling his bucket.

"I don't believe Grace liked my pet snakes," he said. "She might have been jealous of them the way they followed me all over the place. 'Just so they stay outside the basement and the house,' she said one day. But I'd had the snakes before I married her. Yet, I understood how she had never grown up with them and she might not have been exactly chummy with them. So, I heeded her warning and I just let them follow me to the door. I didn't let them go through the basement door with me. I didn't let them come in at the living room door anymore. I kept them outside."

"Spring had passed into summer," he talked on. "Then I missed my snakes. I kept on looking for them to return day after day. But they never returned. 'Funny about my pets, Old Charlie and Emerine,' I said one day when Grace, Willie and I were sitting at the dinner table. 'I never see them. I believe there has been some kind of foul play.' Grace and Willie didn't say anything but when I mentioned my snakes Willie looked at his mother. And I could see some guilt in his roving eye. 'Well, I'd better not find out if anybody killed them,' I said. 'There will be trouble.' The very next day, Willie said to his mother: 'Let's go back to Farlington to visit Uncle Eb and Aunt Sarah. I've had enough of here. I didn't like to live with snakes!' "

"When Grace caught the bus and went back down there I didn't say anything," George said. "But a lot of thoughts went through my mind. I didn't ask her if she was coming back. But I had a feeling she would be back. I knew now who had killed my snakes and I thought maybe she had had that son of hers kill them."

Now we had finished filling George Woods' bucket and had heaped the plums on top until they started rolling off. We stood up straight and threw our shoulders back.

"Well, did they come back?" I asked him.

"She came back but she didn't bring him," he replied. And when she came back I had a little piece of paper waiting for her to sign."

"What kind of paper?" I asked.

"A divorce paper," he said. "I let her go back to Farlington to her own people and that no-good son. And when she signed the paper, she said she had told him to kill my snakes and he was the one who did it. My, I was glad to get rid of her and him. Some strange people in this world. And even when a man lives to be as old as I am, after having all the experiences dealing with people that I have had, a man can get fooled in a woman. I didn't know that she was that kind. From the start I didn't trust her son but I had trusted her. So you see why I am a widower today."

"Yes, I understand," I said. "And I hate that you lost your pets."

He picked up his bucket of plums and I got mine. We walked from under the tree, stepped over the ditch to the lane road where I had parked my truck.

"Now I'll pay you for my plums and get going," I said. "My wife will be waiting to make plum jelly out of these. I'm so thankful you have let me have these." I took two dollars from my pocket.

"Oh no, you don't pay me," he said. "I won't take a cent from you."

"Why not?" I asked him. "I don't expect you to give these plums to me."

"Yes, your bucket and mine," he said. "All four gallons. But you can bring my bucket back when you drive this way again. You're a sensible man. You're a man after my own heart. We see things alike. And you're about the only man I've ever talked to who sees things as I've seen them. This visit with you is worth all the plums on both trees."

"But Mr. Woods . . ."

"Go on and take these plums and do as I say," he interrupted me with a smile. His deep-lined face was smiling all over. And his dim eyes twinkled with light. "And tell your wife if she wants more plums to make more jelly to send you back in a hurry, for the people I've promised these plums to will be coming after them and they won't last long. I think your wife must be an understanding woman to like your snakes. I want her to have all the plums she wants to make wild-plum jelly."

⚵ The Best Years
of Our Lives ⚵

U NCLE Thorny Kirk had sent for me to come and
see him. Aunt Lillie had been gone for four years
now and Uncle Thorny lived with his niece,
Beatrice Birdsong, who was a widowed grandmother.
When Bud Adams had sowed and mowed my fertile
bottomland according to government regulations, so I
could get pay for not raising corn, Uncle Thorny sent
word by Bud for me to come to see him. Only an unfenced
road separated our farms for almost a mile.

"It's time you go see the old man, Shan," Bud said.

And I knew it was time for me to go see him. I'd not
seen him in nearly a year. Five of the months of this year
I'd suffered relapse of an old illness and I'd not left my
home which was twenty-six miles away.

Now, with a good road the distance had grown shorter
than in the early days when I lived with Aunt Lillie and

Uncle Thorny. I went first to live with them thirty-two years ago when I was a very young man. I went there to teach the village school. Since Aunt Lillie and Uncle Thorny didn't have children, I felt like I belonged to them. I loved their old colonial home. And I had the freedom of its many well-furnished but unoccupied rooms.

As a young school teacher I saved money from a small salary and invested it in land that was selling for ten dollars an acre. Here I tried raising cattle, but feeding my cattle in winter was a problem since my soil would not produce well. It was then Uncle Thorny suggested I buy some Big River bottomland. And when the farm that joined him was up for sale he told me to put all I had into the land and to borrow if I had to to finish paying for it. He said the land rose in value one year with another and I couldn't lose money. He was right. I couldn't pay for it with savings and I borrowed and paid for my fertile Big River farm. And after I quit teaching school and became a farmer, I went back to my farm which joined Uncle Thorny's and lay in the right angle with his farm where the Tiber River confluenced with Big River.

Now that I was feeling up to the journey, I got in my farm truck and I journeyed from my Hills and Valley Farm down the hard-surfaced highway which ran parallel to Big River. I drove to Kingston where I turned right and crossed the railroad tracks over to the last vast sweep of level land left between Big River and the railroad tracks. This was a flooded area, too low for building sites. And this was the only part of fertile Big River valley left for farming. About one third of my farm and about one fourth of Uncle Thorny's farm had high acres which were not as productive as the lowland.

Now I drove over a hard-surfaced road, which used to be a dirt lane road, bordered on either side by wild honeysuckles when I used to live with Aunt Lillie and Uncle Thorny. I used to walk down to Kingston in the evening where I went to the theater to see a show. I walked home at night when the moon was shining on the plowed fields and young corn and the wild honeysuckle blossoms. I was a young man then and Uncle Thorny Kirk was then as old as I was now. I was not married then and sometimes I had a date in Kingston. And the next morning when Uncle Thorny, Aunt Lillie, and I sat at the breakfast table Aunt Lillie would want to know the girl's name. And I wouldn't tell her but she always would find out. Uncle Thorny would laugh and say that young days were wonderful but no better than the days he and Aunt Lillie were living and enjoying then. I would like to know how many times after we had finished our bacon and eggs and were still drinking coffee and talking that Uncle Thorny would say: "They're all good years. Just so we are alive and can live them. And I tell Lillie we ought to live them to the fullest."

When I drove the truck around the U circle, I parked near the big sycamore tree where blackbirds used to fly in to roost in such great numbers they broke the smaller limbs of this tree. Here was the big house in front of me, the beautiful place that I had called home for a half dozen of the best years of my life. I looked up at the front window of my room on the second floor. Here is where I had my bed, my clothes, a portable record player, a small radio, my typewriter, and books.

There was something lacking about this place now. The hedge around the yard was not as trim. Aunt Lillie used to spend half of her time digging with a hoe or a small mattock among her flowers. They were everyplace. She had a landscapist's eye when it came to arranging shrubbery and had an artist's eye when it came to matching colors. Hundreds visited her home and yard in spring, summer, and autumn. Aunt Lillie always changed the flower scenery in her yard with each season. So people came to see the new. And each person who came was given a bulb, plant, shrub, or flower seeds from her variety to plant or to set in his own yard. "If you want to have luck with flowers you have to give something to your friends and neighbors," she said. And if no one was interested in taking something home from her yard, she insisted somebody take something before she had bad luck.

Now, I didn't see all those flower beds. I didn't see the blend of color in blossoms of the flowers in bloom. The flower beds were not kept as Aunt Lillie had kept them. There was the bluff that used to be clean but had now grown up until it would take a bulldozer to clear it. This was where the high bottomland broke over and down to the low fertile flooded bottom farmland. This was the bluff between the two levels. And thirty-two years ago when I lived here all the bottomland below at this time of year would have been in knee-high green corn with corn balks as clean as a peeled pawpaw whistle. Uncle Thorny used to ride his horse-drawn cultivator, pulled by his two big horses. And if the cultivator didn't get all the weeds Uncle Thorny got them with his hoe. He husked his corn by hand, leaving the clean long white and golden ears in his cribs. He had corn to sell which brought the highest price per bushel in Greenwood County. Now, in his rich bottomland where he was paid not to farm, wind bent down the grass and passed over and the grass rose again. There was a melancholy wail in the wind as it came up over Uncle Thorny's yard.

Maybe Aunt Lillie's voice is in that wind, I thought as it rustled leaves on her rose vines. How could she ever leave this place?

But the place was not quite the same. The big barn was gone from the high-level bottom and a tall radio-TV antenna reached up into a higher layer of wind, which could blow incessantly and not be obstructed by hilltops on either side of Big River valley. And the small but productive pasture of high-level acres over in front of the house where I used to watch the cows and span of big horses graze had now grown up until it would take a bulldozer to clear those once-green grassy acres. Uncle Thorny had received payments for reseeding that pasture. Now, he could never reseed it again. Beyond the house the wire pen hog lot had gone to rust. Uncle Thorny's blacksmith shop's doors were closed with strips nailed over them. And the roof of the chicken house had fallen in.

It's not the same, I thought as I knocked on the door.

Beatrice answered the door.

"Come in, Shan," she said. "Uncle Thorny is really wanting to see you."

"What's been the matter with you, you've not been down here to see me," he said, as I walked over to where he was sitting on the divan.

Uncle Thorny smiled broadly but his lips held the cigar in the corner of his mouth. The narrow slits of eyes in their deep sockets sparkled for an older man. He extended his hand.

I reached for Uncle Thorny's hand.

The hand I was shaking now had some strength, but it

was softer and smaller than his big fire-shovel hands that did the work of three men on his farm. My hands were not small but his hand would cover my hand when I had lived here and taught school.

"It's good to see you, Uncle Thorny," I said. "A year is a long time but I've been compelled to go slow. I've been inside about five months."

"Yes, I know," he said. "I'm not getting out either these days."

His cane was leaned against the divan. His radio was on a small table before him. And on this table was an open cigar box which contained a few cigars.

"Here is a box of your favorite cigars," I said. "I figured you might be out of cigars."

"Oh, thank you," he said. "You remember the kind I smoke."

"I sure do."

He was as pleased with the box of cigars as a child would have been with a new toy. There was a smile on his face as his big blunt fingers pulled the cigar box lid open. He looked admiringly at the neat layer of fresh cigars and then he smelled of them. He lifted one from the box, pulled the wrapper off, and he took a match from a large box of matches he kept on the small table before him. He struck the match under the table and lighted the cigar.

"Wonderful taste," he said. He exhaled the cloud of mild cigar smoke that swirled upward toward the low ceiling. "You saw what I did to that off-brand cigar I was smoking, didn't you?"

Half of the cigar he was smoking when I went in was lying on a big ashtray and the fire in it had gone out.

"I know a good cigar," he said. "This is a good one."

Uncle Thorny's square face was filled with small wrinkles. His once-brown wavy hair hadn't all turned gray. His hair was only slightly salt-and-pepper colored. But his once-broad square shoulders were bent like a piece of tin. His shoulders were round and his shoulderline was bowed. Each shoulder dropped down from the perfect square. His nicely shaped head that was held to his once-strong body by a short bull neck leaned to one side as he blew another wisp of smoke toward the ceiling.

"We used to be bulls, Shan," he said. "We've lived the best years of our lives. But a good cigar tastes good. I'm sorry your Doc took you off the fragrant weed."

"Yes, I miss my fragrant weed, Uncle Thorny," I said.

"Did he really tell you not to smoke?"

"Yes, he did," I said.

"Maybe you'd better follow his advice. But I sure miss your not being able to smoke the fragrant weed with me."

Then there was silence between us as Uncle Thorny looked me over and smiled.

"I'm sure glad you got down to see me," he said. "It's been a long time, Shan!"

"Yes, it's been a long time."

"See, I can't walk very well," he said. "You remember when the top of a tree fell down and struck me in the head. It struck me on one side and on the other side I had a leg paralyzed for a while."

"Sure I remember," I said. "I was staying here when it happened."

"Well, it was a long time before I got so I could walk," he said. "Then I got so I could work. But I'll tell you, Shan, it takes old Time himself to probe around over your body to find the weak spots when the years pass. Time is better than a doctor to find all the weak spots. Damn, I'm glad to be around. How about you?"

"Yes, I'm sure pleased to be around," I said.

"See, I'm blessed with big windows in this brick house," he said. "I can look out and see Bud Adams when he's cutting the government grass on your farm. Little Bud Adams is a good worker. Yes, you've got a good worker on your farm. I wish I had a man like him on my farm. No, I don't either, for what could I do now with all the products my farm will produce? I'm paid not to raise anything!" Uncle Thorny laughed, then drew a small cloud of smoke from his cigar. "Used to be we got paid for what we produced. Now we get paid not to produce it. The world I used to know has turned around."

Uncle Thorny laughed again as he dangled the red end of his cigar before my face.

"Your Aunt Lillie and I worked and we saved for a rainy day and we didn't trust any promises and gifts," he said. "Now she's gone and I've got enough left to do me two lifetimes. We made it from this farm. Now, my farm will only pay my taxes. It can't pay for its own improvements. The world has changed. Don't people eat anymore? What's happened the government pays us not to produce? We've got more people, haven't we? I've never seen anything like it. I just sit here, look out at the big windows around this room at my land and I remember the time when my father was a young man and plowed these bottoms. That's a long time ago for I'm eighty-six now."

"Have you always lived on this very spot?" I asked.

"Yes, I was born in this house," he said. "Pap might have been born in this house too. I think he was. And my grandfather, Ben Kirk, built this house on the spot where the old house stood. My great-grandfather, Old Ben, came in here when the Indians were around and he built the first house here on this spot. He and my Grandpa Ben cleared most of these bottoms. They raised corn and shipped it on barges on Big River long before there was a railroad here. Shan, I'm the last of the Kirks. I have no sons!"

He knocked the gray ash from the end of his cigar onto the big ashtray on his table.

"Yes, I used to hear Indian stories when I was a boy," he said. "I heard Grandpa Ben and my mother tell 'em and I'm sorry I didn't write 'em down. They've blown off with the winds. Right up there in the bottom is a big Indian graveyard. It's not anything uncommon to plow up Indian bones. No wonder the Indians were disturbed. We even plowed up their graveyards but there were no markers. Well, I guess my people, who were the first to clear and plow this land, will go like the Indians! They're gone forever from here and we'll be gone forever from here when I go! I often sit here and wonder who'll take over next. But I don't think it matters much who takes over. All races of people are here or somewhere else for a while and then they're gone forever."

Uncle Thorny laid half of his cigar on the ashtray. Then he reached down between the divan and wall. He came up with a bottle half filled with wine.

"Does your doctor say you can drink wine?" he asked me.

"He's never said."

"This is dandelion wine we made here in April," he said. "Have a drink of this. Just drink it from the bottle. It's better that way!"

I held the wine bottle up and I drank. Uncle Thorny's

dandelion was better this year than it had been in the years past when I stayed with him and Aunt Lillie. We had dandelion and elderberry wine with every meal except breakfast. And if I had asked for wine for breakfast then I could have had it. I held the bottle up and took a long drink.

"You needed that wine," Uncle Thorny said. "You're starved for wine."

I put the bottle down on Uncle Thorny's table.

"Take another drink," he said.

"Not right now," I said. "I'm afraid I'll feel this long drink."

"Don't worry about it," he said. "If you feel it that won't hurt you. I sit here and take a midmorning swig and I look out upon my fields. And I say: 'Here's to you, Old Ben and Grandpa Ben and Pap! There's no one here to plow. I can't do it now.' And of course they can't hear me for their ears are deaf to sound. They sleep over there at Mt. Zion. I've not been over there since Lillie went there to sleep among us. I never want to go to Mt. Zion again. I spend most of my time in this room and out on the porch."

Now Uncle Thorny turned the wine bottle up and he took a long drink.

"It's good dandelion," he said, wiping his mouth with his big, soft, wrinkled hand. He put the bottle back on the table. "That's about the best. Maybe it does get better every year!"

Then Uncle Thorny laughed loudly at his own joke.

"We've almost finished the bottle," I said.

"Don't worry about it," he said. "There's another full one between the divan and the wall. And when it's gone there is more. Shan, I wonder if there are spirits out there in the winds over the bottoms. I sometimes think there must be spirits of all my ancestors who plowed and hoed this land. And my people loved their animals that worked with them. They must be out there too."

Out across the Big River bottoms sunlight played upon Uncle Thorny's grassy acres. There was a glimmer of haze just above the wilted grass.

"Ten years it's not been farmed," he said.

I heard Beatrice in the kitchen rattling pots and pans. But she couldn't take the place of Aunt Lillie. This house didn't look the same on the inside. The walls of the room where we sat needed papering. And the large panes in the big windows rattled when the wind blew for they needed putty around to hold them securely. They were just about ready to drop from their frames. Not anything was the same.

"Take another drink, Shan," Uncle Thorny said.

"No, I'm feeling the long one I took and I've got to drive my truck home in a few minutes," I said.

"I miss my car," Uncle Thorny said. "I drove it until six years ago. And some fellow came up and hit me behind and tried to say in court I was driving too slow! It caused my lame leg to get worse. Funny how things can happen one after another like the links in a chain. That stopped me from driving."

"Yes, I remember when you had that wreck," I said.

"But they must have thought I was too old to drive," he said.

Uncle Thorny picked up the half of his fresh cigar and lighted it again. There must have been marks under the antique table where he struck his matches. But I knew if

Aunt Lillie was living, she would say: "If Thorny wants to strike matches on that antique table or any piece of furniture in this house that is his business. It's his furniture that he inherited from his ancestors and if it isn't, it's a piece of furniture for which he worked and paid cash. Everything he bought he paid cash for it. He never could owe money in his life. Yes, things have changed from Thorny's world and mine. When one of us goes, it will be awful hard on the other one."

"Uncle Thorny, I want to go upstairs and see my old room, then I'm going to have to be driving back home."

"After that car wreck I started walking with a cane," he said. "I can't go upstairs with you. I wish I could. I've not been up there for years to see how the place looks. But before you go take a little more dandelion."

Then I turned the bottle up and took a light swig. When I set the bottle back on the table, Uncle Thorny turned it up and finished all the wine there was left.

Then I went up to my room where I was looking around when Beatrice came in.

"I want to show you something," she said. "Look over in this room."

I followed her across the hall.

"Look up there," she said.

I couldn't believe what I saw. High up on the twelve-foot ceiling rain had come through the roof and the plaster had fallen. I could look up and out at the sky. This was the last of the old colonial homes on Big River left in our county. This beautiful antique home was old enough to walk with two canes.

"Uncle Thorny can't get anybody to go up there and fix it," Beatrice said.

"I can get somebody to do it," I told her. "I can get Watson Walker."

"Tell Uncle Thorny when you go downstairs," she said.

"I'll do that," I said.

"I've got to go back downstairs and phone in an order of groceries," she said.

Beatrice Birdsong looked like the Kirks. She looked enough like Uncle Thorny to be his daughter. She was tall but she had the square shoulders and the square face. She had the tight lips, laughing blue eyes, waving brown hair that hadn't begun to gray despite her being a grand-mother. She could climb stairs faster than a sixteen-year-old and she was nearing seventy. I watched her hurry downstairs and I knew she was descended from a rugged race of men who had once inhabited this part of America and had cleared the fields, broken the roots with bull-tongue plows, made roads and houses. They had been the first to replace the Indians after they had disappeared. Now, all the Kirks but Uncle Thorny slept in the Big River bottoms with markers at their heads and feet. The Indians slept in unmarked graves and plows had gone over their bones and turned some of them up. But plows wouldn't turn up any more Indian bones now for they were silenced. The government grass grew on these treeless level acres. We cut the grass twice a year but we couldn't feed it to livestock. And the government would not have paid us not to grow corn. This most fertile land in these parts had grown food for thousands of people and had grown feed for hundreds of thousands of livestock. Now, the horses and mules who pulled the bull-tongue plows and cut the roots in a wild soil had been planted in that rich earth and their bones had slithered upwards from the ground to the grass . . . and they were white dots on the green fields. And the people who had pioneered this land were now sleeping deep in the land they had pioneered and made of it a nation. And now, the land itself, loved by man and animals because it had fed them, was taking a rest, and those who had deeds for the land were getting little paychecks . . . dream-colored, fantasy-substance made of paper and about as substantial as the wind.

I stood in the hallway upstairs. Here the doors opened to six rooms. Where had the antique furniture gone that Aunt Lillie had here? Had it gone before Beatrice had come to stay with Uncle Thorny? In one of the exquisite rooms was a pile of rags. In another were disheveled window curtains and piles of nondescripts. My old room was the best kept. My old bed, my table, and dresser were still here. But something had happened to the place with Aunt Lillie gone and Uncle Thorny who couldn't walk upstairs. The upstairs had gone before the downstairs when the downstairs should have gone before the upstairs. Everywhere there were the marks of deterioration. Long unseen fingers had reached from nowhere into the somewhere to mutilate and destroy what once was beautiful, as the beetle will destroy the rose. I had a strange feeling that came over me as I walked downstairs.

"Bee told you there was a hole in that roof up there," Uncle Thorny said.

"Yes, she told me there was."

"Well there isn't," he said. "That roof doesn't leak."

Beatrice came and stood in the dining room door. She didn't dispute what Uncle Thorny said but she smiled when he said it.

"It's the damned . . . the damned . . . you know, that fly over," he said; his voice was like the sound of tin grating over stones.

"You mean, Uncle Thorny, jets that fly faster than sound?" I said.

"That's what I mean," he said. "They've cracked the roof and they've cracked the ceiling. Why do they have to fly so fast?"

"Don't ask me," I said.

"They fly too fast for people and for houses," he said. "As I've said, Shan, we've lived in the best years of our lives. I know I've enjoyed the years. Now, I don't know what to do. I'm not willing to leave the years now. I'd like to know what they'll bring next to us."

"I'm going to have to take off," I said. "I've got to get up to my farm to see about the cattle!"

"Ah, the cattle," he said. "We used to have three hundred head here. We fattened that many from the corn we raised in these bottoms and we sent them down the river to Cincinnati on barges. That was a wonderful time to live. Yes, I remember the tall oaks along the lane road and how they leafed in spring and how the leaves turned color and zig-zagged down from their tall tops after the first October frost! These are things that are good to remember!"

Maybe the payment in life is what we collect in impressive and vague memories, I thought. I said goodby to Beatrice and then I shook Uncle Thorny's big, soft, wrinkled hand. He was still sitting on the divan with his little table before him. This was a small little world compared to the world he had known. But he was staying on the very spot where his ancestors had settled in 1796. He is holding to the dreams of them, I thought as I left the old colonial home and walked toward my little farm truck parked under the big sycamore. He won't have many more years but he has the integrity to stay, not to sell and go to a rest home. While the unseen fingers from nowhere had grasped the heirlooms of colonial antiquity since Aunt Lillie had gone and he couldn't get upstairs even with the help of a cane, he had not budged. The flesh, blood, brain, and heart of his people were made of a richer pioneer dust that was durable, good, and lasting in its day and time. None has since equalled it.

⚚ The Builders and
the Dream ⚚

PA may have had peace in his long hours of hard
work and much walking, but we didn't find peace
where we lived. And more than one time I had
heard Mom say that it couldn't go on much longer. I was
standing under the big persimmon tree near our barn
watching for Pa to come from his work. And when he saw
me standing there he knew something had happened. He
never said a word, but hurried into the house where Mom
was sitting in front of a little fire she had made of green-
oakwood in the open fireplace to kill the chill of March.

"So, he's been here again," Pa said to Mom, while she
looked into the fire and wept.

"Yes," Mom replied.

"He's your brother," Pa said, "and I hate. . . ."

Pa didn't finish his sentence.

"It has to stop, Pa," I said. "If I can't do anything else, I
can throw rocks hard and straight!"

"What was the matter this time?" Pa asked. "Why did he come up here on you?"

"He came to tell me what a bad family I had," Mom said, sobbing like her heart would break. "He talked about the fine family he had. He bragged how his children had worked and how they would amount to something some day!"

"Now isn't that something," Pa said. "Just think he'd come up here and insult you like that!"

"I told you, Mick, how it would be when we moved on his place," Mom said. "Look how he treated John Belcher when he wanted him to move. Look how he treated Frend Nixon. He's always been like that," Mom continued half sobbing. "He gets people on his place and then he bullies them until he gets them off. They can't do anything to suit him. Pap always said Mel was his only overbearing child!"

It was one year ago that Uncle Mel had come to our cottage over on Warfield Flaughtery's farm. He had come to get us to move onto his place. He told Pa about what a good garden he would have and that he would let us have free pasture for our cow and horse. And he told Pa that he would rent him the best ground he had on the farm, and that I could do the plowing and Mom, Sophie, and Mary could do the hoeing in the tobacco and corn, and that we could raise plenty of shares for him and for us. Then Pa went with him to look at the place. When he came back home he told Mom that he had rented and we had better start getting ready to move.

Mom told Pa then he had made a mistake, but Pa said he thought he could get our land paid for in one year. He told Mom he could save half of what he was making on the railroad section. And what we made on the tobacco and what he made in the second year would be enough to build us a house on our own land. Pa's plans sounded good to everybody but Mom.

"I know Mel's dreams and his temper," Mom said. "It won't work, Mick! We'd better stay on here with Warfield. We'd better rent from him."

Warfield was a landlord who drove a hard bargain with his renters. He had charged us extra for our cow pasture and he had charged us cash rent for the house and garden and grain rent for the fields. But the worst thing he ever did to us was to come into the cornfield when Pa was away working on the railroad section and haul out the biggest corn shocks for himself and leave us the small ones at the ends of the fields. Though he did these things, he never had come to our shack and cussed one of us and carried on like Uncle Mel.

"Why doesn't he ever come up here when I'm at home?" Pa said. "He's afraid to come! He gets me gone and then he comes here!"

"Why don't we go down there, Pa?" I asked.

"That's just what he wants," Mom said. Her tear-stained eyes moved in red sockets. "Remember, if you go down there and anything happens, you are paid for! He'll be waiting and he'll do plenty to you!"

"He told me how good this land was," Pa said, shaking his head. "And we had a crop failure last year. It's a white sand under a little loam. His land is no good!"

"And to think of the way we worked last year," I said. "We grew three acres of tobacco, and after we brought it to the market they sent us a bill for thirty-six cents! We didn't raise enough to pay the warehouse costs of handling it!"

And then I laughed.

"It's nothing to laugh about," Pa said. "And we've had to buy feed all winter for the cow and horse and sell the heifers! We didn't even raise enough corn to fatten our hogs!"

"But that's all right," Mom said. "I don't mind that work and crop failure. I mind Mel's coming up here once a week and bawling me out. I can't stand Mel's abuse. I can't go on like this!"

Pa sat down on the split-bottom chair near Mom. And he looked into the fireplace at the little flames.

"If we only had a house on our own farm," Mom said, "we'd move to it tomorrow! And we'd be out of all this misery."

"I just wonder how it will seem to live in our own house on our own land," Pa said. "We've never lived on our own land and in our own house in our lifetime."

"It will be wonderful," I said. I thought about how we had rented land and moved from farm to farm ever since I could remember.

"If we could build us a house better than Uncle Mel's," Sophie said, "that would be the best way to fight him back!"

"You're right," Mom said, thoughtfully. "That's the only way to defeat him. You can't whip him any other way. When he was a young man and drinking, Bill Kazee broke a bottle over his head and forty years later he met Bill Kazee at the Birchfield Stockyard and whipped him. He never forgives nor forgets!"

"But I'll have you to know," Pa said, "I'm not afraid of him. I'm a little man, but I'll fight him all over a mountainside! And I'll fight him the best way to whip him, too!"

"The best way to whip him is to build a house on our own land," Mom said. "I know that would hurt him. He's glad to see us too poor to build a house."

"He wants to hold us here to work for him on the poorest of all mountain farms," I said.

"You're right," Mom said.

That evening at the supper table we talked about a house on our farm. And we talked about it before we went to bed. When we thought about a place to live on our own land, we were so happy that we forgot about Uncle Mel. Mom even dried her tears and her eyes looked bright when she talked about the flowers she would plant in our yard. Pa talked about a meadow, an orchard, a barn, and a cellar. He talked about them as if they were real and we had them and would move tomorrow. I talked about the melon and popcorn patches I would have—two things I had wanted to plant and Uncle Mel wouldn't let me have the land. What we said were dream words but they seemed real to us as we sat around the fire.

That night after I went to bed I dreamed about the house on our farm we had built under a big pine. I worked all night digging stumps from the yard and helping Mom and Sophie set flowers. And then I dreamed about a meadow we cut over with two big black horses hitched to a mowing machine. I dreamed our farm was much prettier and more productive than Uncle Mel's. I dreamed when Uncle Mel came to see our house, he climbed upon the rim of rocks that separated our farms and took one look at our house, our pretty yard, smooth meadow, and dark clouds of stalwart new-ground corn and then he walked away. He didn't even come down to our new house to wish us joy and happiness.

Maybe Mom had dreamed about the house we were

going to build too. For the next morning as she got breakfast, she sang some old songs. Mom usually didn't sing.
And now she was singing before daylight. Pa didn't even
know why she was so happy. And just as soon as he had
gone to work she told me to get on the horse and ride to
Short Branch and tell Grandpa to come up for she wanted
to see him.

Before noon I had Grandpa at our house. And it took
Mom all afternoon to tell him about our crop failures and
how Uncle Mel was treating us. Grandpa sat there silently
while Mom talked. He listened as he stroked his long
white beard. He was a big man with hands like small shovels and arms as big as small fence posts. And his muscles
were still hard from cutting timber, though he was seventy-
five.

"I understand," Grandpa would grunt when Mom told
him how she wanted to get moved off Uncle Mel's place
onto land of our own. And that is about all he ever said
until after Mom had told him everything.

"Yes, you need a home of your own," Grandpa said. "If
I had somebody to help me saw down the trees, I'd build
you one!"

When Grandpa said this Mom hugged his neck and
kissed his face. And Sophie kissed Grandpa and I stood
before him with a thought in my mind.

"Grandpa, I can help you do the sawing and the chopping," I said. "I can do a man's work!"

"Not the way I work, Shan," he said. "But you could be
a great help."

That afternoon Grandpa rode his horse back to the
Short Branch timber tract to get his tools. And when Pa
came home from work I was waiting under the persimmon

tree to tell him Grandpa had been there. Pa knew everything was all right, but he didn't know our plans until
Mom told him.

"Reckon Dad isn't too old to build a house?" he said to
Mom. "Wonder if he can do it with only a fourteen-year-
old boy to help him! And besides," Pa continued, "Mel's
got us bound up with a contract to raise three acres of
tobacco and ten acres of corn on these steep slopes. If Shan
is able to help Dad with the house, who will do our plowing and raise the corn and tobacco?"

"Leave that to me," Mom said.

"You know I have to work on the section to meet my
land payments," Pa said. "If we could just get a good tobacco crop it would help out. And if Dad and Shan can
build the house that will be wonderful. Just think of the
time that will save us. We'd be on our land two years
sooner than we had planned!"

I could tell that Pa had doubts of our building a house.
He didn't think Mom's plan would work. He wondered
about who would do the plowing on Uncle Mel's farm.
Regardless of what anybody thought, we started to make
our dream a living thing. Grandpa and I took our tools to
the woods Monday morning. And Grandpa was surprised
at the way I could chop. He didn't know that every time I
stuck my ax into a tree to notch it or cut along the side of
the log to score it, I thought I was fighting Uncle Mel. And
I *was* fighting him. I knew how jealous he had been of us
when we had made better grades than his children, our
first cousins, in school. We had led our classes and Uncle
Mel couldn't stand it. And Mom could beat Aunt Effie
making clothes. When Mom made dresses for my sisters,
they were the prettiest dresses at school. And Uncle Mel's

girls went home and told their parents and that hurt them. And I knew we could build a better house than Uncle Mel had.

The first week we worked in the woods Grandpa and I cut enough logs to build a house large enough for four large rooms, two downstairs and two upstairs. At first, I thought Grandpa would be too old to chop and work and I tried to do little things to help him. I'd never seen such a chopper. He worked with a nine-pound ax and I worked with a four-pound one. After Grandpa had hewn a log it looked like one that had been planed.

Pa came to the woods to look at our logs and his face was the brightest and happiest I had ever seen. Sophie and Mary cut the sprouts from the old fields and made them ready for the plow. And Pa burned the tobacco bed on evenings after he'd come from work. Everybody but Glenna, the baby, was working at our house. We were fighting Uncle Mel. We wanted to get off his domain and from under his thumb.

After Grandpa had come to stay with us, Mom had thought Uncle Mel would not be back to raise another racket with her. But he came back and told her that where I had taken the cow to the pasture I had let her step from six to eighteen inches out of the path on the grass. And he was so mad about it that his lips trembled when he spoke and the ruler he'd measured the distance of the cow tracks from the path shook in his hand. But when Mom told him that Grandpa was with us and we were building a house, he stopped talking about the cow's tracks and told Mom if we didn't get our tobacco and corn planted according to the contract, he would sue us.

When Mom told Grandpa what had happened, it made

him work harder. And it made my ax sink deeper into the green oaks. It made Pa work harder and later at night. We were fighting Uncle Mel in a way he couldn't understand. And it was a way that cut deep and hurt. For the next time he came to bawl Mom out, he found her plowing tobacco land. And then he started cussing Pa for letting her plow.

"You've made me plow, Mel Shelton," she said. "You, not Mick. You, with your overbearing temper and your mean ways. But we will beat you yet. We'll raise more corn and tobacco than you! So, go about your own business!"

My five-year-old brother, Finn, worked. He took care of Glenna while Mom plowed, and Sophie and Mary cut cornstalks and sprouts and set tobacco. And when Uncle Mel got these words from Mom, he hurried down the path home. He started getting his tobacco ground ready. He couldn't stand for his sister to beat him.

But that didn't stop Uncle Mel from coming back. When he saw how well we were getting along, he thought of something that would give us more trouble. He came to our home and ordered us to put our chickens up. And when Mom asked him why, he said they were tramping the ground—sixty chickens running over forty acres of woodlands and tramping the ground. And we gathered our chickens and took them to our farm. We just put them down in the woods and left them by a few nests we had built on the sides of trees.

"We'll have the house up by September, Sal," Grandpa told Mom.

Grandpa worked harder than ever and I worked harder. Pa came in and plowed the steep ground after working on the railroad. He plowed it so Mom wouldn't have that to do. And he wanted to keep Grandpa and me at work on the house.

Each morning as Grandpa and I went to work, I would take feed for our chickens. I fed them in one place so it would be a home to them. And often I'd find the feathers of one of our chickens in the woods where a fox had caught it.

"We'll be lucky to have half of our chickens by the time we get the house built," Pa said. "Too many foxes, owls, and hawks in that wilderness."

"But our chickens won't tramp Mel's ground now," Mom said.

The last time Uncle Mel came to bawl Mom out, he told her what his boy and girl had done in school.

"Adger and Geraldine passed the examination for high school," Uncle Mel bragged to Mom. "What's that good-for-nothing Shan of yours ever going to amount to? Adger made seventy-six and Geraldine made eighty-one!"

Then he told her how his children would amount to so much more than Mom's.

"There's another examination, Mom," I said. "I'm going to take it and be ready for high school this fall. If we get the house done in time, I'll go if I pass. And if Adger has passed, I know I can!"

So after my days of working with Grandpa on the house, I went over my old books that I had put away because I had had to work. I worked each evening reviewing until late at night. And Sophie reviewed with me. On the day the examination was held, Sophie and I walked five miles to town and took the examination. She made an average of eighty-six and I made an average of seventy-eight. So, I beat Adger and Sophie beat Geraldine and we were pleased. And Mom waited for Uncle Mel to come again so she could tell him. But he didn't come back.

He just slipped around and peeped over into our fields to see how our corn and tobacco were growing. He got his eyeful too. We had a wet season and it grew better than we had expected, much better than Uncle Mel's.

In June we had our house-raising, and everybody but Uncle Mel came and helped us put the logs upon each other in a square pen. And then Grandpa and I cut windows and doors and put the rafters on our house. Next we covered it with clapboards. Then we blasted a big rock and broke the giant slabs with sledge hammers. Grandpa, who was a stonemason, and I chiseled the rocks into shape and built two fireplaces and a stone chimney up through the center of the house. We chinked and daubed the log pen and made a lean-to for a kitchen and dining room.

By August fifteenth our house was ready! And it was the prettiest house in the Hollow. Our neighbors came to look at it. Uncle Mel came only to the ridge of rocks as I had dreamed he would and peeped over. Jad Hix had seen him there peeping over and had told Pa. And Pa was pleased.

There wasn't anything in our contract that said we had to live another day on Uncle Mel's farm after we got our house up and had lived up to our contract with the crops. And we had the best corn crop and the prettiest tobacco that we had raised in many years. The year had been fruitful to us. We had worked for a dream. We knew as we hauled our furniture into our new home that our dream for the future had come true. Uncle Mel never again would come to measure the cow's tracks along the path to the pasture or make us put our chickens up from tramping his ground. Now we gathered our chickens from the woods where they had gone wild. Hens had laid out in the woods and had hatched young chickens. We brought home more chickens, despite the number caught and killed, than we had moved to the wilderness. And we cleared a place for a meadow where we could cut it with a mowing machine.

"I'm leaving my timber-cutting job," Grandpa told me as we worked on the meadow. "I'm staying here with Mick and Sal and clearing land for cornfields and potato patches. I am going to clear a part of this wilderness for them. Then you can go to school. And, Shan," Grandpa said with a wink, "I want you to sink your head into your books like you sink your ax into a green log!"

✠ *Little Giant* ✠

IZZY Stubblefield come over on Hogbranch and he says
to Pa: "Skeleton, I want a boy to work. I want a boy
that will work. One that knows how to work. One
that will earn his salt." And you know how old Izzy is.
He just meant what he said. A long, snake-hipped man
with a corkscrew mustache the color of faded old-field-
blossom. "I don't mind paying a boy ten dollars a month
if he's worth his salt."

And Pa says: "I got a boy here'll do as much as you and
your four boys put together. But I tell you right now he's
worth fifteen bucks a month and his keeping. He's this boy
right here. It's old Lizard-lip. He's my mainstay here. I tell
the rest of the boys he's part water dog, for he can take the
rain. He's part stud terrapin, for he can wade through the
wet weeds. He's part bulldog, for he won't give up. He's
part mule, for he keeps going around these old hills with a

row o'terbacker or a row o'corn. And he's part lizard the way he can scale the trees for squirrels and mast and fruit. He's a humdinger with britches on. He's a boy worth fifteen dollars a month if he's worth anything."

"I'll give Lizard-lip a try," says Izzy. "And if he ain't what he's cracked up to be I'll send him back on you. Son, get your clothes," says Izzy.

I went in the house and I says: "Ma, get my clothes ready. Pa's got me hired out. Fifteen dollars a month." And Ma says: "Lizard, is he going to make a lackey boy out'n you too?" It hurt poor old Ma. Tears come to her eyes. But she got me my clothes.

I just clim upon the mule behind Izzy. Pa reach me my dab of clothes and Izzy spurred the mule with a little wheel on the heel of the shoe. We went right up over the mountain. Went around a lot of ridges and through a lot of drawbars and pole-gates. We swum one river—went down a long tie-road where there's a lot of ruts. Just kept the mule a-jumping every which way. I'll never forget when we got in sight of a barn that looked like it covered a acre of ground. "That's my place," says Izzy. "That's where I'll try the stud terrapin in you. It's on them old hills back o' that barn. That's just one of my barns. I got two more big terbacker barns. We work over at my house. All hands and the cook work to make a living. What time you used to getting up?" And I says: "Two o'clock in the morning." And Izzy says: "That's got us beat two hours. We get up at four." And we rode on down over some old yaller banks to the house. April was here now and green leaves were coming to the sourvines along the old rail fences.

"Well, here he is, Sugarfoot," says Izzy. "This is my wife, Lizard. You'll know more about her by the good biscuits she bakes and the good corndodger she can make. It sticks to your ribs like saw-briers to a bank."

And I says: "I'm glad to meet you, Sugarfoot Stubble-field." Lord, but she was a big woman—big nearly as Pa. Great big arms that could use a ax same as she could bake biscuits. Had on a big plain dress and a pocket for her pipe and terbacker on the right-hand corner of the checked apron. I just says to myself: "I like that woman."

She just smiled at me—one of them big, open smiles that ain't put on. She says: "Come over here to your room, Lizard."

In my room I opened up the dresser drawer and put my clothes in it. I put on my good pants and one of my clean shirts before I met the rest of the family. I'm glad I did. Then Izzy called me out and says: "Meet Mattie Stubble-field. She's my oldest girl. She's going to college." And I says: "Glad to meet you, Mattie." And I was glad to meet her. She was prettier than a striped snake. She had them big blue sleepy-doll eyes and that lovey-dovey look in her eyes. Hair the color of broom sage in September. Skin prettier than a beef-pelt.

Gee, when I saw her I just melted in my tracks. I says to myself: "I may be their lackey boy, but dad-durn my hide and taller I'd like to have that woman just to look at. 'Pon my word and honor she's three times prettier than any big sleepy-eyed doll I ever saw. I can't help it if she's going to college. That don't stand in the way of old lackey Lizard-lip's love."

I just didn't care about meeting nary 'nother soul. I met Izzy's older boy, Reef, and I met the next boy. They called him Doghide. And the next girl was called Lid. She was ugly as a honeylocust in the wintertime. Izzy said it was because she wasn't through growing. Then the next little squirt of a boy called Horsey. And the baby was called Bruce. "It's a real family," I thought, "and I'm glad to be here with them. I'd give my fifteen dollars a month just to kiss Mattie one time. Can't understand how she's so pretty and old Izzy's so ugly. Her brothers are just as common and ugly as I am."

Well, I never thought about my looks until I saw Mattie. I'd look in my dresser looking-glass. I never thought o' why they called me Lizard-lip until I examined myself real close. God, I was a ugly man—I don't lie about it—to love a pretty woman like Mattie.

It just hurt me to think of her going to college and leaving me there with the family. I just felt like a part of that family from the time I went there. I tell you I rolled out'n my bed a hour earlier and fed the mules while old Izzy and his boys were snozzing in bed. I milked the cows. I took the lead row hoeing terbacker and I led old Izzy, all his boys and the rest of the hired help hoeing cane. I showed them what a working boy was. I'd come in at night and cut the stovewood for the women—something old Izzy'd been letting the womenfolks do. We always got the wood for Ma at home. Pa always said a man that wouldn't cut his wife stovewood was a man that bore watching. I done all there was to do loose about the place besides putting in six days a week in the fields. Once Izzy says to me: "Lizard-lip, you are worth your weight in wildcats when it comes to work."

I tell you that pleased me. I just wanted to call him Pa. But I was afraid. I wanted to call Sugarfoot Ma. But I was afraid. I wanted to say of a morning when I et them good big fluffy biscuits: "Ma, your bread is better this morning than it was yesterday morning." I just wanted to do things for her. I could tell the way Mattie felt. She just passed and repassed with me. She didn't want old lackey boy Lizard-lip working for her pap for fifteen dollars a month. She was a girl in college. She wanted a big man out'n some of them colleges with a education. One that could make his living with a pencil behind his ear. She didn't want to marry a lackey boy working in the dirt.

You know how that is. So I just passed and repassed with Mattie. Lord, but I just died for her love. Prayed over her and I even shed tears. Ma used to say I was hard as a rock. Never would cry when Pa whopped me. But I cried over Mattie. She stirred me till my heart fluttered like a bird and the tears just rolled from my eyes like rain out'n the sky.

"Wonder if Kate will be back to college this year? Her old man's money's not so plentiful this year." And she'd speak of Tom, Jim, Charlie, Mable, Kate, Lovell, Cherry, Amos and Alice. She'd just talk about the boys and girls there and wish she was back. She'd talk to Sugarfoot about them. And I'd hear her say to Sugarfoot: "I just wonder about Leonard. Wonder how he's getting along. I've not heard from him now in two days." Lord, but Mattie did talk proper. And she'd get on the saddle horse and ride down to the post office every day and ask for mail. She'd get a letter nearly every day from Leonard. I tell you I didn't like that name. Leonard Pratt was the name. I saw his picture in Mattie's room on the mantel. Had waxy-looking eyes and one of them little cropped mustaches. Big waves of black curly hair and his shirt collar fit his neck snug as you please. Had a big bow tie beneath his chin. And down below was a big lot of fancy writing. It said:

"To Mattie with love—Leonard." Oh, but it made my blood bile to see it.

Pa come at the end of the first month to take my earnings. He says: "Well, Izzy, how's Lizard doing?" And Izzy says: "Skeleton, he's the best man I ever had on this farm."

Pa took the fifteen dollars from Izzy Stubblefield and he says: "Son, since you're so good to work and doing so well I'll keep ten and give you back five dollars. You can buy you a suit of clothes before the summer is over. You can buy your own clothes."

Lord, I wanted to hug Pa's big bull neck. Now I would be able to get ahead enough money to buy me a suit and look a little bit better. Never would look as much like a doll though as that Leonard Pratt. Why, he looked like in that picture he'd just come out'n a bandbox.

Once I says to Izzy: "Looks like Mattie's beau never worked out in very many cornfields and suckered and wormed very much terbacker nor dug the crab grass from its roots." And Izzy says: "It looks to me like he'd break his back if he stooped over to worm and sucker terbacker and his brains might fall out."

I tell you, April and May just passed by like the shot out'n a gun. Maybe it was because I had a big room all to myself instead of piling up three in a bed at home and a shuck-bed at that. Maybe it was because I got to see Mattie every day—the prettiest girl I ever saw in all my born days.

June passed and the corn looked just fine. So did the terbacker and cane. And then July passed. We laid by the corn in July and the cane. We wormed and suckered the terbacker and cut the hay. It was a busy month—and hot.

Boys had to pick blackberries to can. It left most of the crop on Izzy and me. I had most of the work to do because I was Izzy's lackey boy. I didn't grumble. I'd heard Pa say: "A little raindrop beats a hole in a big rock." I thought I might be a speck on the wall in this love affair. You can't tell just how things will work out with a woman. Sometimes a mighty pretty girl will marry a mighty ugly boy. I've seen it happen more times than one. I just kept working and praying through July and August when Mattie was getting ready for college.

I'll never forget when August was over and the corn started coloring. I'd saved eighteen dollars. I asked Izzy for a Saturday afternoon off. And Izzy says: "Go ahead, Lizard." He says to me: "You've been a good boy to work. Never had one better. You've helped me get a lot of work out'n Snake-eye. I'd like to hire you for the next year for the whole year at twenty dollars a month and your keeping and your terbacker and work clothes."

And I says: "Izzy, I'll call your hand on that right now. I'll stay with you and help you run this farm like it was my own. Soon I'll be a free man. I'll soon be twenty-one. Just three more years. Then I can have all my money."

Lord, all the time I was talking to Izzy I was thinking about his girl. I was thinking about Mattie. I was thinking what if I just had that little woman in my arms and she'd be my dough-beater for the rest of my days. Lord, it was a great thought to have, even if it couldn't be true.

I went to town—rode a mule in—and went to the store. I asked to see a blue serge suit in the fifteen-dollar line. Clerk handed me out a beaut. I tried it on. It looked like a darb to me. First long suit of clothes I ever bought and I bought it with my own money. It made me feel big to do it. I took two dollars and bought me a pair of low-cut shoes and I asked the clerk to throw me in a pair of socks. He didn't like to do it but he did. I took the other dollar and bought me one of the prettiest little gray felt hats you ever put your peepers on. I got on the mule and rode fourteen miles back to Izzy's.

Well, I went in the room and I come out all trigged up. I called Sugarfoot out to see me. And that little lovey-dovey of a honey-baby sleepy-eyed doll come out to see me. And Sugarfoot says: "Your pants are a little short and got a lot of peg in the legs. Looks like they've been measured in the water." And I says: "What do you mean by peg, Sugar-foot?" And she says: "See how they blouse out at the hips?"

And Mattie says: "Why, Ma, I think Lizard looks real nice in his new clothes. He's a good-looking boy!" I believe I was the happiest man in the world. I just run in my room and took my clothes off and hung them on a peg in the corner. I went right out and went to work.

I thought that Mattie cast sheep eyes at me two or three times, but when I tried to catch them I saw she hadn't. She was just nice to me because I was her pap's lackey boy. Once Sugarfoot says to me: "You've come nigher being one of our family than any lackey boy we've ever had around this place." And that made my heart thump like a tired mule.

It was along in early September when Mattie started packing for college. I remember the morning Izzy told me to harness the mules and take Mattie to the train. Lord, it tickled me to death to get to do something for her—like help her in the surrey and lift her trunk and her suitcases and boxes at the depot. I run out and geared up the mules. I shined all the brass on the harness. I fixed them right good and swept the surrey out and greased the wheels so there wouldn't be no screaking.

The place wasn't the same without Mattie. I saw it was Mattie that made me like Izzy's place so. It was that what made me work the way I did. I guess that's what made the stud terrapin come out in me, the lizard, the water dog, the bulldog and all the other varmints. It was that beautiful doll of Izzy's. I wanted Mattie. It looked like too, that I'd never get her. Yet I used to hear Pa say: "Long as there's life there's hopes." And, "Long as there's a will there's a way." So I just put up new courage and started work hard as ever. It was crop-gathering time. We had to cut the terbacker and the corn. We had to make the sorghum. Lord, it was a busy time. And when Mattie sent home letters—why, Sugarfoot would read parts of them to us around the table. It made my heart ache. Lots of times I'd have to get up and leave the table. It hurt me so. Izzy would say: "When did she say she's a-coming home?" Sugarfoot would say: "She didn't say." "I'd like to see her," Izzy would say.

One day when we come in from the terbacker patch, hungry as a bunch of hounds, Sugarfoot come up and she says: "Got good news for you, Izzy. Mattie is coming home Thanksgiving and she's bringing Leonard home with her."

Well, it wasn't good news to me. It was like a bullet through my heart. I just hated to see him come. I wanted to see Mattie.

Day before Thanksgiving I had to gear the mules and go to the station after them. I'll never forget it. Off stepped sweet little Mattie with that dood. Lord o'mercy, I wished you could have seen him. Collar so stiff a fly couldn't'a specked it. Clothes fit him to a T. That little mustache all right in place. A big tie all coiled right below his chin.

I walked up and I says: "Howdy, Mattie." And she says: "Howdy, Lizard. I want you to meet Leonard Pratt." And I says: "I'm glad to know you, Leonard." I reached out my hand. He didn't reach me his. Like my hand was dirty. He bowed a little and says: "Glad to know you, Lizard." And smiled a little and showed his big white horse-teeth. He says: "Get my bags over there, Lizard. They all belong to me and Mattie."

Well, I carried them over and put them in the front seat of the surrey. Leonard helped Mattie in the back seat of the surrey, and before I had them heavy grips carried over they were under the heavy lap-robe. I says: "Smoothing irons in there, Mattie, for you to put your feet agin if they get cold." And she says: "Good old Lizard, to think that much of me." Leonard reached over the seat and says: "Here, Lizard, take this." I says: "What is it?" He says: "A quarter for your trouble." I says: "I get paid for doing this. No trouble to me. Just keep your damn' quarter." It made my blood bile. I couldn't keep from saying it. I never looked back. Kept my hands on the reins and my eye on the mudholes. I knew that Leonard was holding Mattie's hands under the lap-robe. I was Stubblefield's lackey boy but I'll be damned if I was that glue-eyed Leonard's lackey boy. He never dreamed that I loved the same woman he loved. And we went over the roads till we got to Stubblefield's house.

Mattie went in while I carried the grips to the house. I didn't know what the family thought about Leonard. I would see that later.

We's a-setting before the fire that night and he said the

wrong thing. He says: "Mr. Stubblefield, how do you vote?" Izzy says: "My son, I've been a lifelong Democrat. I barely ever scratched my ticket." And he puffed his cigar. Leonard puffed his cigarette. He says: "That's the wrong ticket, Mr. Stubblefield. I've been a Republican all my life."

Well, what he said got Izzy riled. It got us all riled. "Well," he says, "I just want to tell you all right now that this family's got a Republican in it. It's got two. It's got two now, and it'll soon have three. I'll soon have my little wifey here seeing it my way."

"Your wife?" says Izzy.

"Yes, my wife," says Leonard. "She's my lawfully wedded wife. I can show you the certificate. It's in there in one of my bags. You are my Poopy-deck Pappie. I'm your son-in-law. We got hitched last month."

I thought I was going to faint. I never had anything to hurt me like that. Izzy just sat there. He didn't say anything. And Mattie says: "I got me a school to teach down at Leonard's home. He's going to review up on his law books and start practicing law."

I got up and left the table. I walked out in the yard and pretty soon Izzy come out.

I says: "Izzy, I think I'll be leaving you. Me and that Leonard can't stay under the same roof. If it wasn't in your house and Mattie's lawful husband I'd ask him out behind the house and it would be man for man."

"You can't leave me in the time o' trouble," says Izzy. "Now is the time I need you. I ain't going to be able to do much work for a while. She's my girl. He's her husband. I got to treat him right. Just got to accept him."

I overheard Izzy and Sugarfoot talking. And Sugarfoot

says: "I don't believe he's much on the work either. Just won't move. All the time a-talking about the course of time and politics. Them boys ain't saying much but they are mad as hornets. They'll just crack his skull with a club or knife him in a minute if he don't shut up around here about politics. They are all riled."

"You can have him for a son-in-law," says Izzy. "I don't want him. And I just double-dare him to call me Poopy-deck Pappie again too. I won't take that off'n no son-in-law."

That made me feel good. I just thought: "I'm not so bad fooled. I see how they feel about him. They are in great trouble. I'll stay on with Izzy for another year."

"I believe poor Mattie's driv' her ducks to a bad market," says Izzy.

"She loves him," says Sugarfoot. "She told me she worshiped the ground he walked on."

"Love, hell," says Izzy. "A feller with his fingernails painted and his hair all curled—how can she love a man like that? How can a Stubblefield take a man like that?"

Now let me tell you what happened before Mattie and that Leonard left. He even asked Ma Sugarfoot to fetch him a drink o' water. Wouldn't put his feet on the ground. Had to wait on him like a baby. And I just thought: "You low-down good-for-nothing doll of a man you. One thing you will do. You won't be too lazy to get a family of children for Mattie to take care of." I hauled them back to the train. Took all Mattie's clothes. I just barely spoke to that Leonard. I felt for his wife. I says to myself: "Mattie, there'll come the time when you'll look to old Lizard-lip." And when they got on the train I waved goodby.

Just to tell you the truth, Mattie made the living until before the baby come. Leonard would get her checks. He done the spending. I know all about it. Bert Springer's wife, Cat, is from right down there at Big Rock and she told me all about it. He'd buy his clothes, beer and just anything he wanted out of her check. And after the baby come—why, he said he was down with his back. He couldn't work. And he wouldn't turn his hand. Mattie had to pack in the water, coal and carry him water to drink. I'll tell you, when Izzy heard about it he was a riled man. He says: "I'm going after my girl. I'm not going to stand this. I can't help it if she did burn herself. I'm going after my youngin. She's my girl yet."

I saw old Izzy was riled. And I says: "Izzy, just let me gear up the mules and take the surrey after her. I can make that trip down there and back today." And Sugarfoot says: "Yes, Izzy, let Lizard go after her." Izzy was riled and Sugarfoot saw he was riled. "Go ahead," says Izzy, "but be damned sure you bring her home."

I never felt happier in my life. It was one time I put the harness on the mules and felt like I was going to heaven— going after Mattie.

Now you talk about spinning over the road. It was fall-time again, and the dust fairly flew. When I got there—I just hate to tell you. But Big Rock—if it's a town worth living in I'm a suck-egg mule. I says to a big long-haired devil by one of the houses: "Can you tell me where Leonard Pratt lives?" And the feller went: "Ha—ha—ha—that pretty boy. That lazy good-for-nothing that lays in bed and lets a poor wife with a little young baby carry up the water —carry in the kindling and coal and make the living. The laziest, orneriest white man that ever breathed a breath of air and I know it—lives right over there. I heard she's going home."

"Bet your happy life she's a-going home if these mules

are able to pull us in the surrey back them twenty miles we just come."

I driv' over to the house—hitched to the fence post. I walked in: "Honey, come on," I says. "Izzy wants you to come home."

Well, the tears streamed from her eyes. Had her baby in her arms. There laid that Leonard in the bed. He says: "She's not going home."

I says: "Who said she wasn't going home, pretty boy? Now if you don't want to get hurt, keep your pants on."

He took me at my word. He kept his pants on. Mattie got her duds packed and I put them in the back seat o' the surrey. Mules just a-prancing to get started back. I got Mattie's little baby in my arms and I took her by the arm. I says: "Come on, let's get out'n this hole."

And Leonard says: "You'll be sorry someday. In the course of times I'll be the biggest lawyer that ever hit these parts. You must remember the women fall for old Leonard."

"Women and be damned," says Mattie. "All I ask of you is a divorce. I've stood all this I can to make a go of it. Waited on you long enough. I'm going back to my people. You can do just as you please. Goodby."

I led her out to the surrey. I helped her up with one hand and held the baby with the other. Then I jumped in the surrey and took the reins. This was one time Mattie sat right up in the front seat with old lackey boy, Lizard. She sat right by me with the baby in her lap. And I patted the mules a little with the lines. And they started twenty miles away toward their barn—just at a high trot.

Mattie says: "Lizard, I'll always love you, honey, for doing this."

And it run through my veins, them words did, like sap in a spring tree.

I says: "I've always loved you. That's why I've stayed with Izzy and worked the way I have. I loved you the first time I ever saw you. But you was a girl in college and I was a lackey boy working for your pa—working for the Stubblefields."

Mattie says: "Well, my life is hurt. Nearly spent. Look at all this. Look—a baby. It will be hard for me to marry again if I ever want to, don't you think?"

And I says: "No. You can get married just as soon as you get your divorce. You'll at least get a man that can work and that will work and make you a living. You'll get one that don't speak proper words and ain't been to no college. Been to a college of dirt, cornfields, terbacker fields and rocks. Through the college of hard knocks. He's part stud terrapin and part water dog, bulldog and lots of other varmints, but he loves you."

I just never looked around at Mattie. She used to have such pretty bloom on her face. Now all that's gone—she's lean and poor as a winter snake. I just hated to look at her and her pretty eyes.

Well, the moon come out on the pretty brown falltime hills. Mattie got a little cold. She got over close to me. I just pretended I didn't notice. But I just eased over to her. Moon so pretty in the sky. And I had to say it: "When are you going to get that divorce?" And she says: "Before farming time this coming spring." And I says: "It's a long time to wait, but if you can't do no better I can wait that long. I've waited longer than this already for this time to come. I'll wait the rest of the fall and winter while the sap is dead in the trees."

And the mules just kept going toward home. A mule knows the road when he's going home. No one else on the road this time o'day. I hooked my lines over the dashboard and I pulled Mattie up beside me. I kissed her right there in the moonlight. And all that lovey-dovey look come back to her eyes. Prettiest woman in the world. Pretty as a big sleepy-eyed doll. I kissed her again.

And then she says: "Pa's got that big farm above the house and nobody on it." And I says: "I'm not a free man yet. I'm still a lackey boy." She says: "Don't worry about that, Lizard."

And it just seemed to me like I could hear water a-beating on a rock. Maybe it was my heart. I pulled Mattie right over in my arms and the mules kept going. It was heaven to me to ride through that pretty moonlight. And I says:

"I know one thing. Izzy will like my politics. He'll like that about me. Might hold it agin me being a lackey boy. But he can tell you that I can run a farm. And just to think, I'll be running one for you and me soon as the sap gets up in the spring and all life starts over again."

⚓ *The Highest Bidder* ⚓

"SUSIE Bell, come to the window and see who is passing the house," I said. "You won't know them!"

"Men passing?" Susie Bell asked.

"Yes, men are passing," I said. "Men are passing by our door in this forsaken valley!"

"Are they good looking?" she asked.

"See for yourself," I replied.

Susie Bell jumped up from the table and ran to the window. She put her face against the windowpane and looked down the path toward the sulphur spring under the beech trees.

"I don't know them," she said. "Who are they, Sophie?"

"Tommie Hacker and Lonsey Ratcliff," I replied.

"You don't mean they're dressed up like that?" she said.

"Yes, they're dressed up like that," I told her. "Didn't

you know this country has been at war. Don't you know that nearly all of the Plum Grove men are scattered over the world. This country is calling boys and old men to work in the mills and factories. Lonsey and Tommie have found work at Big Etna Furnace in Toniron, Ohio!"

"I've not seen a well-dressed man since Kim left," Susie Bell sighed. "I've not had a date. Let's call them up to the house. What do you say?"

"Suits me all right, but we'll make the Sperry girls jealous," I said. "They are goin' there now to see the Sperry girls. I hear they are going to marry 'em. You see they are goin' to the Pie Supper tonight at Plum Grove."

"I'm goin' to ask them up to the house anyway," Susie Bell said.

Susie Bell went to the door.

"Hello, Lonsey," Susie Bell called.

"Was that a voice I heard?" Lonsey asked Tommie. He turned and looked toward the house.

"Sure was a voice," Susie Bell called back to him. "Won't you and Tommie come up to the house a while? Looks like you're all tuckered out."

"We're not used to these mud paths up and down these hollers and over these hills!" Lonsey said. "We're not used to them any more."

"It's sure hard on good shoes and good clothes," Tommie said. "I don't mind if we do come up a while."

He whispered something to Lonsey we couldn't hear down under the leafless beech trees by the sulphur spring. Then, they started toward the house.

"Goodie, goodie, gee," sighed Susie Bell. "Good lookin' men I see!"

Susie Bell ran across the big front room and clapped her

hands. She laughed as she ran about the room. "Let the Sperry girls be jealous of us tonight," she said laughing. "We'll make them jealous. We'll make them plenty jealous."

Tommie and Lonsey walked up and Lonsey knocked at the door.

"Come right in," I invited them.

"How are you Lonsey?" I asked. I took him by the hand and I squeezed his hand as I greeted him.

"All right, thank you," he said. "Just worried a lot with this old country mud! It's almost ruint my shoes."

I turned to shake Tommie's hand. Susie Bell had him by the hand. She was shaking his hand and holding to it.

"Why of course, Susie Bell, I remember you," Tommie said.

"Don't you remember when we used to go to Plum Grove School together?"

"I should say I do," Tommie said. "You were the purtiest girl in that school. I never dreamed then that you'd ever call me into your house."

"I know but things have changed a lot since then," Susie Bell said. "Our country has been at war. So many of the boys have gone. So many of them will not get back you know. We don't have the big parties and the company like we used to have."

"How right you are!" said Tommie. "Girls used to wouldn't look at me. Since I went to the Big Etna Furnace and got me a job of work and made big money, they're after me now. I'll tell you all the girls are after me!"

"Let me shake your hand, Tommie, since Susie Bell has turned your hand loose," I said. "I thought she was goin' to hold you forever!"

"Yes, let Sophie shake your hand," Lonsey said. "Let old friends unite here this evening."

"Tommie and Lonsey, I want to ask you to supper," I said. "I know you are hungry after climin' that big hill over by Tom Griffith's. I know it was hard pullin' up there in this March mud."

"Yes, see these ten-dollar shoes," Tommie said. "Look at them won't you! I got so hot I pulled off my topcoat and let the tail of it drag in the mud. I'll have to have my topcoat cleaned."

"Too bad, but supper is gettin' cold," Susie Bell said.

"I know," Lonsey said looking toward Tommie, "but we must—"

"Now, Lonsey, you and Tommie just have to eat with us," Susie Bell interrupted. She had come over to spend the night with me since Ma and Pa and the children went over to Lucasville, Ohio, to see Uncle John. "We're goin' to the Pie Supper tonight. We have the best pie baked any-one could ever put his tongue to."

"Come on to supper," I said. "Don't be bashful. We'll show you just how we can cook."

"Well, my dear, it's just as you say," Lonsey said. "We are very hungry but we are supposed to be moving along. We are supposed to be—"

"Oh, I know," interrupted Susie Bell—"but we have vit-tles on the table. We have good hot coffee too. And we will let you sample one of our pies."

"All right, I'm ready," Tommie said.

We walked into the dining room. We sat down at the table. Lonsey pulled his chair up beside mine. I looked at his white silk shirt with wide blue stripes running up and down the front. I looked at the gold crowns around the broken teeth he had in front before he went to the Big Etna Furnace. He wore a double-breasted blue serge suit. A gold watch chain dangled across his vest. He wore a big fob on the chain with Martha Sperry's picture in it.

"You've changed a lot, Lonsey, since you left these hills," I said.

"Yes, my dear Sophie, since I've been making big money I've changed a lot," he replied with a smile. "I've been shovelin' iron ore all the time I could get and then doublin' over on the other fellars' shifts all I could. I've been working nearly day and night. I'm in the big money! Just as I tell the boys! 'Fellars, I'm shovelin' gold-dust with a golden shovel.' "

"And I am too," Tommie said. "I'm Lonsey's partner. We room together. We work together. When he buys a pair of eight-dollar shoes, I buy a pair of nine-dollar shoes. When he pays four dollars for a silk shirt, I give five dollars for one. Shucks, I never thought we'd have times like these when I used to be out here on these hills hoein' corn for fifty cents a day. If I paid fifty cents for a shirt in them days I thought it was big money."

"You are certainly dressed fit to kill," Susie Bell said. "You're the best-dressed men I've ever seen among these Plum Grove Hills."

"Thank you, honey," Tommie said. He was happy. "I've always said when I got to the place I was making big money I'd have all my teeth crowned with gold—just like Lonsey there—of course my teeth are good but I'll have 'em crowned anyway because I think gold teeth are pretty."

"Now help yourself to the beans Lonsey," I said. "Here take a good piece of corn bread."

"Thank you, I've not had a good piece of corn bread

since I've been away," Lonsey said. "We eat what is called light bread. It won't stick to the ribs like corndodger. I'll tell you that right now."

Tommie and Lonsey filled their plates with fried middling meat, brown soup beans, fried potatoes and corn bread. They shoveled the grub into their mouths like they said they shoveled ore. They ate like they were almost starved.

"Not too much, don't put away too much grub, Lonsey," Tommie said. "Remember, we're goin' to the Pie Supper tonight. We're goin' to eat pies tonight. We got to leave some space to hold pie."

"Right you are Tommie," Lonsey said.

"Yes, you've got to sample a piece of our pie to see if it's not the best before you leave this table," I said. "You've got a good taste in clothes and you ought to have good taste with pie."

Lonsey bent over at the table and laughed.

"Yes, darling, I'll sample your pie," he said. "I'll tell you what I think about it."

"And Tommie, you must sweeten my coffee," Susie Bell said.

"All right, honey," he said reaching for the sugar bowl.

"No, darling, you know that's no way to sweeten coffee," Susie Bell said.

"Then how do I sweeten your coffee, darling?"

"Put your finger in it," she said.

"All right, darling," he said.

He put his finger in Susie Bell's cup of hot steaming coffee.

"Ouch! God," he hollered, lifting his little finger from the steaming hot coffee.

"Sweetenin' coffee," Lonsey said. He bent over the table and laughed. Susie Bell took his little finger into her hand.

"Did it hurt you, honey?" she asked him. "I'm sorry about it."

I laughed at Tommie as he bent over toward Susie Bell when she was holding his burned little finger.

"Old hot coffee burnt my Tommie's little finger," she said. "Shame on old hot coffee."

"And if I'd a-got my ring down in that coffee, it would a nearly burnt my finger off before I could a-got my finger out or the ring off," Tommie said. "It might a-turned the gold in my ring too."

"Try my pie, Lonsey," I said. "It's not hot I'll have you understand. It is cool and sweet."

I put a piece of pie on a dessert plate and placed it by Lonsey's plate. Lonsey took his fork and cut off a bite. He lifted it to his lips. He chewed the pie and looked at me. He chewed and looked at Tommie and Susie Bell.

"Honest people, that pie's so good that it melts in my mouth," he said. "I never tasted anything better."

"That's the kind of pie we're taking to the Pie Supper tonight," Susie Bell said. "I mean if we can get there! You know the road is dark and it's awfully rough walking. And to tell you the truth, it's dangerous for two girls to go that far by themselves."

"Yes," said Lonsey, looking at Tommie.

"And it's started gettin' dark already," Tommie said. "See that quarter moon comin' up the blue sky!"

"Yes, I'll haf to light the lamp before we can finish our suppers," I said.

"Ain't you gals sparkin' a couple of war birds?" Tommie asked me.

"We used to but we ain't heard from them since the war's over," I said. "Don't know whether they got killed or not. I guess they did or we'd have heard from 'em."

"It's been so long I've just longed to see a well-dressed man," Susie Bell said. "I've been hungry to walk beside of one and let his strong hand take hold of my arm again. But the boys are all gone. Just strips of boys and old married men here now. Soldiers haven't got back yet. It's not often we see men like you. No wonder you get the girls!"

When Susie Bell said this Lonsey and Tommie looked pleased. They looked at one another and then they looked at us.

"It's about time we were startin' to the Pie Supper," Susie Bell said.

"You'll need help with pies as good as this one," Lonsey said. "We don't want you to stump your toe on a rock, and fall and spill the pie, do we Tommie?"

"I should say not," Tommie said. "We'll take you to Plum Grove if you don't care!"

"But all the girls will be jealous of us," said Susie Bell.

"Never mind about that for I know right now whose pie I aim to get," Lonsey said. "I'll get it too. It takes the money at a pie supper. And I've got the money. They can't run the bid too high for old Lonsey now! It will be my pie."

"We'd better be on our way," I told them. "We'll haf to hurry. Night is comin' fast. The mud has frozen along the path now and won't stick to our shoes. What do you say we get ready and move along?"

"Suits me," said Lonsey. "I'm ready!"

Lonsey got up from the table and put on his topcoat. He

put his white scarf around his neck. He pulled gloves from his topcoat pocket and gloved his hands. Tommie rose from the table and slid his arms into his topcoat sleeves. He wrapped his neck with a white scarf and gloved his hands.

"Here's my pie, darling," I said to Lonsey. "Be sure you don't drop it."

"Here's my pie," Susie Bell said to Tommie. "I'll help Sophie close the doors. We must be movin' along."

When we started down the path by the sulphur spring, Lonsey took me by the arm. He held me tight enough to numb my arm. Tommie took Susie Bell by the arm. There was hardly room enough for two to walk side by side down the narrow path. Tommie whispered in Susie Bell's ear like he had a lot of secrets he didn't want us to hear. After he'd whisper he and Susie Bell would laugh and the March wind would laugh in the barren beech tree limbs that hung over our path. The stars from the March sky and the little quarter moon looked down upon us.

"What's the money for this pie supper goin' for?" Lonsey asked me.

"Honey, I don't know, but I think it's for the Methodist Church," I said. "I think they send it on for the homeless children in Africa."

"Fine, I guess it's all right," Lonsey said. "I'm a Baptist though."

"You're holdin' my arm too tight," I said. "Give the blood a little chance to circulate. Honey, you are more of a man than you think you are."

"It's shovelin' that ore," Lonsey said. "I'll tell you it's hard work when you get down to the hopper and haf to throw it over the side of the car with a long-handled shovel. It puts muscles on a man's arms. I couldn't feel my strength until I got away. Now, my dear, I didn't know I was squeezin' your lily-white arm! I was just holdin' it naturally."

"Now darlin' when I was a boy hoein' corn for John Stevens here on this creek, I used to come over here every Sunday morning and wade from the mouth of this creek to the head of it huntin' for turtles," Tommie said. "I had me a stick with a fish hook on the end of it. I'd go along and stick it under the edges of the banks. After a while, I'd fish out a big ten-pound turtle. I'd bring old Jerry along and he'd hole a groundhog. So I'd go home with a big turtle and a big groundhog for Sunday dinner. Gee, I couldn't do that sort of thing again."

"I love turtle meat," Susie Bell said. "They tell me you can taste seven different kinds of meat in turtle. I like turtle eggs too."

"Best part of a turtle," Tommie said. "Jist to tell the truth I was always a little afraid of a turtle. When a turtle bites you he won't let his holts go until it thunders or the sun goes down."

"Turtles are good, but honey, I'd rather have pie any old time!"

"Good for you," I said.

"Great, Sophie, my dear, I've just been thinkin' if you love me as I love you, I can truly surely say that you are the only girl I'll love and care for anymore," Lonsey said.

"It's awful soon for you to say that," I said. "You almost bring the blood to my face. You make me blush. I've heard you're in love."

We walked down the valley past the Hylton house, over

the frozen crust of mud. Then we passed the old sawmill and the Collins' barn. We walked up the hill past the coal mines and over the top of the hill, through the Collins' orchard to Wheeler's woods. We walked down a long narrow path under the giant oak trees. The bright stars in the heavens above looked down upon us through the barren tops of the oaks. The wind blew through the oak tops and made a lot of lonesome sounds. It felt good to have a date again—to walk beside of Lonsey Ratcliff.

"I see the lights from the Plum Grove church house," Susie Bell said. "I hear Fatty Holbrooks. He must be auctionin' off the pies now! Let's hurry and get out there."

"Yes, we just have that field to cross and we'll be there," Lonsey said.

We hurried across the field. Lonsey held my arm with one hand and the pie in the other hand. Tommie held Susie Bell's arm with one hand and carried her pie in the other hand. I wish you had seen the crowd when we walked up to the church house door—a crowd of young strips of boys that had smelled of a moonshine jug and thought they were drunk. They had been working on the farms and didn't have over a quarter or fifty cents in their pockets. They were standin' on the outside waitin' for some homely girl's pie that wouldn't sell for more than fifty cents. Then one would bid and buy himself a pie.

I wish you could have seen the difference in the way Tommie and Lonsey were dressed. The boys just looked and looked at them. They didn't know them. They didn't know that Tommie and Lonsey used to live among them and dressed like they did. Now they had been away to Big Etna Furnace and had made good. They'd come home dressed in fine clothes with money bulging in their pockets

—money they wanted to spend. When we walked in the house, the girls looked up from everywhere. We could tell they were jealous of us. But we didn't mind.

"Do I hear fifty cents fer this pie?" Fatty Holbrooks asked. "Come on boys! Come on! Jist a half-a-dollar! Open your hearts and your pocketbooks and eat beside a purty gal!"

There was silence in the room. I saw the Sperry sisters over by the stove. They were looking at us. Their black eyes were shining. We could see that they were mad as hornets.

"Fifty cents takes the little girl's pie," says Fatty. "Come and get it young man!"

A tall boy wearing blue overalls, a white shirt and a jumper walked in from the outside and took the pie. It was Fronnie Leadingham's pie. She walked over across the room and sat down beside him. They began eating pie.

"All right boys, all right," Fatty said. "Martha Sperry's pie. Do I hear a bidder? Do I hear one boys? Do I hear one? The purty little girl over here on my right."

"Five dollars," said a voice from the outside of the house.

Lonsey raised his head. He looked around.

"Don't you bid on her pie, honey," I whispered.

"Five dollars I hear," said Fatty. "Not enough for a good pie and a pretty girl. Not enough—do I hear a higher bidder?"

Fatty looked at Lonsey. I could see his eyes set way back in his head were beaming beneath the oil lamp on the wall. His hands were up in the air. He held the pie with one hand and he waved the other hand and hollered for another bidder. There wasn't another bidder.

"Come, young man, and take the pie for five smackers," he said.

No one came to get it. Fatty hollered for him again. He didn't come.

Martha looked over at me. She looked hurt. She looked like she could wring my neck like a chicken's neck if she could get hold of me. Little Murtie Sperry was looking at Tommie. Tommie was trying to miss her keen black piercing eyes, but she had them fastened on him.

"It just seems to me that we'll have trouble before this pie supper is over," Tommie said.

I never said anything. I kept my eye on the Sperry girls —all reared back looking mean as snakes—their collars high upon their necks, wearing big brown coats with bunches of white percoon in their lapels, black hats with big hatpins running through them.

"They may pull the pins out of their hats and take after Susie Bell and me," kept running through my head. I looked for them to do it every minute.

"Well, the five-dollar bidder must have left the hill," said Fatty. "I'm goin' to give him out comin'. Do I hear another bidder for this pie?"

"Fifty cents," said a boy from the outside. "That's what I bid before and that's what I'll bid again. That's all any pie is worth!"

"That fellar was just tryin' to run it up on me a while ago," Lonsey whispered.

"He knew I had plenty of money. He knew I could buy all the pies here tonight."

"Honey you're not buyin' 'em all," I said.

"But I'll buy yours at any cost," he whispered.

It made me feel good. Everything was working out just

right. I wondered if Martha Sperry was sorry the way she'd done me once—took my fellar and bragged about it all over the district. Now the people would talk.

"Bidder the pie is yours for fifty cents," Fatty said. "Come and get it."

I wish you'd have seen the fellow who bought Martha's pie. He was teaed to the gills on moonshine. He took in both sides of the aisle. He walked up and got the pie. I laughed to myself so Martha couldn't see me. He walked up and got the pie from Fatty. "Let's eat, honey," he said. "Where air you sugar babe."

"I'm right here," Martha said. "But I'm not eating with an old walrus like you."

"So much more for me," he said. "I'll eat the pie by myself. I love pie. I've got a pie-mouth." Then he let out a big horse laugh. You could hear him all over the Plum Grove church house.

"Not good enough for the army," I heard a man say. "Off in the head and a glass eye. He was exempted. That's old Charlie Keaton!"

"Now boys, little Murtie Sperry's pie," Fatty said. "Do I hear a bid? Do I hear a bid?"

"You hear twenty-five cents," said a big man in the church house. He was old enough to be Little Murtie's Pap.

"That's Widder Man Hatton biddin' on your old gal's pie, Tommie," I heard Susie Bell whisper to Tommie. "Don't you bid. Let 'im have it."

"Do I hear another bid?" Fatty asked the crowd. "That's too little for a good custard pie."

"Too little me eye," said Widder Man Hatton. "That's a God's plenty for a pie."

The boys laughed on the outside of the church house. I

could hear them laughing everyplace like that was something funny. Little Murtie looked like she could bite a
spike nail in two as big tubby Widder Man Hatton wob-
bled up and got her pie. He walked back and sat down
beside her.

"I'll shore eat half of my pie," said Little Murtie. "I'll
get this much satisfaction out of it. And, Widder Man Hatton, I don't want you to get nary bit over half of it
nohow."

All the crowd laughed. That give us a chance to laugh.
We laughed and laughed. Tommie forced a laugh. He
looked and looked at Murtie. People looked at Tommie
and then at Murtie. Susie Bell looked at Tommie and then
at Murtie. Susie Bell didn't know whether to laugh or
not.

"And now I have Susie Bell Turner's pie," said Fatty.
"Do I hear a bid?"

"Five dollars," said a voice from the outside.

"Ten dollars," said Tommie.

"Fifteen," said Lonsey. Lonsey laughed.

"Twenty," said Tommie.

"Twenty-five," says a voice from the outside.

"Thirty," said Tommie.

"Any higher," asked Fatty Holbrooks as he wiped the
sweat from his fat brow.

"Thirty-one dollars," said Lonsey.

"Thirty-five," said Tommie.

"Any higher?" asked Fatty. "Boy, that's the way I like to
see you bid. The young man is goin' to have his honey's
pie!"

"Any higher bid?" Fatty asked. "Does another young
man want to eat pie with this young man's sweetheart?"

There wasn't another bid.

"Come and get the pie," Fatty said.

Tommie walked up and reached Fatty a twenty-dollar bill, a ten-dollar bill and a five-dollar bill.

"It's a costly pie, Son," said Fatty.

"A dollar a bite," said Tommie with smiles. "But I don't mind. I've got the money. I don't mind helpin' the church."

"And now, boys, I have the sweetest smellin' persimmon pie here you ever smelled," said Fatty. "Do I hear a bidder? Persimmon pie! It's something new—I've heard of 'em but never tasted one."

"Twenty dollars," said Lonsey.

I felt so good when Lonsey started bidding my pie off at twenty dollars. I looked to see if the Sperry girls were watchin' us. Little Murtie was eatin' pie with Widder Man Hatton. She wasn't lookin' up at the crowd. Martha had her back turned. I think she was poutin' at us.

"Thirty dollars," said a voice from the outside. His voice came through the window beside us. I thought I'd heard this voice before.

"Thirty-five dollars," said Tommie. He was sittin' beside Susie Bell who was holding her pie.

"Fifty dollars," Lonsey said.

"Sixty dollars," the voice came through the window.

"Seventy-five dollars," said Tommie.

"I'll raise you twenty-five dollars," Lonsey said. "I'll make it a round hundred dollars!"

"Is that man made of money," Alf Turnispeed said, "One hundred dollars for a pie. More money than brains! Who'd ever dream of anywhere in this world a pie would sell for a hundred dollars—let alone here at Plum Grove when you can buy twenty acres of land for that!"

"Do I hear a higher bidder?" Fatty asked. Fatty was wiping the drops of sweat from his brow with a bandana.

The room was beginning to fill up with staring people. Young men walked in from the outside to look at the pie.

"It's your pie, young man," Fatty said.

Lonsey walked up the aisle. People stared at him as he walked. He took the pie from Fatty's hand.

"Two dollars a bite for that one," said Fatty.

"Four dollars a bite, for I'll take big bites on that good persimmon pie," Lonsey said. "I never et one before but I know it's good. Look at the little girl who made it!"

"Who's that rich man?" a man asked.

"His face looks familiar," said another. "But I don't know him."

"That ain't old Lonsey Ratcliff, is it?" whispered another.

"Nope, you know it ain't," whispered someone else.

"Wish I'd a-paid more now," said Tommie. "Work is good. Everybody is happy. Plenty of money. The world is full of money. This war has brought prosperity to the people left at home."

"So war does bring prosperity to the people at home," said a man dressed in uniform with an overseas cap on his head. "A war on and you at home. You ain't nothin' but a damned slacker! We go fight the war and you stay at home! You take our girls and make the money!"

"Rodney, when did you come?" I asked. "Or is this your ghost?"

"No, Sophie, it ain't my ghost," he replied. "I'm here in flesh and blood. I come out on the Old Line Special this afternoon. I heard there was goin' to be a pie supper here tonight. Thought I'd get back to my old stompin' grounds and see some of the old timers. I didn't think I'd run into you here with these damn slackers!"

"Honey, I thought you was dead," I said. "I've not heard from you in eight months."

"Oh, Kim!" Susie Bell shouted. She run out into the aisle and put her arms around Kim's neck. "Kim, I thought you were dead!"

"If I were dead I suppose you'd pick up a thing like this," Kim replied angrily. "Ask him why he isn't fighting? Yes, ask the upstart! Yes, he can give twenty-five dollars for a pie and his friend can give a hundred dollars for my old pal's girl's pie. But what can we give—a dollar a day and our rations! Big shots, these slackers, dressed so fancy in the best clothes and wearing rings and watches!"

"Tough guys," said Tommie. "War birds!"

"I'll show you what a war bird is," Kim shouted.

"Whow!"

One lick was sent to Tommie's chin. Tommie fell sprawled out in the aisle.

"That's what a war bird is," said Rodney. "My old pal, Kim, has showed you. A war bird is one who fights. He usually has good fists, too!"

Little Murtie bent over and laughed. Martha stood up and held to her seat, for she was shaking all over with laughter. The people stood and looked on. It was a fight and they liked a fight at Plum Grove no matter if it was in the Plum Grove church house.

"And this is for you since my old pal has put that slacker under the sweet peas," Rodney said.

"Whow!"

He hit Lonsey smack on the chop. Lonsey fell sprawling like a toppled tree down on top of Tommie, who lay flat face down on the floor.

"One hundred dollars for a persimmon pie," Rodney said. "My wife-to-be made it! I dreamed while I was in France, Belgium and Germany of a log shack with her— back among these hills—back where peace comes with the plow. Peace is everywhere here. I've dreamed and dreamed about a home I could call my own. I've prayed to live to get back to these Kentucky hills. I'll be damned if a slacker does give a hundred dollars for her pie. I'd see him in hell before I'd let him eat it with her!"

The crowd gathered in around us. Little Murtie and Martha Sperry were still laughing as they looked down at Tommie and Lonsey sprawled senselessly on the Plum Grove church house floor. I never saw two girls as well-pleased over what had happened. I could hardly keep from crying to see Rodney again. He looked so good. He looked a little tired. I'd seen so many uniforms during the war when the Plum Grove boys were back on furloughs that Rodney's uniform didn't look too good to me. The war was over now. I was tired of uniforms.

"Little girls, would you give me the flowers on your coats?" Rodney asked Martha and Little Murtie Sperry.

"Sure will," Martha replied quickly.

"That percoon looks so good to me," said Rodney. "It brings back bygone days when I was a boy among these hills! Bid these bouquets of percoon to the highest bidder, Fatso!"

"I sure will," he said. Fatty acted like a scared rabbit. His bright squinty eyes were jumping around in their sockets.

"Shore I'll bid 'em off to the highest bidder!" Fatty said.

Fatty stood upon a bench. He held a bouquet of percoon in each hand.

"All right folks, who'll bid on these flowers," Fatty asked.

"Two dollars," said John Worthington. "I had four boys over there. Joe can't be here. He's planted out there behind the church house."

"Five dollars," said Rodney.

"Twenty-one dollars and fifty cents," said Kim. "Don't anybody go any higher. This is on me. Put them on my comrades Joe Worthington's, Niles Jackson's and Bill Hilton's graves right out there in the Plum Grove graveyard."

Kim walked up and got the flowers. The crowd cheered him as he went.

"Where's persimmon pie?" a man asked.

"Under the sweet peas yet," said another.

"Come on, Rodney, let's go home!" I said.

"All right," he said.

I took him by the arm. I felt good to be with Rodney again. I didn't care for Lonsey. I loved Rodney. I just hadn't had a date in so long. It looked good to see the boys again. Kim took Susie Bell by the arm. He held the flowers in the other hand. We walked down the aisle.

"If the boys don't come to, you can have their funerals preached right here," Kim said. "The church house and the graveyard behind the house are right handy."

I saw Martha go over and pull on Lonsey's arms. Little Murtie was down on the floor rubbing Tommie's chin. The persimmon pie was all over the church house floor. I held to Rodney's arm. Susie Bell held to Kim's arm. We walked out of the house and left the crowd looking at the Sperry girls working over Lonsey and Tommie.

☆ A Pilgrim
Out in Space ☆

"**G**o, Willie, to the store and fetch back a dozen-and-a-half of hen eggs," Reverend Ezekiel Wrenhouse said. "We want them for breakfast. Our hens have all gone to settin' at the wrong time."

I wondered what Mrs. Wrenhouse would do for her breakfast. The Reverend always ate a dozen eggs for his breakfast, besides the pancakes, sorghum molasses, and hot biscuits. Then he would drink a pot of hot, black coffee. I didn't ask him if he wanted more eggs. I left him standing in the door when I went after the eggs.

If you could only see Reverend Wrenhouse then I wouldn't have to try to describe him to you. He is as different from any other man of the Word as any man I've ever known. When he stands in the door of his house you can't squeeze a knife blade between the top of his head and the doorcasing. He is that tall. And he is big with it. When he walks out of the door both of his shoulders touch the door facings. He has to tilt his shoulders to one side to walk out straight. He says he's just sixty years old. He wears a big moustache. He has big hands. One of his hands is big enough to cover the big family Bible. I've never seen a preacher as large as The Reverend Ezekiel Wrenhouse.

Reverend Wrenhouse moved from the mountains down to Lennix County. He said he left ten children back in the mountains. I don't know how many he left. I'm just telling you what he said. He said seven of his children were boys and three were girls, and that they all were married and lived back in the mountains. He said he had to leave the mountains for a reason. He never told me, but I think I know the reason. Reverend Wrenhouse was shot in the leg. At the big reunion he argued with another preacher over baptism. Reverend Wrenhouse stands for sousing them under. The other preacher said sprinkling was just as good. They got to arguing and got mad. The other mountain preacher pulled a gun and shot Reverend Wrenhouse in the leg. He limps today on that leg. He beat up the preacher who shot him. They had Reverend Wrenhouse in jail over it. He left the mountains. Now he is with us. I have been working for him ever since he's been here.

I walked up the road by the creek to the store. It was a nice ten-minute walk in June. The bees were working on the morning-glory that hung over the fence. Birds were singing in the trees. The sun was bright and warm. The pumpkins bloomed in the potato patch by the garden. Bumblebees buzzed around the big yellow blossoms. Big four-winged snake feeders whizzed up and down the creek.

You walk up the road by the creek. Then you come to a little bridge. It is a wooden bridge. You cross the bridge and walk upon the side of a hill under a beech grove and you will find two stores. These are the only stores for miles. They keep everything from medicine to mowing machines. The Bridges keep one. The Litterals keep the other one. When I walked up the bank I saw a crowd of men standing in front of Litteral's store. The Reverend always had done his trading at this store. The men just stood there. They didn't speak. They looked mean out of their eyes. Their lips were dropped down like mule lips. I spoke to them and walked into Litteral's store.

Jerry Sprouse said, "You wouldn't buy nothing from that store, would you? It's not fair to the Government of America! Look at his window! He hasn't got the bird in it! Where is the Blue Eagle?"

I said, "Reverend Wrenhouse sent me here. I didn't have any choice. I'm working for The Reverend. I've come to get what he wants."

"Go on and get it," said West Yates. "Just go on, Willie, and get it! That will be all right for us."

Fonse Litteral put a dozen-and-a-half eggs in a sack. I went out the door. The whole crowd of men moved up to meet me.

"What did I tell you?" Jerry Sprouse asked. "Let me see what you have in that sack. Why can't you buy your eggs from Bridges' store right over there? It's not ten steps away."

"I got them where Reverend Wrenhouse told me," I said. "I've not got a choice."

"But we have got a choice," said Jerry Sprouse. "You'll get your eggs from now on at Bridges'. See the bird in his window! See the Blue Eagle! Let me see the eggs you got in that sack nohow."

"I'll bet they're not any good," said Walt Sperry. "Look and see, Jerry!"

"They looked like good eggs to me," I said. "We've never gotten any rotten eggs from Litteral's store yet."

Jerry Sprouse grabbed my sack of eggs. The men crowded up close to me. There was Alf Tyler, Mort Sperry, Dave Smith, Kirt Blevins, and Ray Atkins.

"You're shore going to carry these back in a different way," said Jerry Sprouse. His black eyes were shining beneath his bushy eyebrows. He was chewing tobacco and spitting as he talked. Some of the ambeer caught on his black moustache and dripped off as he talked.

"Get down that road," he said to me. "Run for your life. You low-down pup. You don't know right from wrong yet. We'll teach you right from wrong."

"Wow." An egg took me on the shoulder and splattered all over my shirt. "Wow." An egg hit me on the back of the head hard enough to make me dizzy. The egg splattered all over my head. Another egg hit me and then another. I ran down the road as fast as I could go. Eggs hit all around me. The men laughed. They laughed fit to kill at my running and the egg yolks all over my clothes—raw eggs running down my face and dripping off like the ambeer from Jerry Sprouse's black moustache.

I thought, "What will Reverend Wrenhouse think? What will The Reverend do about this?"

I was nearly out of breath when I got to the house. I was scared. I ran into the house with egg dripping from me onto Reverend Wrenhouse's floor. When I ran into the front room he was reading the Word.

"Willie, what on earth is the matter with you?" Reverend Wrenhouse asked. "What on earth has happened? Where are my eggs?"

"A crowd of men standing in front of the two stores tried to make me buy from the store that has a bird's picture in the window," I said. "It's the Blue Eagle. Bridges has it in his store window. Litteral won't have it. I went to Litteral's store because you've always sent me there. They told me not to buy from the store that didn't have a bird in the window. So I bought there anyway. When I came out of the store they took my eggs and ran me down the road with them. They broke every egg I had in the sack throwing them at me."

"Nana, get Willie some warm water," Reverend Wrenhouse said. "I want him to wash the eggs off his face and out of his hair and eyes. He will have to change his clothes too. I'll go up to the store. I want that crowd to egg me! I'll give them a few eggs they can't carry home."

"Be careful, Zeke," Mrs. Wrenhouse said. "Remember, you are a preacher and that you are not as young as you once was. Remember how you had to lay in jail back in the mountains over beating Bully Thombs up over the Scriptures."

"I am a preacher, but I can still take it on the chin," he told her. "I can fight for what I believe. I can stand up and give blow-for-blow. I can still shoot a pistol. My eye is good. My aim is true. I'm going to see into this egg throwing. I want that crowd to attempt to run me away from the store. They can jump on a boy. Now let them jump on a man of the Word! I've fought over the Word, and I can fight over an egg!"

Reverend Wrenhouse pulled his pistol from the nail over the head of his bed. He squeezed out the door with the pistol in his hand. I saw him as he walked up the road on his lame leg. He was walking toward the store.

Mrs. Wrenhouse poured a pan of hot water for me from

the teakettle since the yellow of the eggs had run down from my hair into my eyes until I couldn't see. It had blinded me. She led me to the wash pan. I washed the eggs from my eyes, hair, and face. Then I changed my clothes. When I came down from my room upstairs, Mrs. Wrenhouse was standing by the window waiting for Reverend Wrenhouse.

"Mrs. Wrenhouse, I've stayed here four years and I never knew Reverend Wrenhouse had been in jail before today," I said.

"Willie, The Reverend is a fighter," she said. "If he's to meet the Devil in the big road he'd pull off his coat and fight him. No one knows what I've been through living my life with him. He was jailed for six months for beating up the man who shot him in the leg. It was over baptism. The Reverend believes they should go under in a running stream of water because Christ was baptized in the Jordan, which is a flowing river. The man who shot The Reverend said a pond was all right. They started quarrelin' and The Reverend got shot. After he was shot he took the pistol away from the man and pistol-whipped him real good."

"How long was The Reverend in jail?" I asked.

"He was jailed for six months but he only had to stay three," she replied. "The Reverend is a big eater too. He has always been able to eat an egg for every inch he measures around the waist. He hardly ever eats half that many for breakfast though. The jailer got a dollar a day for keeping each prisoner. He was losing money when he had The Reverend. He put in fifty dollars on his fine to get him out of jail. He was layin' his fine out in jail because he didn't have the money to pay it. Soon as The Reverend got outen jail we moved here. He said he would be a pilgrim and start life over again by going to a new county. So we are here and we're into trouble again."

We stood at the window and waited for The Reverend to come back down the road. I looked at Mrs. Wrenhouse. She wasn't a big woman. She was just a little woman drying up like a late summer shriveling crab apple. She looked like the wind could blow her away. The Reverend was so big. I just thought about her being so small to have ten children back in the mountains. Her hair was gray. She smoked a pipe and watched for The Reverend.

"Don't reckon he'll get hurt," I said. "He's among a bad bunch up there."

"The Reverend has been in tougher places than this," Mrs. Wrenhouse said. "He's always held his own. You can't whip a Wrenhouse. They are fighters from the old school and the old law—an eye for an eye and a tooth for a tooth. Very seldom one ever takes to the Word and starts preaching. But when one does he'll fight over his beliefs. No crowd of wild, reckless boys will stop one of his sermons either. I've seen that tried more than once."

We saw The Reverend coming down the road. He had his gun in one hand. He had a poke in the other. He was limping. His head was bare. The wind was playing with his white hair and his moustache. We stood at the window and watched him walk through the gate, under the oaks, and up to the porch.

"Too bad," he said, "our old hens don't lay enough eggs for our own use. It just caused me to have to flatten out Jerry Sprouse with my fist. He's cold up there on the ground yet. Boys are working with him. I went in at Litteral's store and bought a couple dozen eggs. When I come out I says, 'Boys, you have me outnumbered, but the first man that tries to take these eggs he dies like a dog or I do. Don't think that because I'm a man of the Word I won't let you have it. I'll do it if you try to take these eggs. You can jump on a boy. Now jump on me. I'll buy from where I please.' Not one offered to take my eggs. I left them working with Jerry. He tried to keep me from going in Litteral's store. As I come along I stopped and looked at the eagle in Bridges' store winder. It's some kind of a mark. I feel that the evil days are near and we shall feel them."

"What does Wyatt Bridges mean?" Mrs. Wrenhouse asked.

"I don't know, Nana," replied The Reverend. "I feel like the Word can solve it. That bird is a token. It will come to me. I'll pray hard for a vision. I don't see what a bird has to do with a fellow buying eggs. I've never heard of it before. I'll say again the evil days are nigh. I've been a Democrat all my life. I helped elect the President of the United States. If he had anything to do with that bird in that store winder I can help take him out. I'll fight him to the bitter end. The Word will tell the tale. I'll pray for the Vision tonight. You make me a biler of strong coffee for supper. I'll have to work fast. I'll pray hard."

Reverend Wrenhouse ate a big supper. He ate a plate of soup beans, fried potatoes, hog liver, and sauerkraut. He drank a quart of buttermilk, ate a half pan of corn bread, and drank a boiler of black coffee. He smoked one pipe of crumbled leaf burley. He refilled his cob pipe and smoked it empty again.

"I'm worried for these signs show bad times ahead," Reverend Wrenhouse said. "The evil days are nigh and we shall find no pleasure in them. But they are here. I can see it plain as the night falling around me. I must get in the back room and meditate on the Word. Is my red pepper in the back room?"

"Yes, it's in there by the Holy Bible," Mrs. Wrenhouse replied.

"All right, Willie, you do up my part of the work around the barn tonight," Reverend Wrenhouse said. "Milk the cows I milk, feed the hogs I feed, and feed the mules and water them. Get in wood and water for the night. I have much praying to do. I must pray for the Vision."

"All right, Reverend, I'll do your part of the work," I said.

When I passed The Reverend's window going to feed and milk I saw him rubbing red pepper on his lips to make them smart. He always did this when he thought hard on the Word. The Reverend judged everything by the Word. I went on to the barn and finished the work. When I came back by The Reverend's window I saw him under the light of his lamp. He was bending over the Word. He was reading. I could hear him praying. I went in the house and put the milk in the kitchen. Then I went upstairs to bed.

I couldn't go to sleep all night for The Reverend's praying beneath me. I could hear him pray loud. Then his voice would get low. I couldn't tell what he was saying. The thick upstairs loft was between us. There are two lofts with sawdust packed between them. The Reverend says they will keep the upstairs cool in summer and warm in winter, and they do.

The next morning when I went down for my breakfast, The Reverend came in to eat. He looked tired and sleepy.

"I got the Vision last night," he said. "I prayed to the

Lord. The Lord answered. Let me tell you about it, Nana. I've got the whole thing worked out here. It's the Mark of the Beast. I tell you it's the Mark of the Beast, Nana. The evil days are nigh. They have come upon us."

The summer sun was shining in at the window. The morning sun had just climbed above the hill and looked down on the house. The Reverend had ten fried eggs on his plate. I had six for my breakfast. Mrs. Wrenhouse was dauncy. She had only three. Then he ate pancakes with butter and sorghum molasses, a half of mince pie, a quart of rich sweet milk, gravy, hot biscuits, and hominy. He never ate less than a dozen small biscuits for his breakfast. He would slice them while they were hot and spread fresh yellow Jersey butter over them.

While we ate our breakfasts The Reverend told us about his vision. He would drink coffee after breakfast and talk. He would drink a pot of black coffee.

"I prayed hard for the Vision," he said. "I prayed for light. I got the light. I got the key to all these misdoin's. First I saw in a cloud of light before my eyes a triangle. Across that triangle was a crossbar. This triangle was coming toward me. On it rode three heads. Two were the heads of men. One was the head of an eagle. The eagle rode in front on the point of the triangle. The faces of the men rode on the rear points of the triangle. It was shaped like the letter A. A double pair of wings was attached to this triangle at the crossbar on either side. It sailed over me like a bird. A figure rose from the face on the man on the rear left-hand side of the A. It sparkled and went on through the dark."

"I laid there in bed. I waited in the dark. The sign returned. I saw the letter B as plain as I see this cup of coffee before me. The straight line of the B come toward me. On each end was fastened a double pair of snake feeder's wings. In the middle of the B sat the head of the eagle. On the left end of the B was the head of a man. On the right-hand side of the B was the head of a man. The face of the man on the right-hand side had a smile on his lips. They were spread from ear to ear. The man on the left-hand side looked like the head of a bull. From the blue bill of the eagle there sprang a figure of fire. It was the figure two. It sparkled and rode away on the letter B that was carrying the faces of two men and the eagle. It did not return."

"Then, if A was 1, and B was 2, C would be 3. All the letters of the alphabet would have a number. That would be my chart. That would be my code. I got outen the bed. I didn't spare any midnight oil. I worked all night. I have it all right here. It is as plain as the nose on your face. It is the Mark of the Beast upon us. Do not be surprised if the rain does not fall and our crops burn to the ground. Do not be surprised if torrents of rain fall and wash the corn from the hillsides and the terbacker out by the roots. Do not be surprised if the cattle take the bloody murrain and die. The evil days are here. They are marked with the Beast. I have the Word right here for it."

"Now, Willie, you will get the long ladder from the barn loft this morning and paint this code and this revelation on the back of the barn so that all men may see when they pass the road. This county has voted for the Mark of the Beast once. If I live, it will not do it again. I voted for it. But if God will forgive me for making that one mistake, I'll never do it again. There's a bucket of white paint in the barn loft. Get it and we'll paint today. We'll not go to the fields. The fields won't matter anymore. Something will happen to the fields. You will see."

I got the long ladder from the barn loft and carried it around and set it up back of the barn. I took the gallon of white paint and the brush to the top of the ladder. I started painting the words and figures on the dark oak boards. The Reverend stood on the ground and called the letters and the figures out to me.

"I'm too heavy to get upon the ladder myself," The Reverend said. "I'd love to paint these words and figures with my own hands. Now, Willie, be careful and don't fall. Put the key up first. You know your AB-ab's by heart, don't you?"

"Yes, I do," I told him.

"Then paint them in a straight row across the back of the barn. Start with figure 1 under A, 2 under B, and so on over to Z. Get the key up first and put it crosswise on the gable end of the barn. Get it up as high as you can."

So I painted:

A B C D E F G H I J K L M
1 2 3 4 5 6 7 8 9 10 11 12 13
                N O P Q R S T U V W X Y Z
                14 15 16 17 18 19 20 21 22 23 24 25 26

"That looks good," The Reverend said. He stood down on the ground smoking his pipe. "You can see the letters and the figures very plain from down here on the ground. They show up pretty against the dark oak planks. Now we must get to the most important part. Put these letters and figures up and down the barn right under the key."

The Reverend called them off to me from his paper, and I wrote them down with the paint brush on the hard seasoned oak planks.

F 6	P 16	O 15
R 18	R 18	F 6
A 1	E 5	
N 14	S 19	A 1
K 11	I 9	M 13
L 12	D 4	E 5
I 9	E 5	R 18
N 14	N 14	I 9
	T 20	C 3
		A 1
		D 4
D 4	O 15	C 3
E 5	F 6	___
L 12		78
A 1	T 20	
N 14	H 8	
O 15	E 5	
R 18	U 21	Results
O 15	N 14	267
O 15	I 9	321
S 19	T 20	78
E 5	E 5	___
V 22	D 4	666
E 5		
L 12	S 19	
T 20	T 20	
___	A 1	
267	T 20	
	E 5	
	S 19	
	___	
	321	

Just as we got the figures on the back of the barn and the letters painted there so pretty and white on the dark hard seasoned oak boards, a car drove up and stopped. There was a fellow in it smoking a cigar. He had the top down. The wind hit him. His face was tanned. He wore a little brown hat tilted to the side. He looked at the barn and started laughing. He would look at the painting I'd done on the back of the barn then he'd holler and laugh. The Reverend turned and looked at him.

"What's tickled your fun so?" Reverend Wrenhouse asked him.

"I've been about all over the United States and I was across the pond during the War," said the man. "I've never seen anything like this before. I didn't think a thing like this could happen in America."

"It's not so very funny," The Reverend said. "You wouldn't think that a bird in the winder of a store would keep you from going in a store and buying a dozen eggs either. It's the Mark of the Beast. The evil days are upon us. I don't suppose you ever read the Word."

"The Word," he said as if he didn't understand.

"Yes, the Word," The Reverend said. "The Bible!"

"Oh, yes, I read it," the man said.

"Then read Revelations, 13th chapter and 14th verse," Reverend Wrenhouse warned him. "See what 666 means."

"I can't understand all of this," said the stranger in the car.

"Neither can I, but I'm fighting it to the bitter end," said Reverend Wrenhouse. "I'll fight it until I die."

"We are having good times," said the stranger. "I sell tobacco. I'm all over the country and I know. We're having the best times this country has ever had."

"You will see that we will not have good times," said Reverend Wrenhouse. "The Mark of the Beast is over us. The evil days come nigh. We shall have no pleasure in them. The evil days are not far off, my friend. You must remember what I am telling you. You will laugh at me. You will think I am crazy. But I'm not as crazy as you think. Among these hills will be the last place in America that the face of an eagle will find a roost in store winders. It will be the last place where the Mark of the Beast shall thrive."

"Have it your way, Pop," said the stranger in the car. He stepped on the gas. He laughed louder than the noise from his racing engine. He laughed as he drove away.

"The man is outen his head," The Reverend said. "He believes in idolatry. He believes the President of the United States is a Higher Power. He's not God yet. He's what you'll find in Revelations, 13th chapter and 14th verse."

Underneath the letters and the figures I wrote this on the barn:

Revelations, 13th Chapter.

14th Verse. And deceiveth them that dwell on the earth, by the means of those miracles which he had the power to do in the sight of the beast; (the President's great power at the beginning of his administration) saying to them that dwell on the earth, that they should make an image to the beast (the Blue Eagle), which had the wound by a sword, and did live. (The attacks of a minority of government officials who voted in vain against these measures.)

15th Verse. And he had power to give life unto the image of the beast, (until the Supreme Court declared it unconstitutional) that the image of the beast should both speak, and cause that as many as would not worship the image of the beast should be killed. (If you did not accept the policies, sign the code, and place the Blue Eagle on display, you would be killed from a business and financial standpoint.)

16th Verse. And he causeth all, both small and great, rich and poor, free and bond, to receive a mark in their right hand, or in their foreheads;

17th Verse. And that no man might buy or sell, save he had the mark, or the name of the beast, or the number of his name.

18th Verse. Here is wisdom. Let him that hath understanding count the number of the beast: for it is the number of a man; and his number is six hundred threescore and six. (666)

"Now the people shall know the truth," said Reverend Wrenhouse. "There it is in black and white on the barn. The people who pass this road and who can read shall know the truth. Willie, I want you to paint me a chart so I can use it when I preach. I'm going to spread the Word. I'm fighting this thing to a finish. I'm not afraid. I'm not afraid of man, the Devil, or the Mark of the Beast. We'll let the weeds grow in the corn and the terbacker for something will happen to them anyhow. The government may stop us from raising corn and terbacker. It can do anything. It is the Mark of the Beast."

I took a roll of roofing paper and started work to repaint the code and all The Reverend had worked out from the Word. The coal-tar roof was black. I used the white paint and painted the letters and figures smaller with a smaller brush. The Reverend could roll it up and put it in the back of his buggy or express when he went to preach. He could unroll it in the rain and the water couldn't hurt it. The paint would stick. The roofing was the very thing. It took me two days to get the scroll fixed for Reverend Wrenhouse. He used his cane for a pointing stick when he referred to figures or letters. He practiced a few times before he was to preach. He would point with his cane and preach. His face would get red. His eyes would look mean. He practiced one day in the rain to see if the scroll would stand water.

The big raindrops hit the coal-tar roofing. The letters stuck there where they were painted. Reverend Wrenhouse got wet as a chicken in the rain. He stayed in the rain and preached. He was getting ready for his drive in Lennix County against the Mark of the Beast.

"Lennix County voted for the Mark of the Beast before," said Reverend Wrenhouse. "But they will not do it again. They will see the fruits of their folly. They will see the evil days. They will feel them. They are nigh."

The Reverend Wrenhouse would have me to unroll the chart in the schoolhouse, the church, or the grove—wherever he was preaching, and that was wherever he could get an audience. I would unroll the bolt of roofing and set it against a wall or some sprouts and the Reverend would take his cane and start pointing to the letters and the figures. He would speak hard and fast. He was a big man and his words were just as big and as powerful. He would preach and sweat. It was summer and the nights were warm. The lightning bugs would fly among the green leaves on the trees above us.

"I'll leave you here, Nana," The Reverend said. "Somebody might try to burn our house. The pistol hangs on the nail and it's loaded. I have the other pistol with me. Too many people in this county have stood for the Mark of the Beast. By next election a lot of the people in this county are going to change their minds. This county will vote against the Mark of the Beast next election or I'll be in my grave. I'm a fighter and I'll go down fighting. I've never been whipped yet. I've seen so many men of the Word who are afraid stand in the shadow of a tree and cringe. Just cringe and cringe. Here is one that will not if I die tomorrow. I'm going out here and preach in dangerous places. I've been sent word not to come. But do I fear? No. I go. What have I to fear?"

I would harness the mules and put them in the express. I'd drive the mules and The Reverend would ride beside me on the front seat with me over this rough terrain with his hand on his pistol. During the summer we went to every church, schoolhouse, and big grove in the county. The Reverend would go and preach if only six people would come out to hear him. He would have me unroll the bolt of roofing where he could expose his letters and figures on the Mark of the Beast.

"This is the plague of our country," The Reverend would cry to the top of his voice. Then he would stamp his big feet on the leaves or the floor of the church. "We must root it out and burn the roots first, then the trunk and the branches. It bears no kind but evil fruit. People, the evil days are nigh. They are upon us. I do not hoe my terbacker on the hillside nor my corn. You shall see that the Mark of the Beast will control them. There is no need. There is no need to do anything but fight this plague. If we can't uproot it one way I say to you that we take our guns and upend it. We can fight. Who has ever heard of such among the hills before? And, men, you and I voted for it. I did. I don't deny it. I'll be one of the first to vote against it now."

Autumn came and we went somewhere every night for The Reverend to fight the Mark of the Beast. The winds and rains, the snows and sleets did not stop us. One night when The Reverend was preaching on Gear Branch in a schoolhouse the lights that hung over our heads were shot out. Men stood out in the dark and shot the lights out.

The Reverend said, "Down flat on the floor, everybody! Down on your bellies!" We lay down on the church floor. The bullets passed over us. Many of the men in the crowd crawled out the door with The Reverend and emptied their pistols at the patches of blasting fire. We heard the men run screaming through the brush around the church. If anybody was killed we never heard of it. We saw a lot of fellows going around limping afterwards. We didn't hear of any funerals.

After the shooting was over, The Reverend finished his sermon. He often would preach until midnight. Then we would leave the crowd, carry the roll of roofing and put it in the express. We'd unhitch the mules from a tree and start home. We didn't light our pipes or show any fire. We thought we'd be harder to hit in the dark. But we were never shot at. We traveled the roads summer, autumn, winter, and spring. We went through the drifts of snow on a sled. We had straw on the bottom of the sled. The Reverend wouldn't give up. Snow, rain, sleet, mud, and guns didn't stand in his way. I've seen him take one poke with his fist and flatten a man out cold on the floor and go on preaching.

One night when we were gone from the house Jerry Sprouse and a bunch of men came to The Reverend's barn and tried to wash off the words we'd painted on the barn.

Mrs. Wrenhouse started emptying her pistol at them and they took off up the road toward the storehouse screaming. Someone shot a hole through the eye of the Blue Eagle in Bridges' store window.

"One dead bird," The Reverend said.

I had seen and heard a lot of preachers but The Reverend Wrenhouse was the greatest and most dangerous preacher I ever knew. He wasn't afraid of anybody or anything. He would fight at the drop of a hat. He wouldn't use his gun unless he had to. His wife would use a pistol too. She could shoot nearly as well as The Reverend. I've seen them shoot at a nail head in a plank in the barn. They'd stand ten steps away and drive the nail in the plank with bullets. It didn't pay for anybody to try to push them. People got afraid of them in this county. But The Reverend made a lot of friends. He had a lot of followers. Many of the neighbor men quit working in the fields and started going with us.

We had meetings at The Reverend's house. We had meetings in his barn. We had them by the river. We had them everyplace. The Reverend would say, "If I get killed, or if I die, men, you take up this fight! Don't let Lennix County vote the second time for the Mark of the Beast that is upon us."

We had meetings all winter and up until late the next spring. One day when we had been over on Sand Suck and The Reverend had eaten eight eggs and a chicken for dinner (all but its wings—The Reverend never would eat the wings of a chicken), he came back home sick. He lay down that night and said he felt bad. I unharnessed the mules, watered and fed them, put them in their stalls before I went upstairs to my bed. I asked The Reverend how he was feeling.

"I'm feeling all right," he told me. "I'm a pilgrim out in space. I can see the Vision. I can see the heads of two men on the letter A. I can see the heads of two men on the letter B, but the head of the eagle is gone. The men are here yet, though. I can see them plain as day."

That night The Reverend died. In two days we buried him. We had a big funeral up on the hill above the house under the oak trees. Nearly every church in Lennix County sent one person or a group of people to The Reverend's funeral. The whole hillside was covered. But we put Reverend Wrenhouse under clay—no more nights of preaching, no dozen of eggs and a chicken (all but its wings) at one meal for him. It was all over for him. It didn't matter now.

In November of that year he would have been proud of Lennix County if he had been alive. Lennix County went two to one against the Mark of the Beast that The Reverend preached about. The adjoining counties all went two to one for it. Maybe all The Reverend had said had had something to do with changing the people—the way he used his fist and pistol and the way he preached. I know he wasn't afraid of the Devil, the Mark of the Beast, or men. He was the only preacher I've ever seen in my life that I was afraid of.

I often think about him when I help Widder Nana with the hogs and the cows—how he had to squeeze through the doors and how he could shoot. We miss The Reverend so much. I hope he's not in a place now where he has to fight the Mark of the Beast. I'll say wherever he is, he's one preacher who can stand up and tell 'em and take a lick from a man and give a lick. He'll be good timber for the Lord. He'll be a lot of help unless he disagrees with the Lord.

~ *The Twelve-pole Road* ~

"**I** AM goin' to see Uncle Zeb," I says. "We've lived within sixty miles of him all my life and I've never seen
him." Uncle Zeb lives on the twelve-pole road west
of Fernton, West Virginia.

"You'll find Zeb is one of the cleverest men you're ever
about the house of," says Pa. "But you'll find Zeb is a
dangerous man that can't be pranked with. Don't play any
tricks on your Uncle Zeb. He's gettin' to be an old man
now. He's startin' down the other side of the hill."

I take the Greenbriar bus to Wormwood, Kentucky.
The bus driver is a white-headed man with a gray suit and
black seams up his pants legs. A girl with painted lips and
painted cheeks sits on the seat behind him and talks to him
all the way to Wormwood. He turns and talks to her. He
shows his little white mice-teeth and grins at her with a
little mousey-grin. She smiles and puckers up her store-
bought lips.

"Say, do you know where the twelve-pole road is?" I ask. "That's the place I want to go."

"Now, let me see," says the driver. "The twelve-pole road. I have heard of the twelve-pole road. Now let me see. Do you know anybody around the beer j'int at Jarvis, West Virginia?"

"No, I don't know anybody around a beer j'int in Jarvis, West Virginia," I says. "I've never been there in my life."

"That's where the twelve-pole road comes in, I'm sure," he says. "I don't know exactly. I can put you out there and you can soon find the twelve-pole road."

We go like a shot out of a gun. We roll around a curve and pop into a little hinky-dinky place about as big as Sand Suck. And the bus driver snaps his black eyes and says, "I think here is where you'll find the twelve-pole road." The girl looks at his black eyes and whispers and he looks back at her and grins. I step out the door and the bus goes on. I don't know whether I am in the right place or not. The stars and moon are above the place. There is a light here and a light there.

I walk over on the street to a house that has vines around the front porch. A man sits under the porch light. He is partly bald. His face is red as a turkey snout and his hands are big as fire shovels.

"Pal, can you put me on the twelve-pole road?" I ask.

"Go two miles straight up the main highway to Knows Drug Store," he says. "That's where the road comes in. The drug store is on the left side of the road and you can't miss it. Wait thirty minutes and you can catch a bus up there."

"I just got off a bus," I says.

"Just got off?"

"Yes, I just got off. The driver told me I'd find the twelve-pole road right here."

"That fellow ought to lose his job!" he shouts. "A man that don't know no more about the twelve-pole road than that! And don't know where the twelve-pole road is on a little bus run between Wormwood, Kentucky, and Fernton, West Virginia! You'll just have to walk two miles up the road the way the bus went. Just a little extra walk."

"What time is it?" I ask.

"Wait till I look at this old turnip," he says. "She's allus right with the mill whistle. Five, six, seven minutes till ten. That's right if ever time was right. This old turnip ticks the truth. Where are you goin' up there on the twelve-pole road? It's a tough creek, you know."

"I'm goin' up there to see Zeb Powderjay," I says. "He's my Uncle and I've never seen him in my life."

"Zeb Powderjay," he repeats. "I ought to know him. Seems like I've seen his name in the paper. Didn't he get in some kind of trouble once? Didn't he kill some man up there about two years ago? 'Pears to me like that was Zeb Powderjay."

"It may have been," I says. "You know, I don't know much about these kinfolks. I never saw them in my life."

He says goodnight to me. I say goodnight to him and start two miles up the road to the drug store on the left. It seems like four miles to me. The moon and stars are above me. The wind is over me. The cars whizz by me like one bullet after another. I have a letter in my pocket to show I am a Powderjay if Uncle Zeb happens to ask me who I am.

I walk into the drug store. A girl comes up to the counter. "Give me a light beer, please, and a black cigar,"

I says. She looks at me and smiles. She hands me the light beer. It is pretty, with foam running over the mug. The cigar is black as a sweet-gum leaf rain-soaked on the ground. I light the cigar and sip the beer. "Can you tell me the way to get to the twelve-pole road from here? This is Knows Drug Store, isn't it?"

"Yes, this is Knows Drug Store," she says. "Come to the door and I can show you better than I can tell you. See that lane there? It takes you out across the tracks to the fillin'-station at the left. When you get there you'll find a brick street. It takes you north to a concrete road and then you walk half a mile to a dirt road. That is the twelve-pole road."

"Thank you," I says.

"You're welcome," she says.

"I'm tryin' to find Zeb Powderjay's place," I says. "He's my Uncle. Do you know him?"

"I should say I do," she says. She walks back to the druggist. He is a small peep-over-his-glasses, mushroom-cheeked, dough-bellied man with a gourd-shaped nose, thin lips and flour-poke-pale face. She whispers something to him. They look at each other and grin. I cannot understand what the talk is about. I finish the beer and leave the empty mug on the counter. I puff the cigar as I walk to the road that leads to the filling-station at the far end of the lane. They are laughing in the drug store. I can hear them as I leave. I go again into the darkness. "Hell, I ought to have come up here in the daytime," I think. "It will be midnight when I get to Uncle Zeb's place."

I walk out the lane. I find the filling-station. I turn north up the brick street and find the concrete road. Over to my right I see a crowd of boys lying on the grass. They have a jug beside them. They laugh and laugh after one of them stops talking. I walk up the road with stars and moon above me. The wind is hitting me in the face. It is a good cool wind to breathe. I meet a boy coming down the road. "Pal, can you tell me where Zeb Powderjay lives around here?"

"Turn to your right, follow your nose," he says. "Three pipes of terbacker the way the wind blows."

"None of that smart twelve-pole talk around here or you and me'll tangle right on this road." He goes down the road and I go up the road.

I meet another fellow on the road. "Pal, can you tell me where Zeb Powderjay lives around here?"

"Yes, he used to live the fourth house on the left atter you leave this concrete road," he says. "But since his wife died, he's sold that place up there for eight hundred dollars and he's moved right around here close to us. I'm goin' around there now. Don't you want to walk around with me? Just about half-mile, I think."

"I'm lucky to find you this time of night," I says. "I've been in a notion just sleepin' somewhere on one of these hills and waitin' till mornin' to go see Uncle Zeb Powderjay."

"Is he your Uncle?"

"Yes, he is, and I have never seen him in my life. He's got three boys, hasn't he?"

"Yes, he has. There's Frank, Preacher, and Millbrook."

We walk down at the end of the street. There are many small houses along a broken street. We walk under the maple trees to the railroad tracks. We walk down the railroad tracks and turn to the left. We walk out a lane where three houses stand in a row. "His daughter, Minnie, lives right here. Zeb eats here. He stays in a little shanty over there on the hill. He might be there. Let's get Minnie up and see."

"Rap. Rap. Rap. Rap." The dog barks. No one stirs. "Rap. Rap. Rap. Rap." The dog barks louder. There is a light.

"What do you want this time of night?"

"Is Zeb Powderjay here? A boy out here akin to him wants to see him. Says his name is Quinn Powderjay."

"Uncle Mick's boy. Heard of him but never saw him. Come on in, Quinn. Your Uncle Zeb is sleepin' up there in a shanty on the hill. He don't have a bed up there. You'll have to stay here with me tonight."

"I'll go up there and see him first and then I'll be back," I says. "I'll be back in about thirty minutes."

"Say, I don't like to fool around the old man's place after night," says the boy with me. "He's dangerous as a cocked gun. You know he kilt a man here just about two years ago. The fellow took to the brush, naked as he could be. He had a bowie knife and was jumpin' up and down in front of Zeb's wife and daughters, naked as a picked chicken. Zeb took his pocket knife and went up on the hill atter him. It was some knifin' fight. He stabbed Zeb but Zeb won out. Zeb cut him to pieces. He cut Zeb in a lot of places and Zeb was a year gettin' well. I tell you it won't pay to fool with Zeb Powderjay. You can go about the shanty and do the hollerin'. I'm afraid to mess around there atter night."

There is the shanty in the moonlight just above a scrub whiteoak tree the barb-wire fence is nailed onto. It is a little barnlike shanty out in the yard. Above the shanty is a cottage painted white. "It's been awful nice of you to help me find Uncle Zeb's place," I says "I'd never found it."

"Oh, I'm glad to help you out. Just don't mention it."

"What's your name?"

"Tom Smith," he says. "It's nearly midnight and I got to be goin'. I work in the tie-yard. I stack cross-ties. A body that does that all day's got to get some rest. What do you do?"

"I teach school."

"Teach school?"

"Yes, I teach school."

"How much do you make a day?"

"I get paid by the month. I don't get paid by the day. Make a hundred and twenty-five dollars a month."

"My God! I never thought you was a schoolteacher. I never thought a Powderjay would teach school and make that much money. I make two dollars and forty cents a day. I thought I made good money for ten hours."

I can see Tom Smith in the moonlight, his dirty brown hair, his pimpled face, his rounded shoulders and faded clean blue work shirt. I can see the oak tree in the moon-light, the shanty on the hill where Uncle Zeb must now be sleeping, and the white cottage above the shanty. There's an old gate swinging to the tree, sagging limp in the moon-light when the wind blows.

"You can go up there and knock," says Tom. "I must be gettin' out the lane. Goodnight."

"Goodnight to you."

I walk up the hill to Uncle Zeb's shanty.

"Hello, Uncle Zeb!"

"Howdy do. Who are you?"

"I'm Mick Powderjay's boy. His oldest boy."

"Have you got somethin' to show me who you are?"

"I've got a letter in my pocket."

"Come to the door, Son, and be recognized. I didn't believe one of Mick's boys would ever come up to this God-forsaken twelve-pole road."

"I'm Mick's boy all right."

"Come on in, Son."

I go in the shanty. Here is Uncle Zeb—a tall big-boned man with big cheek-bones, hair as white as clean sheep wool and about as thick, a big nose, blue walled eyes clear as a mountain stream and with a piercing look that goes all over you in a few seconds—Uncle Zeb is bent with the weight of the years as a beanpole bends with a heavy load of pole-beans. "Let me see that letter with your name on it," says Uncle Zeb. "You know I got to be sure about things. I've had a little trouble around here and I'm not takin' any chances. You can't tell about people. I've lived among them four-score and one year. I had to get rid of one a couple years ago. I don't take any more chances." I show Uncle Zeb the letter. He takes my hand in his big hand. "You're a lot bigger than your Pap," he says. "You look a little like the Powderjays."

What a mess of a shanty! Whiskey bottles are stacked. Ridgemore bottles, Kentucky Bourbon, Rock and Rye—bedclothes, fruit jars, furniture, clothes, blacksmith tools, harness, hoes, mattocks, hammers, pitchforks, flour sacks, coffee sacks, scythes—almost everything you can mention around a farmhouse, all thrown in one heap in Uncle Zeb's shanty.

"Caught me in a mess here since your Aunt Mary died last year. Just moved down here and I can't get possession of my house. They wanted eighteen dollars for possession of my house. I told them to stay just where they's at. A bunch of wimmen in there. You know if it was men I'd put them out'n there. You can't do much with wimmen! Their time is up the fifteenth of this month and they're goin' out then."

"What did you say, Pa?"

"That's my youngest boy, Frank," says Uncle Zeb. "He stays with me."

I look down on a mattress spread out on the floor. Frank is rubbing his eyes and yawning. He is a big dark-skinned man about thirty-five years old. He acts like an addled snake.

"Get up," says Uncle Zeb, "and meet your first cousin, your Uncle Mick Powderjay's oldest boy, Quinn."

"Glad to meet you, Quinn."

"Glad to meet you, Frank."

"First cousins and you never saw one another in your life," says Uncle Zeb. "It's a shame, but we never get back to Kentucky since we come to the hills o' West Virginia. It seems so far away since we lived in Kentucky. It was hard to break away from down there—thought I'd die for about five years. Now I've got used to the drinkin' water here, and the people."

"Pa, you got anything left in that bottle over there? Offer Quinn a drink. I'd like to have a little snip too. Midnight and a body up. A drink is good at midnight."

"You don't need any more of that licker," says Uncle Zeb. "You've got to wall rock on that fill tomorrow for the W.P.A."

"Are you a Democrat?" I ask Uncle Zeb.

"You bet your bottom dollars. I am a Democrat and all my boys are Democrats," says Uncle Zeb. "You don't have to tell me. I know what all the rest of the Powderjays are. My own Pap was a Republican. But he turned over to be a

Republican back there when Tillman and Hayes run for President—Pap was a strong Democrat but he got it in his head that Tillman sold out when Hayes beat him by one vote. From then on Pap voted the Republican ticket. Pap was that way. When he thought his party sold out it made his blood bile. When I got old enough to vote, I started votin' the Democrat ticket. I've voted it all the time. It's horse, dog, and cat around here between the Democrats and Republicans."

"I vote the Democrat ticket, too," says Frank. "I ain't got much of a job. Oh, I shouldn't say that. It's good while it lasts. It's like licker and a lot more things. It's gone too soon. I get forty cents a hour for five hours a day. I get five days a week. That's forty dollars a month. Don't keep me and Pa in good licker. Guess we can drink bad licker a while, though, till times get better and we can make better money and buy more and better licker."

"I vote the Democrat ticket because I believe they are better to the poor man," says Uncle Zeb. "I think the Republican Party is for the rich man. Hell, got a lot of poor people in this country. You can almost count their ribs." Uncle Zeb just stands up and lays it off with both hands. Frank sits on the edge of the bed. He rubs his eyes. He yawns.

"Your Pap, Little Mick, is a Republican, ain't he?"

"Yes, he's a Republican."

"I heard that he was a red-hot Republican," says Frank. "Poor man ain't got much of a chance under either Party unless it changes a lot."

Frank pulls out his pack of stud tobacco. He rolls a cigarette. He rolls it in a piece of brown paper. "Haf to smoke these until I get a pay, then I'll get me some ready-mades."

Frank rolls the cigarette. His big fingers have a time sealing the paper that he moistens with his big bearded lips. The pencil-sized cigarette is hard to hold with his big fingers. Frank strikes a match and lights his cigarette. He puffs the blue smoke that thins through his nostrils in two tiny half-blue streaks. With words now of satisfaction since he got a draw of cigarette smoke, Frank says, "I hear you've got a fine education and that you have amounted to a lot. I hear you are a schoolteacher down there in Kentucky. I'm glad to know some of us have done something. I heard you was well thought-of and that's one reason I've never hoboed in there. Thought maybe you might be too big-headed. Guess you are all right, though." Frank puffs the cigarette again and again. As he draws from it, it disappears by fractions of inches.

"We got a old-age pension law through up here," says Uncle Zeb. "I thought maybe I'd better look into it. I'd just as well have it as a lot of them that would get it. Then I saw that it run from one to twenty-five dollars a month— and if you owned a little property you just got a little pension. If you had a little less property you got a little more. You had to sign your birthright away to get it. I just left it for the next man. Damned if I would even fool with it. Not long as I'm able to work. I did a good day's work yesterday. I finished wallin' a forty-foot well that I dug. I can do five times as much work as any of the Gover'ment men they got workin' over there. They don't know how to work. Peck and piddle, that's all they know. I'd a-loved to have seen 'em go out when this country was a little younger and needed men. I'd a-loved to have seen 'em buck up against big hillsides of timber to cut thousands of acres of trees. They wouldn't have pecked and piddled around."

"What time is it?" Frank asks.

"This apple says it's one in the mornin'," says Uncle Zeb.

"We'd better find Quinn a place to sleep," says Frank.

"Well, let's go down to Minnie's and get him a bed. He can sleep down there," says Uncle Zeb. "You know since Minnie's mother died and her husband died we take our meals with her. We live right up here, you see, and that makes it handy. She looks after our clothes and keeps them mended and cooks our grub. Hell, I don't have to marry some old worthless woman to get somebody to cook for me."

Uncle Zeb lights the lantern. The red flame leaves the match-stem and climbs off on the lantern wick. Uncle Zeb lowers the lantern globe and the flame quivers in the wind. I do not need any lantern. The moon is shining. "If you don't mind, Pa," says Frank, "I'd as soon sleep. I've got to work tomorrow, you know. Got to lift heavy rocks and chisel on them."

"You've got to play, you mean," says Uncle Zeb as we leave the door. Frank goes back to bed.

"Goodnight."

"Goodnight," says Frank. "I'll see you tomorrow at breakfast down at Sister Minnie's."

When we go down to the house, Cousin Minnie is up. She says, "I knowed Pa didn't have a bed for you and you'd be back here. So I just set up and waited for you to come down to bed."

We sit on the porch and Uncle Zeb says, "No, Quinn, this country is changin', and it is changin' fast. A man can't do a day's work in five, six, seven, or eight hours. It takes ten hours or more for a man to do a day's work. But they ain't enough work for men to do unless they cut the time down. Old as I am, I can see that. I used to work day and night. I used to raft logs down the Big Sandy and on down the Ohio River to Louisville, Kentucky. I took big rafts of 'em, me and your old granddaddy—the best old son-of-a-bitch that was ever on that river. He could do more work, drink more licker, love more women, outscrap any man on the river. Hell, he was what I call a man out of all the men I've met. What would he do out here five days a week and five hours a day? He'd laugh at 'em."

I remember going to bed—pulling off my pants and hanging them on the back of a chair. I remember the clean soft bed. When I wake up I don't know where I am. I forget about coming to see Uncle Zeb. I get out of a strange bed and put on my clothes. I go downstairs and Uncle Zeb and Frank are waiting for breakfast. Breakfast is on the table—a white fancy tablecloth on the table and the best ham, eggs, gravy—and jelly, oats, and coffee.

Cousin Minnie says, "Just to think; I am your first cousin. I am a gray-headed woman well past fifty years. And here is even my father that you have never seen. And we only live sixty miles apart. Nothin' to keep the families apart only one is a Democrat family, the other is a Republican family. I want you to eat and eat plenty. It might be a long time before you eat with us again. You look so much like the Powderjays."

Uncle Zeb puts away the food. He says, "You tell your Pap I said to send me a jar of honey."

I says, "I can tell you what Pa will say. He'll say: 'You tell that old scoundrel of a Zeb if he wants honey from me he'll have to come and get it hisself.' That's just what he'll say."

Uncle Zeb laughs and his blue eyes laugh. "Just like your Pap for the world."

Uncle Zeb sips his coffee from the saucer. Frank's teacup shakes a little. "Frank is a little nervous," says Cousin Minnie. "He drinks too much licker."

We finish breakfast and Uncle Zeb says, "Well, I got some more work to do on my well. I want to get it finished today. When will we see you again?"

"I've got to go home in a few minutes. When are you and Frank comin' down?"

"Don't know," says Uncle Zeb. "Got to get my place fixed up, a well-box finished, a coalhouse made, and a barn built and a blacksmith shop. Want to get it fixed up and have a right decent place to spend my old days. I must be goin' to my work now."

I says, "I wish I could stay a week, but I got to get back home. I got some corn to plow yet."

"You don't mean to tell me you're plowin' and hoein' corn hot as this weather is, and you a schoolteacher?"

"I mean it," I says. "What's schoolteachin' got to do with it?"

"I believe you are one of the old Powderjays and eddication ain't took it all out'n you. You know, Quinn, let your old Uncle Zeb tell you this and I got to go. But remember this. You can pick up a dog that stinks. Wash him all you damn please and put powder and perfume on him. Then turn him out and it ain't long till he's the same old stinkin' dog he was when you picked him up. That's the way of the Powderjays."

Uncle Zeb gets up and walks out from the breakfast table. He lights his pipe. Frank gets up too, and goes out of the house. He motions for Uncle Zeb. I hear him say, "Pa, I want a dollar. Ain't got a cent and I want a drink."

Uncle Zeb says, "You never brought me back a penny from the last five I give you, and you never brought me back a drink even. Now here is a dollar, but you be damn sure you bring me back some licker." Frank takes the dollar.

I say to Frank, "So long, old Top—come and see me."

Frank says, "I'll do it now since I've seen you. You come back and see me. I'll be down some time this fall when the possums get ripe."

"Goodbye," I say to Uncle Zeb.

"Goodbye," he says. He walks by the garden, a tall man with white hair and bent by the fruit of his season.

Then I say, "Come and see me, Cousin Minnie."

She says, "You're not goin', are you?"

"I have to be goin'."

"Come back when you can. Come back and stay as long as you can. My children are all married off and Tim is dead. I'm left here alone. If it wasn't for Pa and Frank I don't know what I would do." I can see Cousin Minnie standing in the door—her white hair flying in the wind. I walk down the path—out to the road where the tumbling houses face a broken street. I can see before me the roading running up the twelve-pole creek.

ꙮ *Lost Land*
of Youth ꙮ

BERT mused on his own fate as he drove along, looking at the old tobacco barns filled with bright
burley. He observed the tobacco stubble on the
rugged slopes and the little creek bottoms. These were
the same places tobacco grew when he was a boy. But the
valley had changed. The giant timber was replaced by
second growth on the rugged slopes not suited for tobacco. He could remember, and he could see it from the
photographs of memory, the long trains of mule teams
going down the old Lost Creek road with two and three
hogsheads of tobacco on each jolt wagon, pulled by two
husky mule teams, on its way to the Hopewell railway
station, where it was shipped on this branch-line railroad
to warehouses. Now, the railroad was gone. This had
happened, as so many other things, in his lifetime. He had
seen giant virgin yellow-poplars, sixty feet long, pulled

down the Lost Creek road with twelve yoke of oxen. Now, the second-growth logs were trucked away to the mills as the tobacco was trucked away to the warehouses.

Bert remembered in his youth that Lost Creek was a little world of its own. There were two churches and two schools. There was one big store. It was a general merchandise store that kept a little bit of everything: hardware, groceries, seeds, feeds and clothes. It kept everything the Lost Creek people had to have. It was a closed-in world too, due to the roads. It took a man one day to get to Blakesburg by train and one day to return. If he rode horseback it took him four days. Now, Bert had driven in his new automobile from Blakesburg to Lost Creek in thirty minutes. Lost Creek was no longer the little closed-in world he had known in his youth. It was as open as an autumn leaf in the wind to the outside world. A man could even live on Lost Creek now and have his business in Blakesburg.

As Bert drove along observing the wind-ruffling shimmer of golden leaf-clouds slanting upward from the valley toward the bright October skies, he remembered how he had planned to marry Mollie. He had picked out a little farm with more creek bottoms than any other farm on Lost Creek. He had planned to grow more and better burley than any Lost Creek farmer. He was driving past the farm he had chosen now. From the road on the rugged slope above, he could look down at the little creek bottoms. This seemed to him like a long lost dream of his youth. He wondered what would have happened if he had bought these creek bottoms and he had married Mollie. What if he had lived on in this rugged valley of the midday sun? Would he have loved the coming and going of the seasons when he tilled the land? Would he have loved the little joys and sorrows of his people in this little closed-in world? Would he have been happier? Would life have been better this way?

For Bert Hoskins was thinking of his own life and his own happiness. The farther he drove up Lost Creek, the more the world of his youth and his lost dreams returned to him. He remembered how he had loved Mollie, how he had worn out shoe-leather, walking the paths with her going to church, to weddings, corn-huskings, apple-peelings, bean-stringings, candy-pullings, funerals, parties and square-dances. Then he thought of the one little thing that changed his whole life. It was that little something, like the shape of a hand or the curve of a lip that makes a man love a woman. It was that little something like the quivering of a leaf in the soft wind that makes a man decide whether he loves a hill or a valley. This was the little something that caused Bert Hoskins' course of life and love to be changed.

He applied for a position clerking in the Lost Creek General Store. He was one of the up-and-coming young Lost Creek tobacco growers when it happened. When the vacancy occurred, all the eligible young men on Lost Creek applied for the position. When Baylor Landon, a resident of Blakesburg, and the owner of the Lost Creek General Store which was a branch of his large Blakesburg General Store, interviewed his applicants personally, Bert Hoskins got the position. And this changed his whole life.

Baylor Landon, one of Greenwood County's best business men, knew something about men as well as merchandise. Bert Hoskins was such a good worker, so alert to all selling possibilities and so obliging to his customers that when they came to buy at the Lost Creek General Store, they asked for Bert to serve them. He was one of the most popular and efficient clerks Baylor Landon had in either store. He transferred Bert Hoskins after only six months in the Lost Creek General Store to the large store in Blakesburg. While in Blakesburg, Bert was invited to the Landon home where he met Nettie Landon, the wealthy merchant's only daughter. Bert Hoskins didn't return to Lost Creek. He didn't return to his little world of the midday sun. He left the land of his people not to return for reasons of his own. For he married Nettie Landon.

He left behind him Mollie Didway. He left behind him five generations of his people sleeping on the high Lost Creek hill. He left behind him people who talked of his marrying the Boss' daughter and his "getting above" his own people and his world of Lost Creek. Now, Bert was returning for the first time to the world of his youth. He was returning to the old familiar scenes of his first love with Mollie Didway. The Upper Lost Creek Church was in sight. He could see the tall sycamores whose autumn leaves were a cloud of rippling gold in the early afternoon sun. He could see the crowd gathered there like in the days of his youth. The yard was filled with men and boys. He knew the house couldn't hold them all when Lost Creek people turned out to a funeral.

He parked his car at the far end of a long line of cars. Then he walked back to the church. For a minute he stopped and looked at the church. It was much the same as it had always been except it needed a new coat of paint. The grove of sycamores had grown many feet taller. They towered far, far above the church steeple now. They seemed to be struggling to reach as high as the rugged cliffs on either side the valley to get the first slanting rays of morning sun and the last afternoon rays when the sun went over the wall. When Bert, now a handsome well-dressed business man of fifty, walked up where men and boys were sitting on the brown autumn grass, or standing in little groups talking, he spoke to the first group. They greeted him but eyed him as Lost Creek men had always eyed a stranger when he walked into their midst. Not one of the old men or boys knew him. Bert overheard one fellow asking who he was. He heard the man say the stranger looked familiar. He heard him whisper he had seen his picture in the *Blakesburg News* once.

Bert Hoskins walked up to the church door and looked inside. The house was packed with women, girls, children and a few men. Nearly all of the men and a few women were standing in the aisles. Bert estimated five hundred people had come to Lonnie Didway's funeral. Bert watched for a brief time the young couples making love. He heard the older women talking about their housework and their children and Lonnie Didway, a fine and respected citizen, who had passed away. He heard them admit several times Lonnie had lived more than the Bible's number of years allotted to man. They agreed it wasn't too bad after all. Not as bad as if he had been snatched in the prime of his youth, or his middle age when the responsibility of his children would have been thrust upon his wife. So many such funerals Bert had remembered from his youth. Funerals he had attended with Mollie Didway by his side. They had sat in this same church and had made love as the young couples he was watching now.

A strange feeling swept over Bert when he heard the uneven tenor of the country voices singing a hymn to the mournful organ music. He walked away from the door. He hadn't seen Mollie Didway inside the church. He had looked over most of the house. Of course, he couldn't look in many places for the people standing in the aisles had blocked his view. Now, he walked across the dying-brown autumn grass. He walked over and sat down on the gnarled brace roots of the largest sycamore, a place where he and Mollie had sat many times in their young days before this tree was as tall as the church steeple.

And, while the people sang inside the church, while the preacher prayed and preached, Bert Hoskins sat waiting and thinking. He had inherited Baylor Landon's business and his fortune. His only son, Landon Hoskins, now married to one of Blakesburg's most beautiful women, Ellen Sparks, had taken over the business. Bert spent but little time with the business where he had given the productive years of his life. Not all the productive years. For Bert Hoskins was still an active man. He spent his autumns in Michigan and the Dakotas hunting pheasants and his winters in the Florida sunshine deep-sea fishing. But he wasn't a happy man. Something of his early youth kept coming back. He had loved his wife, Nettie Landon. They had gotten along well enough together. They had never quarreled like he had quarreled and "made up" with Mollie Didway. Life in Blakesburg with Nettie had been a pattern and routine life. In material things he had had everything he'd wanted. He had inherited a fine home. He had driven expensive automobiles. He had worn the most expensive tailored suits. Had ordered them from Chicago and New York. He and Nettie had been the best dressed couple of Blakesburg. And, at her death, his son and daughter-in-law had come to live with him in the "old Landon home." He loved his daughter-in-law. She had tried to make him happy.

Two years after Nettie's death, Mollie Didway's husband, Bill Didway, passed away. It was then Bert started speaking more often of Mollie than he did of Nettie to Landon and Ellen. He reminisced over his old courtships on Lost Creek. He told how many pairs of shoes each year he had worn out climbing the rock-bound paths with Mollie. He seldom mentioned Nettie's name. He didn't mention her name enough to suit Landon. Landon had suggested he go to Florida early this year. He had gone to Florida but he didn't stay more than a week. He gave his reason for coming home, deep-sea fishing for the first time in his life had made him deathly sick.

When he returned, he started telling of his youthful romance with Mollie. He described her beauty to Ellen and Landon. He went back to an old album and took her picture to carry in his billfold. He told Ellen and Landon he believed she was the most beautiful girl in the world. He told them about her long black hair, her brown eyes and long black eye lashes. He spoke about her slender body and how she could dance all night with him, how she could climb the steep slopes and work in the tobacco field. His son and his daughter-in-law didn't understand. But they understood on this day when he had heard that Lonnie Didway would be buried. He told them he was going to the funeral. They knew it was his first time back to Lost Creek. They understood, too, the death of Lonnie Didway was not the reason he was going back.

Bert sat thinking about how everything had changed

while the seemingly endless sermon went on. He was thinking about how lonely he was at his home in Blakesburg. It wasn't the same as it had been since his son had taken over. It wasn't the same and it would never be the same. And he thought about how strangely Landon had acted when he knew that he was going to the funeral. Bert knew his son would not tell him what to do. Life was still before him and he had good years ahead. He knew if Mollie felt the way he did, they might be able to share the late summer and early autumn of their lives together since they had missed the springtime and the early summer. His son wouldn't have anything to say about it. He would not ask him to return the business. He didn't need it. And if he did anything at all, it would be something else anyway. He might return, he thought, to Lost Creek now that there was a good road. Lost Creek was the lost world of his youth but he would return to it. He would pick up where he had left off thirty years ago. These thoughts came to him while he sat waiting. He knew what he wanted. He was going after it.

The golden sycamore leaves swept down beside him. They spilled on the dying-brown autumn grass with every little gust of October wind. He sat on the roots of the tree and he occasionally looked up to watch a leaf zigzag to the ground. For no one knew him here. There was no one to talk to unless he let it be known who he was and that he had once lived here. That he had left here thirty years ago. Besides, he didn't want to tell anybody he had been away thirty years for reasons of his own. He didn't want them to know he was here for a motive other than the funeral either. He thought it was better to sit quietly and watch the leaves, flying in the bright October wind like flocks of south-going birds. Better to watch the larger leaves zigzag slowly to the ground. For it had been a long time since he had sat down under a tree and contented himself watching the leaves come down like big drops of yellow rain. The only reason he was doing this was to see the face of one whom deep in his heart he had loved throughout the years.

Bert grew impatient waiting for the sermon to end. The time seemed endless. And he was a man of action. He had worked fast all his life. He had covered ground hunting and he had covered ground in business too. He had driven his car fast. If his car couldn't "deliver the goods" he gave it "a trade-in" on a new one that would. He couldn't sit contented watching the leaves any longer while he waited for the one face on earth he knew he loved. He arose from his uncomfortable seat on the sycamore root and walked over to the church door. The sermon ended just as he reached the door. He didn't have much longer to wait. Just another prayer and another hymn.

Then, Bert watched the pallbearers walk up the aisle carrying the coffin laden with wild autumn flowers. He watched the people file into a double column behind the pallbearers. Bert stood close enough to the door so he wouldn't miss a face. He looked each one over as she came through the door. Many passed and he had not yet seen Mollie. He knew that the years had changed her some. But he had in mind now how she would look. He knew that he would know her. He thought that she would know him. Minutes he stood there, while they kept coming, looking at the faces of the Lost Creek people. But Mollie's face was not among them. He waited beside the door and looked searchingly until the last old man, with a long white beard, walked from the church by the aid of his cane. Mollie was not among them. Then he went inside the church to see if she was inside. The house was empty. Flower petals and clumps of yellow mud from the brogan shoes were scattered over the floor. A strange feeling came over him. He hurried outside the church.

He looked at the procession of Lost Creek people and people from the valleys and hills beyond Lost Creek as they streamed across the valley toward the mountains. The men and boys had left the church yard now and had fallen into the line of march. The church yard was lonely and empty and the dying-brown grass was flattened everyplace where men and boys had sat. He wondered if Mollie had been inside the church.

Then he hurried to join the procession of slow-moving people. When he reached the rear of this great exodus, he walked up beside the old man with the long white beard and the cane. He asked the old man if he had seen Mollie Didway at the funeral. He told Bert that she was inside the church for he was standing at the door when she entered. He told Bert, he knew she was inside the church for he was so close to her that he could have touched the hem of her dress when she walked up the steps. He said Mollie Didway was now somewhere in the line of march. Bert wondered how he could have missed her. He thought she could have been behind someone when she came from the church and that was why he had failed to see her or she had failed to see him.

Bert followed the procession to the foot of the mountain. There the great movement of marching feet came to a halt while a fresh set of pallbearers took over for the first part of the hill. Then the procession started moving again. When the rear of the great exodus reached the base of the mountain, Bert stopped. Not one of the older men or women stopped. They kept moving on. Bert Hoskins was the only one not to climb the mountain. He stood looking for a minute up the steep slope at the great procession of people from the world he once knew, as they climbed slowly in a seemingly never ending line toward the tryst of the blue October sky and brilliant shimmer of leaf-gold clouds.

He knew that he would not climb this mountain he and Mollie used to climb together every time there was a funeral. There wasn't any use. He wasn't interested in the funeral. It meant nothing to him. He thought for a moment, as he stood watching fresh pallbearers take over high upon the mountain, that he would go back to the car. He would drive back to Blakesburg and forget his returning to the land of his youth and his search for the one woman on this earth he knew he loved. But he knew he couldn't forget.

Then, another thought came to his mind. He would wait at the foot of the mountain for this was the only way for them to return. He would wait until everything was over on the mountain top. He would wait until they returned. This would be better. He thought it was possible he had not yet seen Mollie's face. He could have the old man with the cane point her out to him, if he failed again to recognize her.

While he waited the October wind whipped the dead leaves from the black oaks, tough-butted white oaks, maples, beeches and poplars on the mountain slopes. The heavier oak leaves zigzagged to the leaf-strewn ground like slow drops of red rain. And the broad feathery poplar leaves floated over the valley like flocks of golden birds.

This was the first time Bert Hoskins had paid much attention to autumn. This gave him a feeling of sadness. He felt like a stranger in a strange land. It made him feel that the whole world was a mass of dying leaves and that he was definitely a part of this dying world. He could see bright death all around him, in the vegetation on the earth and in the people he knew in his youth when they were all younger and knew each other by name. Now, Lost Creek was a lost world and a dying world. The dreams of his youth were lost and dying dreams. Even the song of the autumn wind was as melancholy to him now as the organ had been when it played hymns in the church. He was a stranger in the lost world of his youth. He didn't know anybody. Not one person had recognized him.

He knew it was a dead and dying world unless he recognized Mollie. He knew, too, he would not ask the old man with the white beard and the cane or any person to point her out to him. He had to find her. He had to know her. She had to recognize him. It had to be that way. And while the mournful autumn wind chanted a dirge for his Lost Creek world he waited. He looked toward the tryst of gold and blue for he heard their voices. He heard the laughter and the shouts of the young children as they were the first to come over the skyline. He could see them against a backdrop of blue and above a shimmer of gold. Then he heard the jovial laughing of men and women now that everything was over and it was time for get-togethers, laughter and fun. That was the way it had been here thirty years ago.

The boys and girls passed him, first shouting and laughing, as they ran into the Lost Creek Valley. They paid no attention to the waiting stranger. They didn't wonder why he hadn't climbed the mountain. That wasn't anything to them. They were having fun. And beyond this autumn was spring for them. Take the good bright days in full stride under the sun. Take them while they were good. Take them while they could. Then came the older people and Bert stood where the path came down the mountain. He stood where he could observe each face. He waited as if he were looking for someone he knew would come down from the mountain. He searched each face. And he searched and searched until the young loving couples came down with arms around each other. Bert Hoskins understood this kind of love. That's the way he and Mollie had come down this mountain together. The lovers passed and behind them were a few old men and women. The old man with the white beard and the cane was the last again. Bert looked up the mountain to be sure Mollie was not walking down alone. She was not there.

Mollie, why didn't I know you, he thought, as he followed the wild procession toward the church, with your indelible photograph stamped in my memory? Where was this beautiful dream of lost youth he had so often contrasted to Nettie? Where was she, his beautiful Mollie, whom he could always fall back upon from his world of reality? Now, the autumn wind, he knew, was chanting a more melancholy dirge than could ever be played on the Upper Lost Creek Church organ. Why had he destroyed this dream? Why had he returned? The answer was simple. He had to return.

⚸ *Holiday with the Larks* ⚸

"**N**ow when you go over to Larks' I want you to act like a little man," Mom said. "I want you to show your raisin'. I don't care much about lettin' you go there to spend the night. There's a lot of talk about that family."

"But Mom, the Larks are our neighbors and friends," I said. "Every time I've been there to stay all night Uncle Rank Larks tells me about how Grandpa Shelton lived as a neighbor to him in Ennis County. And he said when you were twelve years old you slipped off to come to his and Aunt Edna's wedding."

"Yes, I did that with sister Mallie," she said. "Mallie was older than I was. And Ma was dead. That's before Pap married the second time. When he remarried, my stepmother put a stop to that. And besides, I used to tell you to call Rank and Edna, Uncle and Aunt. But I want you to know, we ain't no blood kin. They're a tough set of folks, Shan. They are good to work when they have to work but they are a dangerous people. They take to fightin' from the Lark side. Their youngin's might take to drinkin' booze when they grow up, too. Edna's brothers are all sots. I don't want you to take to their habits. But you'll go over there tonight and you'll soon be in bed. And tomorrow you'll be pickin' wild blackberries all day."

"Yes, Lester told me we'd take two lard cans to pick them in," I said.

"But how'll you get them to Blakesburg?" Mom asked.

"Lester said we'd haul them to Blakesburg on his red wagon."

"But that will jostle them down to the juice," she said. "You might not get a top sale. But go on and learn by experience. You'll never get the experience any younger."

Now I was smilin' because I was happy. I wouldn't have to cut horseweeds beside W-Hollow Creek for the hogs. I wouldn't have to cut green fodder for our two milk cows. And I wouldn't have to carry stovewood from the woodyard in and put it in the woodbox behind the stove. And I wouldn't have to draw up two buckets of water from the well to use in the kitchen. I had so many little jobs to do at home that kept me busy until I didn't have much time for play before bedtime. But this was all right. I didn't have a brother big enough to play with me. He was only four years old and I was thirteen. I had had a brother but the pneumonia fever got him. And I'd never forgot that either. I'd missed him so much. It was a lot of fun to go over to Larks'. I didn't think they were as mean as Pa and Mom had told me. Gee, I liked Uncle Rank and Aunt Edna. I liked to call them Uncle and Aunt more than I liked to call some of Mom's brothers and her sister that. Pa had brothers and sisters but they lived up on Big Sandy River over a hundred miles away and they never came to visit us. They stayed at home, voted the Republican ticket and worked to make a livin'.

Well, Uncle Rank had said so often that he hated the Republicans, all but Pa, and that he thought it was a sin Pa would never be held accountable for on the Judgment that he had voted the Republican ticket and that he wasn't a Baptist because he was a real nice neighbor to live by. He'd told me that many times and told me to follow my Mom's people and be a Democrat and a Baptist and be somebody. Well, I'd never taken much to this kind of talk. I'd rather be a loser and go along with my Pa. He'd never larruped me with a tick or a razor strap as a lot of the Pas had done their sons. And Pa had always been good and kind to animals. My Pa had told me a lot of things and he'd been so good to me I couldn't go against him.

But it was so much fun to go to Uncle Rank's and Aunt Edna's. They had five boys and five girls. But a lot of things had happened to Uncle Rank's boys. Helmar had gone to the Big River Valley to spend a day riding freight trains. He liked to show the other fellows who went with him how he could catch a coal drag going sixty miles an hour. One day he didn't hang on and his legs went under across the rail and the train ground them off just above the knees. Well, we never heard much about a hospital then but they took Helmar to the hospital. And they put his ground-up legs in a box and buried them. Helmar woke up in a couple of days from a long sleep in the hospital and he missed his legs. "What can I ever do without my pins," he said. "I can't work no more. I can't do anything." And everybody believed that missin' his legs so much is what caused him to kick the bucket so young. Helmar was eighteen. Then Fonse was giggin' frogs one night wearing a pair of hip boots and the boat overturned in a deep hole in Little Sandy. And he couldn't get his boots off and no one was able to dive twenty feet to get him. He was found on the bottom of the Little Sandy Deephole with one of his boots cut off with a knife. The knife was opened and clutched in his hand. So, Helmar and Fonse slept on the Plum Grove Hill. Still there was Lester, who was my age. We were born on the same day. And then there was Poss, who was eleven, and Cease, who was nine. Then there were the girls, Tinnie, Mallie and Lizzie, who were married. Nora as well as Tinnie lived at home. Nora was fourteen, just a year older than I was, and she was plump and pretty with clear water-blue eyes. There was one place where I'd rather go spend the night than at Larks'. I'd rather go to Arn's and Peg's home and be with Sparkie. Sparkie and I were born on the same day and were the same age.

When I went to Larks', Lester always bragged about how much more of a man he was than Sparkie. He said Sparkie wasn't tough at all. He said Sparkie just bragged about bein' tough. He said he'd met Sparkie out and dared him to fight. He told me how Sparkie backed down. Well, I never believed this for I liked Sparkie and I liked Lester. Both were my friends. And then Sparkie told me how he slipped his pistol out of the hollow log at the barn once when Lester had come to stay all night with him, and how they went to a green persimmon tree down in Tom Fitch's field. He said he shot a persimmon from the tree first crack. And then he gave the pistol to his friend Lester and

Lester missed with his first shot. Sparkie said he took the pistol with four more cartridges in the cylinder and shot four more times so fast Lester couldn't see the four more persimmons he shot from the tree. He said when he did this Lester took off running for home and that he'd never been back to spend a night with him and he had never been invited to Larks' again. Sparkie said Lester was a big puff of wind. He told me he was a big blow that went around all puffed up with gas like a toadfrog swelled up with wind. He said Lester just couldn't take it.

The soft ground along the path under the oak tree felt good to my feet. Above me the wilted leaves on the oaks were losing their wilt for the sun was going down and the leaves were coming to life again. But the jarflies were singing in the trees. And I was told when the jarflies sang they were singing, "Schooldays, Schooldays." And there was a lot of truth in this, for Plum Grove School always began first Monday after the second week in August, just the right time for us when we had the hoin' and plowin' done and the crops laid by. If farmers weren't through by then, their sons and often their daughters stayed out of school to help lay by the crops. My sisters and I didn't stay out of school to help with our crops. Pa wouldn't let us. He said goin' to school was more important than anything else. And maybe this was the reason I was in the eighth grade and Lester, who went to school with me, was in the fourth and Sparkie, who wouldn't go to school but who lived in the woods, slept in rock cliffs and went up and down the Little Sandy in a skiff he'd made, was only in the second grade. And maybe this was the reason Mom had said so often she wished there were other boys in the neighborhood for me to have for friends.

I would run a part of the way over the path and then I'd walk to rest myself so I could run again. I didn't want to get too hot and sweaty. Mom had me put on a clean shirt and overalls before I left home. Clean clothes felt good against my body. I didn't want to soil my clothes by running too much. Now I was up the hill and I was on the ridge where the path was about level, high up where I could look down at the green valleys below. I'd seen so many things along this road: foxes, groundhogs, squirrels and rabbits, hawks, owls and crows. I'd seen a lot of snakes too. I'd seen so many snakes, rattlesnakes and copperheads, I was almost afraid to walk this ridge path at night barefooted. And I went barefooted from March until frosts in late October or early November. I didn't have to wear shoes but about four months unless we had an early winter and a late spring.

At the end of the ridge path I took another winding path down a steep hill. I went under a grove of gnarled oaks with big roots that stuck above the ground. This oak grove had always reminded me of big snakes. I'd heard there were snakes on this ridge that lived in the rock cliff dens as big as these giant brace roots that kept these oaks from rooting up during the big storms that swept over here. But I had never seen one of the real big snakes like the one Old Pop Akers told me about. "Shan, I was tired and I sat down on a log," he told me. "The big log started movin' with me toward the top of the hill. I just sat there until it reached ridge path and started over for the rock cliffs on the other side for its rock cliff den. I slid off the snake's back and thanked him for my ride."

Now I went down the hill over the crooked path where the sassafras were as thick as fleas on a dog's back. And, the late afternoon wind, which was cool up here, sang as pretty a song as I had ever heard among the sassafras leaves. I was in the head of Rocky Fork of Town Branch, a land so poor, so Pa said, it wouldn't sprout black-eyed peas. And here was land so steep, so Pa said, that a mule's legs on one side got shorter when he pulled a plow around one of these slopes. Pa was about right, for the slopes were almost straight up and down. And right down at the foot of one of these steep slopes I could see Uncle Rank's and Aunt Edna's big brown plank shack. It covered a place big enough for a patch of potatoes. It was beside the Rocky Fork stream that never went dry. This stream flowed under their front porch which was built upon posts. And big willows in their front yard was watered by this flowing stream. Pa had always said it took a lot of water for the willow tree.

"You're a little late," Lester said. "We've been lookin' for you."

"I've come fast," I said. "I've wanted to get here as soon as I could."

"We're all set tomorrow to pick blackberries and make us a lot of money," he said. "I know where the berries grow. We can pick berries by a handful at the time. These are big sweet berries, growing in the shades of the persimmons, pawpaws and wahoo bushes. We're goin' to the Putt-Off Ford County."

"But that's copperhead country," I said. "No one goes there."

"That's just why we're goin'," he said. "That's where the berries are. No one goes there so there'll be plenty of berries for us. I've got it all figured out. I know what to do if a copperhead bites one of us. Shucks, we can't afford to be afraid of a little thing like a copperhead. Not like

Sparkie. He's skeered to death of a copperhead. That's why he totes that old pistol around with him. Take his pistol away from him, he's not tough. He's not half as tough as I am. Say did I tell you the time I played hardknuckle with him?"

"No you didn't tell me."

"Well I barked his knuckles with mine until they bled and he hollered for me to turn him loose. Did I ever tell you about the time we played lapjack? And you can ask Little Ed and Big Aaron Howard about this. They were right there and saw each of us go into the big ring. Little Ed made it with a stick on the ground. He had a six-foot willow limb and I had one six feet long too and we whipped one another until it was a sight. But I whipped him right out of the ring. Say he's not tough enough to reach over and pick up a copperhead by the neck when he's quilled. Ask Big Aaron Howard if I didn't do that once right before his eyes."

"Come to supper, Less," Poss said. "Don't you know supper is ready and everybody is down at the table."

"Let's get to the dabbling pan, Shan," Lester said.

On the high porch was a bucket of water and some lye soap Aunt Edna had made. Lester dipped three full dippers of water into the pan.

"Wash your hands with me," he said.

We smeared the lye soap over our hands and washed in cool water. There was a white meal-sack hand towel hanging on a nail and Lester took it down. He dried on one end and I dried on the other. When we had finished he hung it back on the nail. Then we went into the kitchen which was hot, for the flat-topped stove in the corner was still full of fire.

"Come on, Shan, take a chair and get your feet under

our table," Uncle Rank said. "You've not been to see us for nearly three weeks. We've missed you."

Uncle Rank sat at the head of the table and Aunt Edna sat at the other end. Lester and I sat down side by side. Poss was below us. Nora, Tinnie and Cease sat on the other side across from us. Nora was right over in front of me. And when she saw me she smiled then looked down at her plate. This was what Uncle Rank had called "Casting sheep's eyes." And I later learned when a girl looked at a boy like this it meant she liked his looks.

"Now just reach for the grub like you's one of the family," Aunt Edna said.

Well there was plenty to reach for but I had always thought Mom's cooking was better than Aunt Edna's. There was a full pone of corn bread on a big platter that we broke off in pieces the size we wanted. There was a dish of soup beans. Lester dipped bean soup from the dish and left the beans, broke his corn bread and crumbled it in the bean soup. There were boiled potatoes, green beans cooked with hogjowl and there were pitchers of buttermilk and sweet milk. Then there was a coffee-pot on the table by Uncle Rank's place. And he poured the coffee for himself and others who wanted it. The coffee was so strong here Pa and Mom had always said it made them dizzy to drink one cup. Mom said Aunt Edna boiled the old grounds with new coffee until the pot got so full she had to dump the grounds. Just about everybody around the table drank coffee. Uncle Rank had a mustache cup. Tinnie, his oldest child and married daughter, got him this cup for a birthday present. He was very proud of his cup. He'd told me many times how well he liked it since half the top was covered, just a place for his lips at the bottom and this kept his mustache out of his coffee. He said Tinnie thought about so many things concerning his welfare that his good wife Edna had never considered.

I ate my corn bread crumbled in my soup beans and I had sweet milk to drink. And while we sat at the table Nora said: "Pa, I saw Uglybird Skinner a-layin' down there across the road today. He was so drunk he didn't know me."

"He's a-goin' to get killed one of these days a-doin' that," Uncle Rank said. "I guess he got paid for diggin' a grave. He's a good neighbor but a bad influence. I don't want you boys a-running with his boys. They say that Puss Skinner is a bad'n. And his brother, Little Ted, ain't much better."

I had spent nights with Puss and Little Ted and I didn't think they were so bad. And all of us at my home, even Pa, liked old Uglybird. We liked to hear him talk. He would come and sit in our home out under the poplar shade on a summer afternoon and tell big tales about seein' hants come from the old graves when he was diggin' a new one. He'd told about seeing so many of the people that we had known in our lifetime. And he always said they were saved people, and these were the ones people had doubts about reaching the Gloryland. He told about them returning and smiling upon him and how they disappeared again in thin air right before his eyes.

"The Skinners are a tough set," Uncle Rank said. "I don't want you youngins associatin' with 'em. They have a young girl, that Marie, who will soon be marriageable age and I never want our bloods to mix in my lifetime. They're a people not much given for any good."

"Pa, I don't fool with Puss and Little Ted," Lester said. "Poss and I don't fool with 'em a-tall."

"That's the way I want it to be," Uncle Rank said.

Aunt Edna had not said anything. She seemed to be sitting at her end of the table looking us over. She was watching to see if we ate well. And if one didn't eat at this table he'd have to take medicine after supper. I'd taken her medicine once from a spoon with a lump of sugar afterwards to kill the taste of the medicine. And I didn't want any more of that medicine. She'd boiled up a lot of roots into a dark syrup that was as bitter as gall. I'd rather be sick as to take her medicine again.

"Ma, you know Skinners' house is up where they can see down on us," Nora said. "All they do down there all day long is sit out there under the beech shade and watch us. They know everything we do. And it's a sight how they talk about us. They can even see the clothes we hang out on our line to dry. They even talk about the clothes we wear. I can't get a new dress but what Marie knows all about it."

"Tongue-y people they air," Aunt Edna said. "Their long tongues are dangerous. I don't know what is a-goin' to happen to the world with so many long tongues and all this talk."

After supper was over all the Larks family went out to sit on the porch to watch the dim little stars come into the sky and the moon come up big and bright. But Lester, Poss and I played Hide-and-Find Them. Once when I was finder, I was having trouble finding Lester. Poss told me where he was hidden. And Lester must have heard Poss tell me for he said: "Poss if you ever tell on me again, I'll bust you one right in the mouth. You're as long-tongued as a Skinner. I'll make you lose some of them pearly front teeth."

Uncle Rank heard what Lester said and he got up from

the porch and came out. "All right," he said in his soft voice, "you boys are gettin' tired. Quit for the night, wash your feet in the dabblin' pan and go to bed. Skinners are right down there a-sittin' silently as snakes in the grass a-listenin' to every word we say up here. They heard what you said, Lester, about their long tongues. When we hear about this tomorrow it will be all over the neighborhood we had a big fight up here tonight. You boys have a hard day tomorrow if you are going to make money."

So, Lester, Poss and I went up on the porch and Poss filled the pan with cold water. And we pulled up chairs and put our six feet in the big pan and washed them in lye soap. We dried them on the meal-sack towel. And when we were through, Lester threw the towel on the floor under the table. "Faces and feet can't be dried with the same towel," Lester said. So we went into a room with the windows up where the moonlight came in and each pulled off his overalls and slept in his shirt tail. We didn't wear any underclothes in summer. And we slept on the same iron bed, Poss in the middle and Lester and I on the sides. We laid and talked a while about picking blackberries tomorrow, then the last thing I remember was Lester's saying that Sparkie wasn't tough.

When Uncle Rank woke us, it was very dark in the morning. He lit the lamp in our room. "You boys get dressed and get to the dabblin' pan," he said. "The Old Lady has breakfast ready and I've fed my mules."

Uncle Rank was a teamster who hauled coal on a jolt wagon from the small coal mines to people in Blakesburg. He worked the year round hauling coal for people and crossties from the woods to the crosstie yard. There was a lot of sleep in my eyes until I put cold water from the

dabblin' pan to my face. Poss, Lester and I washed together and when we used the long fresh meal-sack towel,
which was damp because Uncle Rank and Aunt Edna had
used it, Lester used one end and I used the other while
Poss used the middle. It's like three dogs holdin' on to a
bone, I thought. One on each end and one in the middle,
all pullin' in different directions. When we went to the
table Uncle Rank was at his place, pouring coffee for himself and Aunt Edna. There were two fried eggs on our
plates with strips of fat bacon. Uncle Rank had six eggs on
his plate and Aunt Edna had two. There was a big pone of
biscuit on a platter in the middle of the table from which
we broke our own bread. There was a pitcher of sweet
milk. I was the one who drank milk. And there was a quart
of plum jelly and a quart of blackberry preserves on the
table. But when I finished my eggs, part of my bacon and
drank a glass of milk I had had all I could eat.

"You'd better eat more," Uncle Rank told me. "Remember you won't get anything at noon. It will be a long
day out there for you boys. Now, I want you to be careful
about snakes!"

Uncle Rank ate very slowly. He cut his eggs with his
knife and fork. And he'd take a bite of eggs and bacon then
sip black coffee from his mustache cup. After he had finished his eggs and bacon he broke a piece of biscuit from
the pone and spread the wild blackberry jam over it. Then
he got up from the table and looked at his watch. "It's five,
Mother," he said softly to Aunt Edna. "I must hitch my
team to the jolt wagon and start the wheels rollin'. I like to
get to the mine first and load my coal while it's still
cool."

"Your dinner bucket is fixed," she said. "I didn't fix

dinner for the boys because they ought to be home by noon by starting now."

"It won't take them long to fill two lard cans of berries at Putt-Off Ford," Uncle Rank said. "Berries are a plenty for no one goes there. I think you can pick a handful at the time from the vines in the shades of the persimmon, paw-paw and wahoo bushes."

"Twelve gallons and we'll be sure to get ten cents a gallon and fifteen if they hold their shape in the cans," Lester said. "Twelve gallons at ten cents would be a dollar and twenty cents. Forty cents a piece. We might even make sixty cents apiece. We'll divide what we pick three ways even!"

"Mother, where is my rock?" Uncle Rank asked.

"Oh, Rank, I moved it from the chair beside your bed," she said. "It was in the way of the lamp."

Aunt Edna went back into their bedroom and fetched him a round smooth rock as big as a baseball. I wondered why he was carrying this rock in his pocket. I didn't ask but when he went out the door Lester told me.

"Pa is a decent man," Lester said. "He never carries a gun. He just carries a rock."

"Why?" I asked.

"If anybody starts any foolishness with him," he replied. "He never had to throw it at a man but once. Pa nearly killed him."

"Can he throw like that?" I said.

"He kills squirrels in the trees with rocks," Poss said. "He can throw a rock about as fast and as straight as a bullet."

Then we took the two lard cans, put them in Lester's red wagon. We were on our way. Putt-Off Ford was two long country miles up where people forded the Little Sandy River. "A man once lived there who 'put off' doing things from day to day," Lester told me. "They called him Putt-Off Perkins. And when he kicked the bucket, they named the ford after him."

We had walked almost a mile before daylight came. We met only one teamster along the road. He was going after coal. Lester pulled the wagon a while, then I pulled it. And our small buckets that we took along rattled inside our lard cans. And when we reached the Putt-Off Ford County, Lester said: "I know where the berries are. They're in Poodie Greene's old pasture fields that slope down to the river. And right here is where they begin."

Now I knew that Lester had seen blackberries here. He had told the truth. I reached up on the tall vines and took them off by the handful. I filled a little bucket then I carried it to the lard can. Well, we filled a lard can in less than an hour. Lester had his Pa's old watch which he said kept good time. "We'll have finished and be on our way back by ten o'clock if we can fill the second lard can as fast as we've filled this one," Lester said.

No one had picked berries here before. We made our paths through the tall ragweeds. We smashed weeds down with our barefeet. We made paths to the berry vines. At the foot of the hill was a little bottom. And when we had filled one lard can and had the other one half-filled, we had reached the place where the slope gradually began to climb up toward the blue morning sky where the sun looked like a big bright wagon wheel. The sun had helped us by drying the dew on the berry vines and the grass. Now the picking was a little harder, for we didn't have shade from the persimmons, pawpaws and wahoo bushes. Berries grew bigger and better in the loam at the foot of the hill.

"We'll be in Blakesburg with a load of nice berries by eleven," Lester said as he poured the last bucket on, to heap the second lard can. "We want to heap them to allow for their settlin' when we haul them in the wagon."

"Now let us fill our little buckets," Poss said.

"It might not pay us to be piggish," Lester said.

"But let's get them while we are here," Poss said. "Two one-gallon buckets make forty cents more."

"But can we haul them in the wagon?" I asked.

"Yes, there'll be room," Lester said.

So Poss led the way up the hill. He had finished his one-gallon and I'd finished mine. We'd carried them back to the wagon. Then we went back and were helping Lester put the last berries in the two-gallon bucket when Lester hollered. I saw the copperhead reach out from behind a stump and fang his index finger on his left hand.

"Kill the son-of-a-bitch, Poss," he shouted. When the snake let loose, its fangs didn't hold on in Lester's finger. Lester squeezed his finger tight with his right hand while Poss picked up a rock. He threw it as Uncle Rank must have thrown his rock at a squirrel. He smashed its head. "That son-of-a-bitch won't bite my brother Les or no one else again," Poss said.

"Get your handkerchief and tie my finger tight," Lester told Poss. "Don't let the blood get up in my arm."

Poss tore his handkerchief in two and wrapped a part around once and he pulled and pulled each end. "Tight enough?"

"Yes, no feelin'," Les said. "Now to your knife."

Poss cut one way across the bite then the other and the blood spurted.

"It's hard to do, Les," Poss said. "But you're my brother."

He put Lester's finger in his mouth, sucked blood and spat until there was no more.

"You got the pizened blood, Poss," Lester said.

"And it's almost made me have the blind billards," Poss said. "Do you see a stream?"

"Right down there," I said, pointing to a wet-weather stream that oozed from the hill.

Poss ran down to it, laid down on his belly, filled his mouth with cool water which he spat out. He did this again and again but he didn't drink.

"I didn't swallow a drop," he said when he walked back. "I'm afraid of that typhoid."

"Are you sick, Lester?" I asked.

"Hell no," he said. "I'm not Sparkie. I'm tough. I've been bitten by a copperhead once before and it didn't faze me. Pa got the blood before it got in the arm."

I carried the two-gallon buckets to the wagon while Poss and Lester followed.

"I'll pull first," I said. "I'll pull as long as I can."

Morning was still with us and since tall trees grew along this Sandy River road their branches interlocked overhead and made a shade and this helped us. The wagon wasn't hard to pull. So we moved down the road and I was hoping Lester didn't get sick. We moved at a fast pace. I didn't want him to get hot either. Once Poss spelled me pulling the wagon. He took it about a quarter mile. And I guess we were lucky. We'd not gone a mile before Poodie Greene came along in his express wagon, pulled by a fast long-legged mule team. He stopped and asked us if we were headin' toward Blakesburg and Poss said we were. "Put your wagon and berries up in the express bed and climb in and I'll have you there in a jiffy," he said.

Poss and I set the lard cans and buckets up first, then we lifted the wagon up. When Lester started to help I told him not to do it and get hot.

"Why did you tell him not to get hot," Poodie Greene asked. "I tell my boy all the time a little sweat won't hurt him."

"A copperhead fanged my brother on the finger," Poss said.

"My heavens, why didn't you tell me so we could rush him to the doctor," Poodie Greene said.

"Don't need the doctor," Poss said. "We cut the blood off from the arm, cut the bite and I sucked the pizened blood."

"Smart boys," he said. "Whose boys are you?"

"We're Rank Larks' boys," Lester said.

"I'm Shan, Mick Powderjay's boy," I said.

"Oh, I know your Pappies well," he said. "Good men. Where did you get your berries?"

"On you, I think," Lester said.

"On copperhead hill I'll bet," he said. "No one picks there. No wonder you got bit. That's why we don't pasture that slope. Too many livestock got bit and died."

Poodie Greene was now taking us along in a full gallop. The wheels spun and left little thin traces of dust behind them.

"Stop at Marcum's Store in Blakesburg," Lester said. "Our berries will be in fine shape hauling them in this express wagon with springs under the wagon bed."

We were in Blakesburg in a jiffy and Poodie Greene asked me to hold the leather check lines while he ran in the store and asked Applegate Marcum, the merchant, to come out and look at our berries.

"Wonderful berries," Applegate Marcum said. "Never had berries as nice as them this season. How many have you got?"

"Sixteen gallons," I replied. "Will twenty cents a gallon be all right? That's a top price?"

"It sure will," Lester said. "Best berries that ever come off of copperhead hill."

"They picked them where no one dares to pick," Poodie Greene said. "And this boy got bit by a copperhead but he's all right since they tied his finger and cut the bite and sucked the blood."

"Boys that will take a chance like this and work to make money, I'll pay better than top price," Applegate said. "Twenty-five cents a gallon!"

"Four dollars!" I said.

"Divide the money three ways even and we'll come later to pick up the cans and buckets."

Right there he gave me a dollar, a quarter, a nickel and three pennies. And he made the right change for Poss and Lester.

"I'll drive the boys home," Poodie Greene told Applegate Marcum. "You feel all right, young man?" he asked Lester.

"Yes, Mr. Greene, I feel fine," Lester said. "I'm as tough as that copperhead, only he's dead and I'm alive. Brother Poss got him with a rock."

Poodie Greene drove us up Rocky Fork to Uncle Rank's home.

"You all right, Lester?" I asked.

"I'm tougher than Sparkie, Big Aaron and Little Ed and Penny Shelton," he said. "I'm not even dizzy. But if you keep on asking me I might get sick."

"Well, I have to leave you here and get home," I said. "Thank you Mr. Greene for helping us."

"Yes, thank you Mr. Greene," Lester said. "I'll tell my Pa how good you've been to us."

"I'll tell my Pa too about this," I said. Then I started up the long winding path toward the ridge where the sassafras trees were as thick as fleas on a dog's back and where the wind sang as beautiful a song in the sassafras leaves as I had ever heard. I had money to jingle in my pocket. And I knew now that Lester Larks was tougher than Sparkie and all my other friends too, for I had seen him tried among the wild blackberry briars.

Uncle Mel Comes to the Aid of His Clan

A STREAK of fire flashed from Cousin Bob's Winchester while his four-cell flashlight strapped onto the barrel held the sheep-killing dog in a circle of light.

"I didn't get 'im," he said. "Too far away."

My flock of sheep had run into a huddle when they were attacked. They were among the rocks on a high knoll that stuck up like a thumb in the middle of the pasture.

"They select the right place to attack the sheep," Bob said. "It's hard to shoot one among those rocks."

"How many do you think are attacking?" I asked.

"No telling how many," he said.

Bob's father lived on an adjoining farm, across the High East Ridge and down in Tanyard Hollow. The High Ridge was the dividing line between his father's farm and mine. I owned the head of Pleasant Valley, which lay like a bowl that had been cut in two. This part of the valley was up where the tributaries came to form the headwaters of Pleasant Valley Creek. I had eight hundred acres in this half bowl. Here I grazed six hundred sheep.

I had just married Jean Torris, who had been an elementary school teacher in Blakesburg. She and I had renovated an old farmhouse where we lived. I decided the best way to make a living was to have a sheep farm. I discussed this with the sheep men in the Agriculture Department of State University. They showed me how I could make a profit of twenty-five dollars on each ewe. Now I realized when I mortgaged my land as security to borrow money at the bank to buy ewes and bring them all the way from Montana, and to buy the best rams in the Kentucky Bluegrass, that one thing we hadn't discussed was sheep-killing dogs.

"I could have hit that dog if the sheep had stayed back," Bob said. "You know how they panic when attacked."

"I wonder how many sheep got torn up by the dogs tonight!"

"It's hard to tell," he said. "A sheep-killing dog goes from one sheep to another attacking them as fast as he can."

"That's just it," I said. "Tear holes in their flesh and they're bound to die a slow death."

We had six ewes in the barn waiting to be killed to prevent a slow painful death. I just couldn't kill the sheep I'd been among from early winter until beginning spring. I'd not had any trouble with dogs when I trucked them home in winter and put them in a barn lot. I had built a large barn where I had a ramp going from the ground floor up to the loft. These two floors housed the sheep at night and then I turned them out in a five-acre lot where they could get water and where I fed them hay and grain. Not a dog ever dared attack them in the barn and lot which were near the house. The trouble had begun when I had turned them out on pasture in late March. And now there would be more trouble for my ewes were heavy with lamb. When a dog tore up a ewe I was not only losing her but I was losing one or two lambs soon to be born.

Bob and I walked to where we had tied our white western ponies. I had bought a pair of these all-purpose ponies. They could not be surpassed for riding over our rough terrain. Bob, an excellent marksman, came to stay with me to help dispose of the sheep-killers. Night after night, but never at day, the sheep had been attacked. Night after night I was losing from four to six sheep.

"We're going to have to change our tactics," Bob said as we mounted our ponies. "We'll ride down and see what damage has been done."

"How would you change our tactics?" I asked.

"Get two more men," he replied. "Get Finn and Bill to help."

"But they're still in high school," I said.

"This is an emergency," he said. "Our brothers are as good as marksmen as we are."

We rode up to the flock.

"Here's a ewe badly torn and bleeding," Bob said.

We had to remove her from the flock. Bob and I carried her and laid her across the pony's back behind his saddle. We roped her to the saddle. Among the flock we found three more that had been torn. We roped two ewes behind each saddle.

"We can go in, for they won't be back tonight," Bob

said. "After they attack and taste warm blood they're satisfied until the next night."

We rode back to the barn where we dismounted and unroped the wounded ewes. We put them in the barn where they dropped to the ground. They joined the other six mangled ewes we'd kill tomorrow. All the ewes were heavy with lamb. We had plowed a deep trench beyond the sheep lot where we buried them.

"I dread killing those ewes in the morning," Bob said. "It does something to me to have to shoot a helpless mother sheep to put her out of her misery."

"I killed the first four," I said as we walked toward the house.

Bob had his room in our home. He took his Winchester upstairs with him when he went to bed. Jean had already gone to bed. But when I went into the room, she was wide awake. "Did you get any dogs?" she asked.

"No, but they got four more sheep," I said.

"We're going to fail on our project," she sighed.

"Yes, the $15,000 I'd planned to make this year," I said. "I'd planned on a lamb from each ewe. Twenty-five dollars is low for a good spring lamb. About every fourth ewe will have twin lambs. Sale of the wool will feed them through the winter."

"And we have our land mortgaged for them," she said. "We borrowed money to renovate this house. I love our home. I would hate to leave it! I can't sleep for worrying."

"Maybe we can get it stopped before we lose more," I said. "We're going to get brother Finn and Cousin Bill Shelton so we can circle the sheep on tomorrow night's watch."

"We've got our land posted and still the fox hunters

hunt on the North Ridge," Jean said. "Has any dog the right to be on our premises?"

"No, it hasn't," I said.

"Why not ride over the farm and shoot stray dogs?"

"Say that's a real idea," I said.

"It might be a pack of strays doing the killing," she said.

"No, we killed eleven wild dogs over there when they attacked the cattle last winter."

"Maybe more have come to take their place," she said.

"You might be right about that too," I said. "People dump unwanted dogs outside of Blakesburg. They feed from the dump. Then they go up among the Artner Cliffs where the females have pups. They grow up to be wild dogs!"

Early morning after breakfast Bob said he would kill and bury the ewes. He thought Jean's idea of killing stray dogs was good.

"But one thing you'd better do," he told me. "You'd better take a spade and give the dogs a nice burial. You'd better never leave a dead dog for a hunter to find. He might burn your house or barn. This is war."

That morning I rode early toward the flock. Two ewes were limping. I caught and examined them for dog bites. They'd not been bitten but probably had been trampled when dogs had attacked and they panicked. After examining these ewes I got on my pony and rode to the North Ridge where I'd most likely find stray dogs. It was hard for me to kill any kind of an animal. But I was so mad at dogs now it wouldn't be hard to shoot them. I saw a wild dog come up from the Artner Rocks. I shot him from the saddle and roped him behind me. Before I'd ridden another hundred yards I met another stray. I shot twice from the saddle. I roped him behind my saddle too.

When I went home, Bob had killed and buried the ewes and had ridden toward South Ridge since he knew I had gone to North Ridge. When he returned in the afternoon, he had two large black poodles.

"You ought to know a poodle wouldn't attack sheep."

"That's what you think," he said. "I rode toward barking dogs. When I got there three poodles had singled out a ewe. One was nipping at her nose, another at her hips and the third was circling the ewe. First shot I got the one at her nose. The others broke to run but I got the one at the rear and my Winchester jammed."

"The dogs attacking last night I know were not poodles," I said. "They looked like short-haired dogs, curs or hounds."

"Say, we've got a battle on our hands," Bob sighed. "Do you know anybody who can get these sheep-killers?"

"Uncle Mel Powderjay," I said. "He's my father's uncle who used to raise sheep in Scotland."

"Where does he live now?"

"He lives at Twelve Pole in West Virginia."

"Get him here the fastest way," Bob said.

"He doesn't have a phone and I don't have but I know the store where Uncle Mel trades," I told Bob. "Hopkins Brothers. I can ride to Blakesburg this afternoon while you're out and call the store to relay word to him."

"You've not asked me how many dogs I killed this morning," I said. "I brought two in and threw them in the ditch."

"Last month if anybody had ever told me I would have

killed a dog, I'd have called him a liar," Bob said. "Now I don't bat an eye. I aim and shoot!"

"I don't either," I said. "I think of my ewes!"

"I'll give the dogs a nice burial and then I'll ride again while you go call your Uncle Mel," he said.

I went to the house to tell Jean our plans.

"Uncle Mel is seventy, rough as a cob and you might not like his language," I explained.

"I don't mind if he can save our sheep," she said. "He's welcome to stay all summer."

I rode over the Eastern Ridge, down Academy Branch and down the back road to Blakesburg. When I got the call through to Hopkins Brothers Store, I told the man who answered the phone that I wanted him to relay a message to my Uncle Mel Powderjay.

"I won't have to relay it," he said. "He's in the store. I'll put him on the line!"

"Uncle Mel, this is Shan Powderjay," I said. "I'm in trouble!"

"What kind of trouble?" he said. "Hurt somebody?"

"Dogs are killing my sheep and we can't get them!"

"I'll be on my way this afternoon," he said.

When I reached home, brother Finn and Bob's brother, Cousin Bill, had come. Bill had a pump gun and Finn had a full-choked double-barrel shotgun. Each had flashlights with eight-cell batteries that made a stronger light. Jean had supper waiting. Bob and I ate while Bill and Finn sat bragging how they would get the sheep-killers. I told Jean and Bob how lucky I'd been with the phone call.

After supper Bob and I got our Winchesters.

We rode the ponies and Finn and Bill followed. We rode past the rocky knoll. The sheep were not there. Then, we moved to the southern boundary, where the fence cut across the valley. We followed the fence up to the East Ridge. We rode out this road to a place where there were some scattered oaks. Here we found the flock, bedded down for the night.

"We have a problem," Bob said. "Look at this wooded area below us!"

It was almost a jungle with wild grapevine entanglements among the treetops. We dismounted and took our ponies back and fastened their reins to low branches on a pasture oak. When we got back Bill and Finn had come.

"I don't mind taking the jungle," Bill said.

Finn was to go below in the open pasture field. I was to lie on the ground about one hundred yards east and Bob was to take his position about a hundred yards west. We knew to lie breathlessly still, our guns ready for any approaching animal that looked like a dog. I lay flat on my stomach and now and then I'd look at my wristwatch. The hours passed slowly: eight, nine and ten. Slowly the seconds ticked by in that stillness until it was eleven. Once, a pony nickered. I knew Bob would be alerted for he had the watch in that direction. Bill was somewhere down in the dark green forest under the ridge. I didn't know how far he was away from the sheep. A few stars blinked in the sky. A young sickle moon came up but didn't give much light.

I heard a commotion among the sheep. It was between eleven and midnight. I jumped up and ran toward the sheep. If I saw a dog in front of me I couldn't shoot, for Bob was somewhere directly in front. The ewes were panicking.

"Dogs!" I shouted. "Watch how you shoot!"

I shot into the air to scare the dogs. In the dark woods below us a strong light flashed on! Bill shot twice.

"I got a glimpse," he shouted, "a big dog and a middle-sized one and I believe they're hounds. I believe one a black-and-tan hound and one was a bluetick."

"They're no ordinary dogs," Bob said.

"They must have got their taste of blood," I said.

Finn, Bill, Bob and I turned our flashlights on when we went among the flock. We found four badly torn ewes.

It was now midnight and Bob went for the ponies.

"I couldn't get my gun to my shoulder," Bill said.

Again we roped wounded sheep behind our saddles and Bob and I led the ponies toward home.

"You suppose the dogs will return tonight?" Bill asked.

"No, after a taste of blood they're satisfied," Bob said.

We went home, put the wounded ewes in the barn and unsaddled our ponies and put them in their stalls. When we went to the house Uncle Mel was there talking to Jean. On the floor beside his chair laid his turkey of clothes. Beside his turkey lay his Winchester.

"How long have you been here, Uncle Mel?" I asked.

"Just got here," he said. "Took a bus to Cattletown, caught Number Seven down to Blakesburg, got off the train and walked out here!"

Uncle Mel had not removed his large black umbrella hat. He was dressed in a faded blue-serge suit that looked like it had seen its best wear. His blue shirt was clean and fastened at the collar but he didn't wear a tie. His gray horns of mustache looked like the horns on an old bull.

"How did you fellows get along tonight?" Uncle Mel asked. "Did the dogs come?"

"Yes, we brought back four wounded ewes," Bob said.

"They must be smart killers!" he said. "Can you tell me where the sheep bedded down and how you fellows went about guarding them?"

Then Bob told him the story.

"They're smart but I know how to get them," Uncle Mel said. "Tell me how the land lays."

I explained to Uncle Mel how my farm was like a half bowl with a high continuous ridge for a boundary except where the fence cut across the valley.

"Tomorrow, we'll drive the sheep to the center," he said. "We'll let them bed down. Shan, we'll post you by the sheep while we take positions on the ridge."

"With one guarding, dogs will break through," I said.

"They've been breaking through on you," Uncle Mel said. "You'll lose more sheep before we get the killers."

"You're the boss, Uncle," I said. "In the morning do we kill wild stray dogs?"

"Kill every one you find on your property," he said.

Next morning I heard Finn's and Bill's guns at the break of day. While Bob killed four more ewes and buried them in the trench, I rode my pony back to the North Ridge. I killed another stray and strapped him behind my saddle. Then I rode on and came to where Finn and Bill were burying two dogs.

"No wonder you can't raise sheep here," Bill said.

"Can I throw this one in with your two?" I asked.

"Sure can," Finn said.

When I got home Bob had taken his pony and gone. Uncle Mel came in and said he walked to the cone-shaped hill where a dog ran from the rocks and he shot him.

After an early supper, Finn and Bill came to join us. We went to the pasture and found the flock getting water be fore they bedded for the night. Uncle Mel had selected the place where we would corral them. We drove them to the spot where they were content to lie down.

Uncle Mel directed Finn, Bill and Bob to their positions. Bob led the ponies away and tied them to a pasture oak not far from the flock before he went to his position.

We stood watch until two in the morning and no dogs showed up. Then, Bill, Finn, Bob and Uncle Mel came down where I was standing guard.

"What do you think of this, Uncle Mel?" I said.

"Smart killers," Uncle Mel said.

"Wonder if we got the killers among the strays?" Bob asked.

"No, we just got the future killers," Uncle Mel said.

"Now what do you propose, Uncle Mel?" I asked.

"Tomorrow we'll bring the flock back to this same place," Uncle Mel said. "And we'll take our same positions tomorrow night. They'll be back here hungry for blood."

Next day, Finn and Bill went again to hunt for wild strays. Bob and I rode the ponies, he to the East Ridge and I to the North Ridge and Uncle Mel went out with his gun toward the cone-shaped hill. While I was riding out the North Ridge I met young Ottis Skinner with his hunting dogs trotting front and a shotgun across his shoulder.

"What are you doing hunting on this sheep pasture?" I asked. "This is posted land and dogs are killing my sheep."

"Not my dogs," he said. "I've been on this land with them, hunting your woods for squirrels and my dogs never once looked at your sheep."

Ottis Skinner and I had grown up together. Our families had been neighbors until his parents moved to Academy Branch. We'd played marbles, baseball and gone to Walnut Grove one-room school together.

"You're supposed to be my friend, Ottis," I said. "This is posted land and you're hunting out of season."

"You shouldn't have brought sheep here," he said. "This was a hunter's paradise until you got sheep."

"I'm trying to make a living, Ottis," I said.

He walked out the North Ridge toward the gate where he turned over into Academy Branch. I rode out the North Ridge, where I kept thinking about Ottis Skinner's dogs. He had a large dog and a smaller one. On this day Uncle Mel, brother Finn and Bill didn't kill a stray. I thought by killing six strays we might have got the killers.

After supper we drove the sheep back to the flat on the broad slope. They seemed to be eager to return to the place since they weren't attacked the night before. Bob tied the ponies to the same tree. Bob, Bill, Finn and Uncle Mel went back to their positions. I stood guard over the flock. And it was about ten in that dusty light when my flock began to scatter. I couldn't see the dogs among them. But when I shot into the air, two dogs ran toward the closest ravine and I shot at one as he went over the bank.

It was Uncle Mel who emptied his Winchester at the glimpse of them, as they topped the circular bend of the ridge between the North Ridge and East Ridge.

"It was like shooting at ghosts," Uncle Mel said after he came down to the flock. "They're smart killers."

They hadn't been among the flock a minute before I began shooting. Still they split the sides of two and the throats of two more ewes. In a minute, we'd lost four ewes. We loaded these on the ponies, took them to the barn for slaughter and burial.

"How many houses are on the other side of the bend in the ridge?" Uncle Mel asked.

"There are two down on the Right Fork of Academy

Branch," I said. "In the Middle Fork there is one. Then there are three on Main Academy Branch."

"They're at one of the houses," Uncle Mel said. "When I shot they were making a beeline for home."

"What do we do next?" Bob asked Uncle Mel.

"Tomorrow we search for the dogs on Academy Branch."

"Everybody will say his dogs won't kill sheep," I said.

"I'll be the judge," Uncle Mel said. "A sheep-killing dog can't look you in the eye. Tomorrow morning we search for the real killers."

Early next morning Uncle Mel rode a pony and I led the other and walked with Bob, Bill and Finn. First house on Right Fork of Academy, Tillson's, had two dogs, a shepherd and a feist that playfully came to meet us.

"They're not sheep-killers," Uncle Mel said. "Move on!"

Then we went up to the second house where Fonston Hill lived. He had a friendly white bulldog and a cocker. "Not the killers," Uncle Mel said. "Let's move on to that house on Middle Fork of Academy Branch. It's about in a beeline with the way the dogs were heading."

Rank Sparks lived here. He had two lazy hound-dogs that came out to meet us.

"These are not the dogs either," Uncle Mel said. "Now let's go up Main Academy Branch and check the houses!"

The first house was Bundy Callihan's. He didn't have a dog. Then we checked in at Wash Tussies. He had eight hounds. They barked lazily at us when we entered the yard and then laid back down.

"Let me see all their eyes," Uncle Mel said. The lazy hounds looked at Uncle Mel. "They're too lazy to chase a sheep," Uncle Mel sighed.

"Just one more house," I said. "I dread going to Ottis Skinner's since I had a run-in with him today on North Ridge. He was there hunting with a gun and I told him to get out and he got funny."

"Why didn't you shoot his dogs?" Uncle Mel said.

"I told him to get off the place and take his dogs," I said. "We grew up together. We've been friends all our lives."

"He's not your friend,' Uncle Mel said. "I want to see his dogs."

"He lives in that little house up there," I said.

When Uncle Mel, Bob, Finn and I walked up the crooked footpath to his house, his two dogs came running down the path barking at us. Uncle Mel stood still in his tracks looking at the dogs. They stopped, tucked their tails and went up the path to the house.

"We've found them," Uncle Mel said. "Here are your killers!"

Ottis Skinner came out on his porch.

"You want something, Shan?" he asked. "You want something after the way you treated me on the North Ridge today?"

"Yes, we want something," Uncle Mel said. "We want a closer look at your dogs. We're hunting sheep-killers!"

"You needn't come here," Ottis said, raising his voice. "I bought these hunting dogs from Wallie Blue in Remmington County."

"They're sheep-killers," Uncle Mel said.

"Uncle Mel," I whispered, "I borrowed money in Remmington County to buy my sheep. I know a lot of people there."

"You'd better get to a phone and ask someone in the sheep business down there to see if Wallie Blue had two sheep-killers he sold up here," Uncle Mel spoke softly.

"Tell the county sheriff to come up here too for there might be trouble. I have to inspect Skinner's dogs."

I ran down the hill, leaped onto the saddle and rode to Blakesburg.

"Sheriff Darby, hurry out to Ottis Skinner's," I phoned first. "There's trouble out there!"

Ottis lived only two miles out of Blakesburg.

I put in the long distance call to Bill Woods. "Yes, Wallie Blue had two dogs! I don't remember their colors but one was a large dog and the other was a smaller one. They were sheep-killers. But I understood he destroyed them when he learned they were killing his neighbor's sheep."

I hung up the receiver and rushed to my pony. Uncle Mel might have the right dogs. When I got back Sheriff Darby was there.

"I just want to inspect your dogs, Mr. Skinner," Uncle Mel said. "I'm an old sheep man."

"That's fair enough," Sheriff Darby said.

"All right, inspect them then," Ottis said.

"Hold your dog's head for me," Uncle Mel said.

"Come Drive," Ottis said to the larger dog.

Drive came up and laid his head in Ottis's arms.

Uncle Mel stepped up and opened his mouth.

"Here's your killer," Uncle Mel said. "Look at the sheep's wool in his teeth!"

"All right, Fleet," Ottis said. "Come over!"

Fleet came up to Ottis. He held her head while Uncle Mel looked in her mouth.

"Enough wool to make a baby's cap in her teeth," Uncle Mel said. "Here are the smartest sheep-killers I've ever seen. Say you got them in Remmington County?"

"Yes, I bought them from Wallie Blue," he said. "I paid him a hundred dollars apiece for 'em."

"They've killed thirty-nine of my ewes just before they lambed," I said. "They cost me a thousand dollars in lambs, besides the loss of the ewes. I've put in a phone call to Remmington County. I found out about Wallie Blue's dogs. He had two sheep-killers all right, and he told his neighbors whose sheep his dogs had killed that he'd get rid of the dogs. So he sold them to you, Ottis!"

"I'll sue that man," Ottis shouted. "I'm sorry, Shan!"

"It's my duty to take these dogs," Sheriff Darby said.

"The work is done," Uncle Mel said, as we walked down the hill. "I'll go over and get my turkey of clothes and my Winchester and be on the way."

"Not tonight," I said.

"Yes, I've got more work to do," he said.

"You've saved us, Uncle Mel," I said. "How much do I owe you?"

"Not a cent," he replied. "I don't charge one of my clan."

☙ Eighty-one Summers ☙

It was a new, strange feeling to drive my car up the winding Womack Hollow Road. It was a wonderful feeling to move up the green valley, to feel power at my finger tips, my body comfortable and cool. I loved to feel the car swerve just a little around the curves, under the shades of the tall sycamores, oaks, willows, poplars, and beeches. I'd walked over this road so many times before when there was only a path. I'd felt the sting of sweat in my eyes. But my legs were muscled then. I knew the smell of the flowers and the songs of the birds. I knew where each bird's nest was. And I knew what it was to smell the morning-fresh perfumes when dew was on the grass, leaves, and flowers. But now, I knew what it was to enjoy the comfort of a new road and a brand new automobile.

Before I reached the head of Womack Hollow, I had to

make a sharp right turn. As I slowed my car I glanced up to my right and saw old Rock, the white mule I'd sold to Cass Timberlake. Rock was standing in harness, hitched to a root-cutter plow. I couldn't see the plow for the waist-high green corn, but I knew this was the only kind of a plow that could be used on this steep, new-ground slope. And between the handles of the plow stood Cass. He wasn't wearing his old black felt hat today and his hair was as white as the mule. My father told me three or four times that Cass had told him he wanted me to stop, so I slammed on the brakes, pulled over to one side of the road among the wilted ragweeds, and stopped the car.

"You want to see me, Cass?" I shouted up the hill.

"Yep, I do, Shan," he said. "Wait just a minute until I go down to the house!"

Cass Timberlake's shack was down in the little valley between two high hills. This little valley was the first and only one on the right side of the road that dented the western wall of Womack Hollow. The shack was made of rough boards, with strips of batting to cover the cracks. His wife, Bridget, had painted the boards white and the strips of batting brown. It was a pretty little shack, with morning-glories vining up the porch posts and sunflowers in the front yard growing along the palings. There were four hives of honeybees between the shack and the garden. There was a box for martins on a long pole in the front yard and a dinner bell between the forks of a tall locust post in the back yard.

I watched Cass go down the hill at a fast pace, dodging the stalks of stalwart corn as he hurried down to his shack. And, as I looked at him, his white head was against a white cloud. Behind him, a little higher up the steep hill, was the white mule standing just the way Cass had left him. He was bearing his weight on three legs and resting the other, while the rope lines, wrapped around the plow handles, sagged with limpness in the sultry July air.

Sweat ran from my forehead into my eyebrows and dropped down between my eyes. I didn't like to wait in this hot car, parked over the smelly, wilted ragweeds. I wanted to be going. I wanted to feel power at my finger tips and have the cool wind blow through the windows. I was restless to get started. I didn't have long to wait. I saw Cass coming around a corn row from the shack and he was carrying a feed sack in his hand.

"Oh, so that's what you wanted, Cass," I said. I had to laugh. "Why didn't you keep that old sack? I didn't want it back! I intended for you to keep it."

"But the sack don't belong to me," he said. "It's your sack. Since I'm so busy with my corn, terbacker and potatoes, I hated to make a trip, Shan, to your place to return the sack. Not when you passed here most every day in your car. I told your dad to tell you to stop so I could return the sack to you! It's a busy season for me right now!"

"I see it is," I said. "It must be pretty hot up there on the hill plowing."

"Not so hot, Shan, as you might think," he said. "Not hot enough to notice after you get used to it!"

I looked at Cass Timberlake's blue eyes in their wrinkled sockets. His blue eyes were laughing at me. And the white beard stuck to his face, for the sweat had dampened it. Cass Timberlake wasn't a big man. He never in his lifetime could have lifted the end of a small saw log upon a log wagon, as I had seen my Grandpa Shelton do. He didn't have shoulders broad as a corncrib door like

Grandpa. He didn't have big arms and hands like my Grandpa either. But Cass was nearly six feet tall and he had bright eyes, a good smile, and a few of his natural teeth. The hair on his head was as thick and white as clean sheep's wool. His eyebrows were as white as frosted ragweeds over a winter cliff.

"When I get so I can't plow, I don't know what I'll do," he said. "I love to plow and smell the dirt. I love to smell pussley, careless, smartweeds and ragweeds when the July sun is at its best. Love to watch the lizards sunning on the stumps and rocks. There's something about plowing, too, that means corn in my crib when the snows and the rains fall and the season's done. Corn in my crib, Shan, means bread for Bridget and me. Yep," he talked on, "this summer makes eighty-one summers I've plowed!"

I was stunned. I looked again at Cass Timberlake. I didn't say anything. He smiled as he looked at me.

"You don't believe me, Shan?" he said. "I was born in 1868 and this is 1959. So you figure it up. Today is my birthday and Bridget is making me a cake."

"You mean to tell me that you're ninety-one?" I asked.

"I'm ninety-one, Shan," he said. "I've plowed since I was ten years old. I used to plow cattle on the Elliott County hills! I traveled down to this country when I was twenty years old, found Bridget and married her, a girl of sixteen then. And we raised seven children and they raised thirty-five children and these thirty-five children are about all married and are raising children! Bridget and I got the place all to ourselves again!"

My memory flashed back to last year when the state built this road. They had sawed down a giant elm, too big to push down with a big bulldozer. It grew across the road in front of Cass Timberlake's shack. When they sawed the tree down, they left it lay to rot on the ground. But Cass Timberlake didn't let it lay and rot. Bridget, a large, white-haired, beautiful, elderly woman, with a smile on her lips and a sparkle in her eye, helped Cass pull a big crosscut saw through the big trunk. She helped him saw the big body into sections as big around as barrels, but not as tall. The first one sawed from the tree would have been big enough for a small round table. A meal for two could have been served on the top of it.

I passed by one morning and stopped my car while they were sawing. Bridget and Cass were quarreling. He said Bridget was riding the saw and she accused him of riding it. I listened a minute to their quarreling, then they both broke out in explosive laughter. They changed their minds about each other's riding the saw. They agreed that the saw was dull and Cass decided to file it. He was ninety then, and she was eighty-six. Cass Timberlake split the big pieces of wood with a wedge, sledge, and double-bitted ax. He chopped the branches of its bushy top. He cut enough wood from this tree to fill a woodshed.

"When Bridget and I got married," Cass continued, "we built a log house on a farm we rented and moved into it. It was a one-room shack. But in three years we bought the farm. And we added to the shack as our youngins were born. By the time we had our seven we had a pretty good-sized house. We lived on that farm for fifty years. I cleared the farm, made pasture fields and meadows. I loved that farm where we just had a little wagon road up Straight Creek. But after the automobiles got here and everybody started gettin' 'em, and big steel monsters started tearing down hillsides to build a road up Straight Creek and through my farm, I started wondering whether I'd live on there. When the automobiles drove by and clouds of dust blew over our way, Bridget and I agreed to get away soon as we could. We didn't have any more new ground. We'd conquered the hundred acres of wilderness we'd bought. That's why we come up Womack Hollow and bought this fifty-acre farm. There was only a little crooked wagon road leading to it. There was fresh spring water here and plenty of new ground. We never dreamed the big steel monsters would ever come up this narrow valley and build a road for the automobiles to give us their dust. But it's happened here. Shan, it's getting so there's no place to go. Not a place left. Do you know of one where there's plenty of new ground, good ankle-deep leaf-rot loam on top of the soil?"

"No, I don't," I said. "I can't think of one just now!"

"I love to grow corn in it," Cass said. "Corn has strength that's grown in leaf-rot loam. I don't care what people say about it. And the taste of tomatoes grown there is sweeter and better. Shan, new ground has strength, but now it's about all gone! But it is new ground I'm after. That hillslope there I'm plowing is new ground! Look at my dark green corn. Pretty corn, ain't it?"

"It certainly is," I said. I looked up the hillslope at the tall green corn. Old Rock, Cass's mule, was standing quietly resting another leg. Once he stomped at a biting fly and swished him with the brush of his shorn tail. Cass looked at his corn too. His eagle eyes surveyed his clean field that seemed to reach up to the sky on the ridge line above. His tall corn near the ridge line was etched against a white cloud. It was beautiful to see.

"I'm one of the last new-ground farmers left here,

Shan," Cass said as he turned from looking at his field to look at me. "This country has changed. When I first come to Womack Hollow twenty years ago, everybody around here made his living from new ground. They plowed these steep hills, the little bottoms and the valleys. Now, who will plow a steep hillside? The young men don't. They don't even plow the slopes. They don't walk between the handles of a plow any more in this hilly country. They plow the creek and river bottoms and they ride when they plow. If they don't ride, they don't plow! There's only one farmer left around here with me. That's Fred Doore! Old Fred's still farming his hills and growing the best cane and corn in this county! But he's a young man, Shan. He's only sixty-five."

Cass stood behind the palings, resting one hand on the fence and holding the sack in the other.

"I'm about to forget your sack, Shan," he said, handing it to me.

I reached from the window and got the sack that was worth a dime. I threw it over onto the back seat. He had worried more about getting the old sack back to me than I worried about making the payments on my car. But that was the way he lived.

Cass Timberlake didn't have a smile on his face now. He had a faraway look in his eyes.

"I don't understand it all, Shan," Cass said. "So many of the people who worked, farmed, thought, and believed in the way of livin' that Bridget and I do are gone. I couldn't go down there and take that state handout like my children tried to get Bridget and me to do. My oldest boy, Lew, said we'd been eligible for it for the last twenty-five years. I don't want it as long as I can plow old Rock!"

The sweat ran down my face in little streams and soaked my shirt collar. I looked at Cass Timberlake's sun-tanned face and he wasn't sweating. I couldn't mop any more sweat from my face with my bandana; it was already soaked. The sun's rays, slanting down over the growing green waves of corn, heated the steel and glass that enclosed me. Even the springy new seat of my car was wet with perspiration. Honeybees zoomed past us and fussed with each other over the nectar in the white blossoms of Queen Anne's lace and the purple blossoms of ironweed.

"But Bridget and I are holding out on all this stuff," Cass said. "We're not goin' to let it swallow us. And when we find a farm with a lot of good new ground on it, away from a road and automobile dust, we're sellin' this farm and buyin' that one. She feels just like I do about it. We loved this place until the steel monsters come up this hollow, cutting down the slopes with their big blades and rooting up the poor helpless trees! We'll go to new ground where we can raise what we eat and eat about all we raise from that good earth. It'll give us strength. It always has. You can't beat the fertilizer made by the earth itself and tempered by the rain that falls on earth. You can't beat it, Shan. I'll never be a-takin' these pills that give you this and that and have some other kind of strength shot into me with a long needle! When I go, I'll go as the leaf from the tree the frost has nipped."

I fidgeted in my car for I was hot. Cass had held me too long over a ten-cent feed sack. I had helped to get this road. I'd written to the Governor of Kentucky about it. I knew the Governor personally and I got it. The road had softened my legs a bit, put a little weight around my middle, where I sat bent over so much in the car. And I couldn't smell like I did when I walked up and down the little path that was the Womack Hollow Road. I didn't know where the birds' nests were and where the patches of snow-white percoon grew and bloomed in late March and early April. I never had time to find it now and fondle the snow-white blossoms and smell their pleasant perfumes of spring. And I wondered how I ever got around without my car and a good road. My world had changed, too, but I didn't tell Cass. I didn't want to talk any longer. I'd lost all this time because he wanted to return a feed sack.

"It's a hot contraption you're in, Shan," Cass said. "You ought to get out so the wind can blow over you!"

"I guess it would be cooler," I said.

"Shan, you've got to go and I've got work to do," Cass said as he watched me fidget restlessly. "And I've got to get back up there to old Rock. He's had time to rest all four legs now and dream about the big ears of white and yellow corn we'll have in the crib this winter when the cold November rain falls and the snows come! Corn for old Rock and the cows, and corn to make the finest new-ground corn meal in the land! Talk about good hot corn bread with strength and yellow butter to go with it!"

"You make me hungry, Cass," I said. "Come to see me. Bring Bridget!"

"I'll do that," he said. "Stop again and see me!"

I looked once from the side windows as I got started. Cass was walking up the slope across the corn rows toward his mule and plow.